NO ONE KNOWS ABOUT US

NO ONE KNOWS ABOUT US

A Short Story Collection *by*

BRIDGET CANNING

BREAKWATER

BREAKWATER
P.O. Box 2188, St. John's, NL, Canada, A1C 6E6
www.breakwaterbooks.com

COPYRIGHT © 2022 Bridget Canning

ISBN 978-1-55081-950-2

All of the characters and events portrayed in this book are
fictitious. Any resemblance to actual persons, living or deceased,
is purely coincidental.

A CIP catalogue record for this book is available from Library
and Archives Canada.

We acknowledge the support of the Canada Council for the Arts.
We acknowledge the financial support of the Government of Canada
and the Government of Newfoundland and Labrador through the
Department of Tourism, Culture, Industry and Innovation for our
publishing activities.

PRINTED AND BOUND IN CANADA.

Canada Council   Conseil des arts   Canadä   Newfoundland
for the Arts   du Canada   Labrador

Breakwater Books is committed to choosing papers and materials for
our books that help to protect our environment. To this end, this book
is printed on a recycled paper that is certified by the Forest Stewardship
Council®.

To some great friends
who spark many stories:
Angela, Bryhanna, Christa,
Deirdre, and Grant.

CONTENTS

SEEN

To: Irene Hogan
From: Dennis Power
Date: January 13 / 2018
Active 1 hour 13 minutes ago

Irene,

I know this is coming out of the blue. I'm in Hawaii and they've announced a ballistic missile is headed towards us. We have been told to seek immediate shelter.

We haven't talked for a long time. I want you to know I never stopped thinking about you. Every day I'm sorry I didn't do things differently.

I love you, Irene. I've missed you.

Yours,

Dennis

IRENE IS IN HER KITCHEN. She makes a cup of tea while the radio blares coverage of the false alarm in Hawaii. Reports say it was a button pushed in error during an employee changeover. She listens to a woman's voice full of tearful vibrato: We came here for our honeymoon. At first, we thought it was a hoax, an Orson Welles thing. Then everyone was panicking. We didn't know what to do. We stayed in our hotel room. We called everyone we loved.

How do you feel now, the reporter asks, knowing it was all a mistake?

Right now, I'm just happy, the woman says. I'm with my husband and everyone knows we're safe.

Irene gazes at her phone. Reading Dennis's message produces a notification that it has been seen. Her name and tiny profile avatar sit below it like a punctuation mark. The radio commentator remarks how tensions between North Korea and the US translate into fearful governments. Hawaii is no exception. Everyone exists in a heightened state of readiness.

Irene moves into the living room and settles on the sofa. She turns off her phone before she checks what's new on Netflix. It's too easy to end up looking up reviews of the offerings. She prefers to watch and see for herself.

Later, she accidentally watches a bad film. She only wants to read the description, but her finger slips and hits play. Shag it, she figures.

The movie is chock-full of the kind of tropes they'd discussed in the film studies class she took last year. The male lead returns home after running away from his emotions. He hungers to reconnect with the woman he mistreated. But when he approaches her at a party, she tells him to go to hell and storms off. He grabs her arm and peers into her gorgeous enraged expression with absolute sincerity. Irene imagines her classmates' responses: Oh look, woman says no, buddy won't stop, woman rewards his persistence. What tripe. No wonder no one understands consent.

But Irene tries not to get frustrated with bad writing anymore. These types of films demand a little suspension of disbelief in exchange for cheap escapism. In real life, actual drama is rare, even when things end abruptly. Back when she decided not to forgive Dennis, the last time, she simply pretended he was dead. If she saw him around, it was an apparition. She wasn't about to start talking to ghosts.

And at that point, they weren't talking anyway, so it was straightforward: no greetings or eye contact. When she explained the theory to her roommate and her friends, they all played along. There were many satisfying moments of bitchy aloofness: Don't look now. Phantom Dennis at three o'clock. Alert the Ghost Guard.

Years later, when he was elected to city council, she was so accustomed to considering him gone, she hardly recognized his new image. Goateed, got-what-you-need, hemp-ware Dennis really was dead. Councillor Dennis Power was sanitized with hair products and glossy slogans: Put Power in Ward Four. Vote Power for Change. Name like that, people think you're born to it.

Irene knows for the movie to reflect reality, the man and woman would have to be filmed from opposite sides of the room. They'd stay close to their friends. If the woman became separated from her clique, the man might approach or wave. A stiff exchange would inform him she's not inter- ested. He would then retreat to his friends with ego safely bubble wrapped. No highjinks or oracle-like supporting character who sees through their walls to recognize two matched souls and speak a truth to pierce their bruised pride. No perfect storm of coincidence—a broken elevator, a random blizzard—to trap the couple so they squabble it out until finally succumbing to exasperated, angst-oiled, long-overdue humping.

When the movie ends, she scores it thumbs down. It is satisfying to tell the algorithm how she feels.

The next day, at the centre, Irene does a quick survey of the activity areas. The newest ECE, Ashley, plays a Raffi CD for the preschool group while Nyana gets the snack ready. The smell of sliced apple lingers in the hallway. Irene inspects Room 2. She makes sure the dates are clear in the cleaning schedule and the art supplies look tidy. These are details that attract parental scrutiny.

In the staff room, Ed and Mackenzie discuss the news. It was the second time buddy made that mistake, Ed says. Staff was told it was a drill, but he just didn't get it. Must have been worse than Pearl Harbor there.

Reminds me of when I worked at Tim's, Mackenzie says. If you ordered your coffee black from this one girl, she'd still give you a double-double. Just try it, she'd say. It tastes really good.

Irene listens as they segue into more tales of dummies from past jobs. She clears her throat and sips her tea with deliberation. They are getting back to work as she enters her office.

She sorts through her day planner and inputs calendar

reminders to her phone. Parents will soon be making plans for their kids' spring activities. She needs to send out ads for Gotta Have Art! Winter Programming: indoor painting sessions, workshops with visiting artists, all the free city-sponsored events. She scans her inbox: messages from parents, inquiries about new admissions. Her eye catches on an email from Carla Warren at the Department of Arts and Tourism. Message sent yesterday at 4:53 p.m.

Dear Gotta Have Art! Administration:

The Department of Arts and Tourism is dedicated to supporting the vitality of the arts and art-related organizations in the province. We have recently processed over one hundred applications and reports for sustainable funding from a wide range of not-for-profit programs in communities all over Newfoundland and Labrador.

Due to inaccuracies in reporting data, we have revoked the 2018/19 funding for Gotta Have Art.

Carla Warren has supplied a screenshot of the offending form, with $3,685.77 highlighted in neon yellow. It is in the profit column when it should be one grid over in discrepancies. In the actual accounting spreadsheet, the totals boxes at the bottom of the page contain the correct amounts. But here, Ed slipped.

On the phone, Irene hears her own voice tighten as she fights the urge to curse: what does the mistake matter if the totals add up? Oh my, no, the secretary says. The provincial auditors hold us responsible for any discrepancies in the paperwork. They take the allocation of tax dollars very seriously. Also, it's unfair to the non-profits who did report their finances accurately.

When Irene asks why the government is treating community groups like they're competing parties, she is directed to contact her MP. Carla Warren's auto-reply boomerangs back announcing she's on leave for the next three weeks.

The current Gotta Have Art! funding comes from three different sources. It allows for Irene's coordinator salary, one assistant, four part-time teachers, rent, and whatever supplies they can't gather via donation. Their current capacity is forty-five and as they base tuition fees on income, the waitlist is always over a hundred names long. This was the year Irene hoped to expand—the grant proposal was peppered with accolades from students and parents. In a bigger location, they could double their size, maybe become a community centre. They could provide night classes: crafts, home repairs, film studies, Adult Basic Education. There could be a kind of barter system of shared knowledge and needs. Students could collaborate on murals, a jam space, a community garden. She keeps lists of ideas in a notebook by her bed: ESL classes or language exchange meetings. Collaboration with local art galleries and the Native Friendship Centre.

The loss of funding will mean at least one immediate layoff. The staff currently consists of young music and visual art teachers who haven't found formal positions and are filling the blanks on their résumés with non-profit experience. She has already been finding it hard to retain staff—last week, she overheard Ashley complain about the lack of benefits, how she really needs something with more security. But Irene had been confident that if things kept going well, they would be known as a good place to work. And just last month, the centre received a nice write-up in the *Telegram* about their dedication to income-based tuition and using art education to build self-esteem in at-risk children. She posted it on their Facebook page. It was shared twenty-one times.

With Ed, her frustration melts when his voice cracks. Oh Jesus, Irene, he says. I'm so sorry.

It's okay, she says. An honest mistake. You're doing the work of three people. We'll get this fixed, don't worry. The whole thing is ridiculous.

Ed's fists clench. This is some sadistic bureaucratic horseshit, he says. He shuts the door when he leaves. She stares at the spreadsheet until her eyes invent patterns with its formatted squares. A cat face. A heart shape. A stairway to heaven.

Twitter and CBC NL reveal two other arts and cultural organizations have also lost their funding. Responses rack up: *This is loss of jobs over mistakes made by busy volunteers / The government is treating allocated arts funding like the artists are threatening them with sharp objects / This attacks what is vital to the economy in this province / Yeah, well, lazy welfare artists leeching tax dollars should be accountable to the penny.*

Irene scrolls other headlines. Local news has collected the scattered Newfoundlanders in Hawaii, including St. John's Deputy Mayor Dennis Power. A photo from his Twitter account shows him and his sun-kissed family, smiling on a beach. Both Dennis and his wife wear pressed white linen, her tidy yoga legs silhouetted against the sand. The twins grin up from a sandcastle. A tiny Newfoundland flag impales the top. Dennis's caption: *Hug your loved ones today. An experience like this makes you realize what's most important.*

Irene cannot recall the twins' names but remembers her initial feeling when she first learned of them, respectful relief they hadn't gone the alliteration route. She can't imagine a Dennis Power naming his children Johnny and Jenny or something. Not even this corporate changeling version of him would do that.

After supper, she does the trail around Quidi Vidi Lake because it's mostly flat and good for a circle of brooding. The funding decision could have been fixed with a courtesy call. Basic communication, a little tolerance for human error. Now, even if the decision is changed, how is she ever supposed to trust them?

She yanks her toque over her ears. No one wants to spend money in winter. She thinks about how in the spring, Queen Anne's Lace sprouts along the wooden walkways. Dennis used to call them Cat Piss Blooms. Sometimes, back then, they would make their way to his place in Pleasantville this way, and they did it in one of the gazebos a couple of times. She remembers wiping old cigarette butts off her pants when she pulled them back up. And there was one time on the leg extension machine in the outdoor gym, the metal legs digging into her shin, the creaking of the hinges echoing around them. That was fucking dirty, he said afterwards. I hope you liked it.

The last time they were together was at that apartment. He had just returned from Halifax and had an assortment of his regular party favours, as well as some new ones. He hadn't called her, but when he walked into the bar, he came straight over, all swagger and c'mon, we goes. Back at his place, she sat on the kitchen counter as he lifted his powdered house key to her nostril.

Why are we still doing us like this? he said. I didn't know if I'd see you tonight.

You tell me. You're the one who doesn't call.

I never heard from you either. Why are we still just carrying on? We should just be together already.

She stayed composed, but her legs swung back and forth off the counter edge. You're the one who plays games, she said.

That's true, he said. But you like it.

What's changed then?

I don't want to play anymore, he said.

Then his roommate came in, Joel or Jake or something, a massive guy who looked like his ancestors wrestled bears for pocket change. Dennis pointed at Irene and said, Have you met my new girlfriend? And Joel or Jake said, 'Bout fucking time. And later in bed, when they were coming down, she asked if he still meant it and he held her so tight when she closed her eyes it was as if their bodies merged into a single line.

Forty-eight hours later, Dennis Power and Bianca Feehan were on the edge of George Street. Him helping her on with her coat, shrugging into her, something muttered under his tongue making her eyes glitter. Irene was about to say his name when he spotted her. His face gave nothing, not even surprise. She watched them get into a cab.

It was the next day Irene killed him in her mind. She lay on the living room floor while her roommate Andie handed her cigarettes and brushed her hair. She cried and laughed while Andie invented causes of death: accidentally snorted

Ajax. Drowned by the East End mafia. Tried to fuck a mirror. And fifteen years later, at forty-one, Dennis Power is an occasional twinge: his voice on TV or radio crackling in its fresh coating of polished urgency, a flash of disdain over his new townie brogue. Changing the channel and feeling the satisfaction in that—pressing a button on him. A gesture he'd appreciate.

Back home, she rereads the message. She takes a screenshot and sends it to her Dropbox. She polishes her fingerprints off the screen until it shines like an offering. She watches the interview again. Flying back on Friday, Dennis says. No place like home.

That night, Irene lies naked on her bedspread. She takes three selfies. It's been some time since she's really looked at her body beyond a passing wince at a ripple of cellulite. When she lies on her back, her breasts stand up nicely, hips slimmer than she'd imagined. In her early thirties, she welcomed finally liking her body, but that feeling has slipped as work has taken over good habits. But she still looks smooth and firm. Crush-worthy. Touchable and untouchable at the same time.

On Friday, she prepares for the airport. A strong silhouette is important. She wears her long black coat that cinches in at the waist. It takes an hour to do her hair and face.

Dennis and his family descend the Arrivals escalator to a media flutter, predestined by his travel-update tweets. Irene finds it hard not to check out the wife, vacation tan immaculate in white slacks and a crisp blouse. Irene wonders how she packs for travel—she must possess in-depth knowledge of fabrics that don't shrivel with ten hours of flying and how to pack just the right amount of the best facial rejuvenation potion to get it through security.

Dennis carries his daughter and pauses at a reporter's microphone: She's all tuckered out. There are chuckles and handshakes. When he spots her, his gaze bounces immediately to someone else: Oh hello, great to see you. They shift on to the luggage carousel. Irene watches his back, two horizontal creases through his navy blazer, his posture set in focused neutrality.

She leaves in the midst of an exiting crowd. In the parking lot, she scrambles to get into her car. She should avoid being noticed as the sole occupant of the vehicle. She catches a glimpse of her face in the rear-view mirror and she should really do something about her eyebrows and what the fuck, this is some stalkerish shit. Dennis didn't skip a beat back there. Everything with her was always a joke to him. Maybe he is the kind of bastard who sends one last poke in his final hour. Maybe the message was copied and pasted to a list of women. She pictures Bianca Feehan tearful over an iPhone. Christ almighty.

Irene sends the email on Tuesday. It is mostly formal and to the point. *Gotta Have Art! is an organization in need of expansion. Meanwhile, there are so many vacant spaces in the city which should become useful and appreciated in the ways they deserve. What's the point of having a warm safe place and not using it? Attached is information on Gotta Have Art! Perhaps we can meet to discuss potential vacant properties. If you or any other city official requires more, please feel free to ask.*

Dennis responds by the end of the day with an invitation for coffee. He says they can talk and possibly go see a property which may fit her organization's needs. *Wear your walking boots. See you soon.*

The café is busy and the bustle of getting their drinks prolongs their mutual silence. Dennis nods as Irene goes over the centre's funding predicament. Whatever product he uses in his hair dampens it in the front so his scalp is visible underneath his fringe. Otherwise, he is immaculate: pressed grey suit jacket, smooth hands, the scent of something subtle and expensive. She wore all black hoping to look chic and bohemian, but now the variations between shades stand out; the leggings are faded, the sweater is pilly. None of her blacks match. She has non-profit written all over her.

She arranges the paperwork on the table. Dennis alternates between sipping coffee and making notes. Eye contact is purposeful and fleeting.

I've heard good things about your organization, he says. I didn't realize you were involved.

Yes, from the beginning.

Good on ya. St. John's needs more options for kids and parents. I'm actually working with a proposal for a new daycare centre in City Hall.

Well, I hope you don't drag off my ECEs, Irene says.

Dennis's face kind of stalls. Why did she say *drag off*? What I mean is, Irene says, all that municipal money is pretty enticing. I can't compete with those bells and whistles.

He pulls a folder from his briefcase and opens it. Her email and enclosed articles have been printed and tagged with neon sticky notes. Of course he has a secretary. Probably an assistant too.

It's too bad about the province's decision to get nitpicky, he says. It reeks, actually.

Reeks of what?

Something higher up. Decisions to put the money somewhere else. Art's an easy target. I've been doing this for over ten years now and Irene, you wouldn't believe the pork-barrel, back-scratching, nepotistic disgrace—I mean, I imagine you do know, I'm not trying to mansplain anything to you. But there are so many in all levels of government who are little more than loan sharks and frauds. I spend too much time in furious heartbreak over this place.

He blows a slow ripple over his coffee. Her skin involuntarily crawls. She is reminded of being in a coffee shop with Andie, back when Dennis was newly dead. Andie spotted him across the room and drew a little cartoon ghost on a napkin, a tiny zero for a mouth with a speech balloon: *Boo! My asshole-shaped mouth makes me extra spooky!*

We may be able to scrape by without the grant, she says. But we'd definitely be better off in a larger space. There are families on the waiting list that can pay.

Yes, I'd love to get more groups into vacant public properties. We can put together a proposal.

Thank you, Dennis. This has been a scary experience.

I can imagine.

I bet you can.

He swallows the last of his coffee. Suddenly everything is final. He speaks into his lap as he shuffles the folder back into his case. The building I'm thinking of used to be an elementary school, he says. It's a short drive if you want to follow me.

Irene leans over the steering wheel as she drives. This

would be a terrible time for a fender bender or an encounter with a careless pedestrian. She pulls in three parking spots away from his car. The only sounds as they cross the parking lot are the remote beeps of their cars locking.

The old school is one storey, a long, faded building with dated forest-green trim on the windows. Graffiti tags and cigarette butts. One storey means accessibility. Students could paint murals outside, colour and whimsy to draw the eyes of passersby. The street is busy; she passes here regularly and had forgotten about this place. Refreshed and reused, it would get noticed.

There's a new condo nearby, Dennis says. Lots of bus stops.

Maybe we can see in through the windows.

One of the councillors knows the manager, he says.

Keys jingle in his hand. She watches as the lock opens easily, like it's been oiled with use. He enters without looking back at her.

The entrance foyer is cold air and sawdust. Dennis's footprints uncover white tile under the layer of grime. She follows the shape of his shoulders. He moves into a small auditorium. Good for games and small concerts, he says. The first thing visitors see.

The hardwood creaks under their feet. There is a small makeshift stage at the end of the room. Irene walks towards it with purpose; she is grateful to have something to focus on.

I hope you don't mind me showing you this place right away, he says. It came to mind when I read your email. But the guy who loaned me the keys said the CNIB have also shown interest.

So, art education versus the blind. Not sure about those odds.

It doesn't have to be odds. We just need a strong proposal. I've had luck with a number of projects so far. There was a lot of pushback on the roundabout, but I managed to change minds.

The stage is ancient plywood. Irene runs her hand along the edge worn to a shine from a thousand bums of the past. She leans against it and surveys the space. The place is dirty, but there are no signs of water damage. Funding for repairs is a whole other process and committee. It could work. It could work really well.

She averts her eyes as he approaches the stage. He is a pendulum sway of coattails. He takes the steps and examines the room from centre stage. He clears his throat, but his voice is still tight and careful.

I realize my message must have taken you off guard, he says. I've been feeling embarrassed about it. Which is terrible, isn't it?

It's okay. People do things out of character when they're afraid.

He steps closer. Is he going to touch her? But you see, Irene, he says. It's actually the most in-character thing—most true thing I've done for a while.

She looks back. He stands about six feet away. How many other grand speeches were made on this stage? It is the east and Juliet is the sun.

Am I the only one you messaged?

What? Of course. Seriously, you think that?

Can you blame me?

I know. He steps forward. I'm sorry. I was very prideful

back then. It was foolish.

There is a loud crack and a high-pitched sound. An animal, some kind of rodent under his foot. Then her mind recalibrates; it is Dennis who makes the sound, pulling his foot from a fresh hole in the stage floor. The cuff of his trousers is shredded and red. Ow, ow, ow, ow, fuck.

Oh shit, Irene says.

She clasps a hand over her mouth. Dennis's lips form a perfect "o." Andie's voice: *Look at his arsehole-shaped mouth.* A giggle emerges and hiccups from her.

Dennis angles his ankle to see the damage. His face is grape-rage. And she laughs, he says. Of course, Irene finds it funny.

She guffaws, her nerves are an avalanche. *Finds it.* Dennis Power's natural tongue bleeding back to life. I'm sorry, she says. It just scared me. The floor must be rotten. She pulls a packet of tissues from her purse.

Don't bother.

Don't be cross.

I'm not cross, he says. I'm disappointed.

About what?

Dennis paws the wall as he backs down the steps. She's standing before him. He won't take her hand. It was always a job to get genuine kindness from you, he says.

You're in pain. Let me help you.

Why? We both know what this is about.

He limps towards the foyer. Oh look, she says, Dennis suddenly changes his mind. As soon as it's not fun, off he goes.

Jesus. You think I don't feel like shit? I wrote you that message when I thought I was going to die. You didn't even respond.

I knew you were safe by the time I saw it.

Oh well. Shag it then.

You're married. With kids.

He opens the door and fumbles with the keys. Outside, a fresh dusting of snow covers their cars.

What happens now?

Send me what you need. I'll get my team on it.

Thank you. Thank you, Dennis, you didn't have to do this.

Sure. Sure I didn't.

She waits until he is gone to get into her own car. The snow starts to cover his trickles of blood.

She submits the proposal later in the week. He responds, cc'ing another councillor and a Lena Hartery she assumes must be the assistant. She adds Ed to the exchange on her end. The neighbourhood is notified and, overall, supportive. Now everything is transparent: here are our quarterly expenses; here is our payroll, current rent, tuition scale, our long-term business plan. Here is how we match provincial curriculum standards, here is a comparison with a similar project in a similar place. Here are our hands, our bodies, our eager mouths.

Then the CNIB gets access to a space at the university and Gotta Have Art! charges ahead. Irene and Ed sit in the back of City Hall and pump their fists silently as the vote passes. I am pleased to support such a progressive project, the mayor says. It is a triumph for both the arts and for revitalizing local properties.

The move is planned for early summer. Irene consults with the Gotta Have Art! staff and they agree to celebrate at the Jungle Jim's on Torbay Road. It's close to where Nyana and Ashley live and fits their student-sized salaries. Irene orders appetizers and a jug of strawberry peach sangria. Ashley snaps photos and asks Irene if she wants pics for the Facebook page. She takes a few of each person and group selfies—everyone wants one, phones lined up on the table. They smile for all the cameras, their faces luminous with hope and sweet wine. Irene tells herself to wait for tomorrow to post them, if at all—you never know what might make a parent uptight. And as warm and happy as she feels, she leaves with Nyana, who needs to relieve her babysitter. No one really wants to party with their supervisor and Mackenzie's getting loud. Ed's eyes are growing playful.

The next morning her phone isn't in her purse. The zipper on the pocket is open, maybe it fell out? She retraces her steps. At Jungle Jim's, the waitress retrieves it from behind the bar; someone found it on the bathroom floor. Irene thanks her and leaves. The smell of brunch eggs pings her stomach.

No new messages. She begins a text to Ed, might be good to check to see if everyone got home okay. At the top of the list is a message sent at 12:17 a.m. Unknown number. Three photos sent. It takes Irene about twenty seconds of staring at the first one to recognize her faded bedspread and then her own flesh. Breasts arching towards the camera, lip-sticked lips parted in a cliché. Then in the second, her face fully visible, her eyes over-intense. Her fingers making a journey south.

Her hands shake so much it takes multiple attempts to

tap open her applications. There are no new posts or tags, no notifications besides birthdays. No new emails sent. No cryptic messages.

If they wanted to, they could have deleted the text after it was sent—just taken the photo for themselves and she wouldn't have known anything. She considers how last night, she put in her code repeatedly for Ashley to take photos. Swipe, swipe, zigzag. It kept locking up. She changed the setting so the touch screen was available longer. Then it just has to keep being touched to stay touchable. Ashley smiling and nodding, not meeting Irene's eyes.

If she calls the number from her phone, what would she say? They'd have the sound of her voice too. They might recognize her number and taunt her, breathe heavy. She circles the Torbay Plaza parking lot looking for a phone booth. She drives to the Tim Hortons on Major's Path. Inside, she buys a donut to break a five and asks for more quarters and realizes she doesn't know how much a pay-phone call costs anymore. The guy at the cash has three inflamed pimples on the ridge of his chin and doesn't close his mouth when he's not talking and he doesn't know where a phone booth might be. Everyone has cellphones now, he tells her. Thanks, she says.

She tracks one down by the library, an actual phone booth. Inside, it smells like someone just finished smoking. She dials and it rings twice. Then a man's voice: Hello? Small children in the background. Hello? Hello?

If you're there, I can't hear you, he says. This is a private number. Who are you looking for?

She waits, listening. Speak up if you have something to say, he says. It's rude not to respond.

She hangs up. The receiver is sticky. It's starting to snow again.

In her car, she starts the engine and lets it warm up. Snow collects on the windshield, filling up the blanks. She goes through the events of the previous night. There is enough data on her phone to check her work email.

Ashley has sent a message: *Sorry for the last-minute notice—we were having so much fun last night, I couldn't bring it up! I'm starting a new position with City Hall on Monday. It needed to be filled immediately. Thank you for everything, Irene. I've learned so much at GHA.*

Irene replies. *I understand, Ashley. Everybody has to do what they have to these days. I'm sure your new employer will appreciate what a hard worker you are. Good luck.*

She sets a reminder to call a sub for Monday and pulls out of the parking lot. She keeps the radio off to better focus on the road. She'll get home before the snow gets too bad. The beat of the windshield wipers is slow and steady and she uses their rhythm to pace her breathing. She finds herself thinking of a few winters ago, a night her car was broken into. She had parked downtown and thought she'd locked it. But she didn't notice anything gone; all he did was rifle through the glove box. Later, the cops called because they arrested a guy who'd been breaking into cars all night. Nothing he took was of much value: he'd snatched an expired motor vehicle registration card with her name on it. He's done this before, the officer said. When it starts getting cold, he figures out how to go away for the winter. Nothing major, just enough so he might stay safe and warm.

At home, she busies herself around the house. She sets an assortment of simultaneous tasks to keep her on a rotation of occupation: laundry, dishwasher, soaking the pots, putting the kettle on. In the kitchen, she tunes the radio to local news. Two masked men held up a bank outside town and escaped on skidoos. The mayor has announced a ceremony for the new daycare centre opening at City Hall. NDP demand inquiry into the new provincial budget.

In weather, the forecast calls for mild temperatures, a break in the cloud cover. Irene feels a loosening of tension at the possibility of an early spring thaw. She turns off the kettle right before it whistles.

WITH GLOWING HEARTS

ROY HAD CAROLINE AT HIM all week to clean the bathroom. The Post-it notes on the fridge screeched in red Sharpie: DO IT ROY, IT'S NOT FAIR. NEVER ONCE IN EIGHT YEARS, WTF!

He got it done Saturday, every little bit according to her instructions, circles of Comet bleeding away the soap scum in the bathtub. Look Caroline, he said, you could eat off that porcelain.

Seriously, Roy? she said. Get over yourself. Doing a drop of housework doesn't make you some kind of Renaissance man.

Then that was a racket and she pointed out how she's cleaned the bathroom every other time throughout their entire marriage and she doesn't make an announcement afterwards because he takes it all for granted, like the way he seems to believe clean underwear magically walks itself into his dresser drawers and he shouldn't be bragging about having to be told and taught how to do a single goddamn household chore. And all Roy could say was Fine, Caroline, you're right. Fine.

When he woke up on Sunday, the residual guilt and

annoyance was still potent, like a damp stain in his chest. He looked at the clock and it was before seven, twenty-four hours until up and out and back to the stack of invoices on his desk and fake Monday pleasantries and Kerry Osgood's staff meeting on this month's promotions. He got up and slunk around the house in his bathrobe. He checked his Hotmail account. A Groupon message in the junk folder said, *These Deals Want to Meet You*, and he thought, Like fuck they do.

He dressed and drove to Bowring Park. It had been rain, drizzle and fog all week in the shrinking daylight of November. Surfaces were dewy with frosty ambitions. The park was full of families and couples with dogs; everyone seemed to be trying to move as much as possible without getting wet.

He considered the long-dormant idea that maybe he and Caroline should have had children. They agreed long ago they didn't want them, but now it feels like at least there'd be something to collaborate on. Something to blame for weight gain and bad backs and diminishing *cool*. Something to force a stop to Caroline's seeking out of potential middle-aged kindred spirits for them to spend time with. Like last week's supper at her friend Wendy's house. Wendy and her husband, Larry, are also childless. Caroline said it would be nice to socialize with adults who don't constantly refer to their offspring.

Back in the 90s, Larry was in one of the more popular local grunge bands, some one-word name synonymous with downtrodden. Now he was in IT and only played reunion shows here and there. Roy listened as Larry drank brandy out of a snifter and complained about hipsters, millennials, and modern music: the auto-tune and bouncing asses. He was all pursed lips and reddening face, his faded punk now a kind of rock-and-roll petulance. And everything Wendy and Larry had was quality, the charcuterie and booze, but the conversation was so much work. Caroline and Wendy talked about their jobs and Larry asked Roy about hockey, because doing the books for Osgood's Athletics Supply suggests he would know about sports. Since then, Caroline had mentioned upcoming Christmas get-togethers. Roy might be a jerk for already designing excuses.

He edged around a puddle in the park's main walkway. He sighed and it came out as a bellow so loud the Black couple in front of him turned and the man said something in another language that sounded like swearing. Here is Roy, some white, middle-aged fop, flopping around by himself on a Sunday. How is it that even at his age it is still so difficult to ignore what others might think? He headed towards the duck pond, mashing leaves underfoot, trying to blink away a sudden stinging flood of memories: *Here's the time in grade ten you called Jean Dobbin. You hung up when she answered and she star-69ed you. Here's the time you printed off that poem for Caroline at work and someone got to it first and pinned it to the bulletin board. Here's a list of words and names you've mispronounced in conversation: potpourri, psoriasis, Sade, Bruce Cockburn.* A knot started along the left side of his neck and shoulder blade, right on his cringe nerve.

Roy continued along the path to the duck pond where everything opens up. Clusters of families feeding birds, couples taking photos by the statue. And Doug Cluett.

Doug was all by himself. He stood back on by the pond, contemplating the water. Roy regarded Doug and thought about how Kerry Osgood goes on about positivity and feeling grateful. Roy felt grateful he could recognize Douglas Cluett's arse a mile away and therefore plan a route of avoidance. Gratitude entering the universe, like a kind puff of smoke.

It's not always easy, working with Doug. Kerry Osgood occasionally said something in this vein when the guys were on a Doug Rant, usually on a day when his BO was particularly potent. Doug was fat and getting fatter, but lived in cheap track suits, the kind with reflector stripes and vinyl swish. Whenever they ended up on the sales rack at Osgood's, Doug liked to snatch them up with his employee discount. Sometimes, when Doug was stinking up the stockroom and Roy had to do inventory, he imagined pools and eddies of sweat in the crevices of Doug's body, sealed under the polyester veneer like when Caroline covered bowls of leftover soup with Saran Wrap.

Roy adjusted his sunglasses and cap. He took the wide path around the duck pond where there are enough trees to stay out of sight. Doug stared at the ducks and kind of hopped from one foot to the other, like he was getting ready to kick one.

What a sin for you. Caroline would say you're being judgmental. But a day at Osgood's without Doug was like a catchy song you hadn't heard in a long time. Everyone spoke easily, openly. They smiled more. When Doug was absent, no one had to smell his stink or hear him think, hear his two-cents clatter on every comment made. You couldn't say TGIF without his personal declaration of laziness: *Know what I shoulda done? Stayed home in Botwood and gone on the pogey. That's the Newfie dream my son.* And Kerry's calm firmness: *Now Doug, a lot of people don't like that term*, and Doug nodding until she's out of sight: *Fuck 'er if she can't take a joke.*

Doug spat on the ground. He removed something white and soft from his pocket, face tightening as he regarded it in his hands. Roy thought about kidnappers and bottles of chloroform. *Sure, why would you need a life of crime?* That was last week, Doug's interjection on a conversation about a local robbery. *If I got on the welfare, I'd have enough for rum and smokes and I already makes home brew. Only crowd you need to rob is the government.* Then he hitched into laughing, loud enough in the stockroom for customers to overhear.

Doug pulled the white object onto his head. It was a bright white headband with a blue and green insignia. Roy pulled out his phone and filled the camera zoom with Doug's big sour head. The headband bore a Winter Olympics 2010 logo, but there was something different about it. One of the ones with a special design, created just for the torch-bearers.

Special like the essay Kerry Osgood's daughter Bethany wrote, back when she was in grade ten. There was a contest. Students had to choose a line from the national anthem and write about its significance or something like that. Bethany's essay was so good it won her a chance to carry the torch for a symbolic section of its starting journey across Canada. She also received a pile of Olympic swag, mugs and badges and a bright white Olympic track suit, covered in symbols and corporate logos. After Bethany showed it off in school, Kerry coaxed her into displaying it on one of the store mannequins. When customers walked into Osgood's Athletics Supply, they were greeted with the official Olympic torch-bearer outfit and a mini-shrine to young Bethany, her photo for the *Telegram*, a copy of her winning essay. Roy remembers how Doug was unimpressed: *I'd be rotted if the Olympics came here*, he said. *Too many people from countries you can't trust, walking around like they own the place.* Everyone told him to shut up. Shut up, Doug, for Jesus' sake.

Later, between spring cleanup and inventory intake and stock switchover, the outfit disappeared. New spring running gear was put on the mannequin. Bethany's things were supposed to be put aside. There was a lot of discount Olympic gear that month. Kerry fumed over the possibility it may have ended up in the bargain bin.

Roy watched Doug smooth the headband against his forehead. He took one, two, three photos. If Roy talked to Kerry first, she wouldn't let on that it was him. Submitted to her anonymously, she could say. There is a zero-tolerance policy on staff theft, Doug. This is hard not to take personally. This belonged to a child, Doug. This was something my daughter worked for.

Doug tugged his track jacket down and exhaled. He started running. Pigeons scattered. Ripples ran through his body with each step. Two teenage girls jolted out of his way. One whispered something and the other barked in laughter. Doug's face reddened. He forced his shoulders back. His track jacket rode up, exposing the pale curve of his underbelly, swaying and vulnerable. He kept going.

Roy put his phone away. He took the path by the river back to the parking lot, stopping twice to wipe his eyes under his sunglasses. All the recent rain made the river wild and heavy and deafening. He stood on the bank and tried to listen for other sounds, but it was hard to hear anything above the relentless pounding of the current. Two ducks swam along the edge from eddy to eddy, beating their feet to gain momentum. He stood and watched them until he realized he was shivering. It was like the river had put him in a trance. He took out his phone and sent a text message to Caroline: *I'm out and about. We need anything at the store?*

He returned to the car. Somehow, the overcast sky had managed to warm up the front seats. Roy let the heat replace the chill in his spine. His phone pinged with Caroline's response: *We need milk and eggs for the week. Come home out of it. I made pancakes.*

GUTLESS BRAVADO, PART ONE

THE CHURCH HAS ONE OF those billboards with the change-able letters for posting platitudes. I read it out to Jerry as we pass. *You know that little voice inside, that gut feeling? Listen to it. God finds ways to speak.*

Interesting thought, I say.

I turn down the volume a touch so I can focus on what I mean. Sometimes I do the same thing when I'm trying to park. Makes me feel like a chump.

The stomach is a bag of nerves, I say. More so than the brain. I read an article about it. Gut feelings are caused by these microbes which give emotional cues that structure the brain. These scientists did MRI scans comparing gut bacteria to brain behaviour. When they switched the gut bacteria of anxious mice and fearless mice, their behaviour changed. Pretty cool.

I hit the indicator. Across town to the overpass to the Trans-Canada Highway, the bypass road is the first exit. The turn signal sounds like a thumb popping a jar lid. Jerry stares straight ahead in the passenger seat.

The ancient Egyptians were in touch with that, I say. When they mummified a body, they would take out the internal organs and put them in clay jars, for the dead person to have in the next life. But the brain, they hooked that out through the nose. They thought the brain was just for balance. Thinking and understanding, that happened in the belly.

Jerry inspects the weather. It will be dark soon. We've had three straight days of monochrome, overcast sky. At the end of each day, it goes straight from grey to black, like it gathers dust during the day, and with evening it's a clean slate.

Might rain soon.

We've been driving all day. I can drive for five hours without stopping, but today I take a break every two hours. Too much to do and I need to have my wits about me.

I used to get nervous about driving in the rain, I say. Especially when it was foggy. The fog blankets surfaces. You can't see how slippery the road is. When it rained, every hydroplaning story I knew would come to mind. I'd check the forecast; if I saw that grey cloud icon, my tummy would curdle.

We cross the overpass. Not many cars on the road. Grey days mean stay inside and get things done. Or do nothing without feeling guilty 'cause you didn't get off the couch and make the most of nice weather.

One time I called in sick for work because I didn't want to drive in the freezing rain, I say. That was back when I was driving back and forth to Bull Arm. I felt guilty about it. Using up a sick day.

The GPS tells me to take the next exit to the bypass road. It will be a half-hour drive from there. Things are on schedule.

That job was stressful, I say. And Max made everything worse.

Jerry's lips jut out, parallel to the brim of his cap. His profile is like the edge of a cliff, a place to ponder the situation with his own tumultuous innards.

Max. What a little brute. One of those guys who love to make you uncomfortable. Like, he would fart just to gross you out. You'd be in an elevator with him and see his face screw up, like he was concentrating. That was him, trying to fart. People made excuses for him, said he was trying to be funny. But he got off on causing discomfort. The way he'd stare and not look away. How he'd rumble phlegm in his throat and spit whenever one of the foreign workers was around.

I shift in my seat at the thought of Max. The seatbelt against my scar makes it itch. I work my hand under my sweater and rub the puckered flesh. I don't like to scratch it directly. The skin feels too new.

On my first shift with Max, I had on a T-shirt from a concert: The Shins. He had never heard of them. What's that? he said. Besides a good place to hit you. He mimed cracking me in the shin. He did the same thing every time I walked past him; he'd swing at my legs with his welding gun: Here comes the shins. I joked that it was a good thing I didn't wear a Hole T-shirt. He didn't get that. Guess he never heard of that band.

If the boss wasn't around, Max told stories. He wore camouflage gear a lot; he said it was so he could sneak up on pussy. He joked that when he lived in the trade school residence, he threw a woman out in the hallway after he was done with her. Didn't even give her time to dress, just tossed her clothes out after her and locked the door.

The bypass road has been groomed for spring and summer; the foliage is cut back along the sides of the pavement. Ravaged dirt and tree stumps pepper the arch of the ditch leading to the trees. Makes me think of my scar, the torn-up strip. Mostly healed, but I still get tingles from time to time, the invisible openings and closings, the settling cellular connections.

Max bragged about nights downtown with his buddies. The time they got thrown out of this bar. The time they ran out of that bar without paying the tab. The times they found a solitary guy and chased him. Herding faggots, he called it. First, I thought he was bullshitting, but I heard things over time. Like that he got kicked out of residence 'cause he shaved a cat and fed it LSD. And later, he stalked an ex-girlfriend and she had to get a restraining order. He messed up the car of a guy she was friends with by burning thermite through the hood. Used a magnesium ribbon and a blowtorch from the site.

A car approaches in the opposite lane; its headlights flash, once, twice, three times. Warning signals. Maybe cops or a moose. I tap the brake lightly. It's nice when other drivers give you a heads-up. But there's the awareness of being noticed.

Then he brought Julia to the staff Christmas party. I remember feeling sorry for her. Her hair hung in long thin wisps down her shoulders. Just the ghost of hair, really. And she had a bug-eyed look about her, like she was on the alert.

At the bar, I noticed her earrings, little dangly things with pink crystals attached to square nuts. I made them myself, she said. I'm doing the machinist program out in Placentia. I like working with metal.

You ever do any welding? I asked and then she started to say something, but Max came over. She went still, like a statue. Bracing herself.

That summer, she almost burned their house down because of Max's hockey card collection. He was drinking outside with his buddies, beers out of a cooler. He brought out his collection to show off: his signed Guy Lafleur and Brett Hull. The next morning, Julia went out to clean up and the hockey cards were at the bottom of the cooler, soaked in the melted ice water.

She took the cards into the house and laid them out to dry. But they started to curl on the edges. She took heavy books off the shelf and put the cards inside, so they would stay flat. Then she turned on the oven and put the books on the racks. In her mind, this would dry them out. And she knew once he was angry he'd find a way to make it about her.

Something large and dark stirs in the ditch. I pump the brake; Jerry jerks forward and resettles. The large, bulbous head of a cow moose lifts and stares at us. She stands about three feet from the road. Cutting the underbrush back was a good idea on the Department of Highways' part.

We glide by. A brown flicker on the left. The calf bounds onto the road, heading for Mom. I watch him in the rearview mirror; he stops at the yellow line, the mother clambers up to meet him. They nuzzle each other, brown silhouettes against grey.

Max complained about Julia afterwards. That bitch is a real dummy, he said. But I understand why she did it. That's what happens when you're scared. You can't think straight. You'll do anything to not feel scared. I had started feeling that way about Max. It got to a point that if I knew he was on my shift that day, I could hardly eat my breakfast. Belly seized up at the thought of him, I'd choke trying to get cereal down. He drove a silver Dodge Ram with oversized tires. The bumper sticker read *Let's play carpenter. First, we get hammered, then I nail you.* The sight of it in the parking lot gave me instant gut rot.

But this is what I mean. These physical triggers, their purpose is to reinforce the reality of fear and shame. Love pangs and anxiety flutters. Nervous diarrhea even: we've evolved so that they serve a purpose. You might wonder what happens when they go away.

The light is fading. I press the gas. The brown shapes shrink behind us. Ten minutes, the GPS says.

It started for me with little twinges of discomfort I'd get when swallowing. At first, I blamed it on stress. But Dad had the cancer. Uncle Rob had the cancer. The endoscope was hell; doctor had to put me under to get it down my throat. The whole stomach has to come out, he said. Full gastrectomy. And when they took my stomach out and studied it, they found sixty-one precancerous lesions. A hidden ambush, right there.

It's still hard to eat. Gotta do tiny bites and if I swallow too fast, it comes up. No stomach means there's limited space for food to go. And there's little processing before stuff hits your bloodstream. My first bite of cake gave me instant queasiness all over.

When I went back to work, they had to find something for me to do. They got me to do presentations: Occupational

Health and Safety for new hires. I told myself public speaking would be scary. But the fear didn't happen. When my stomach was present, I would have hidden in the bathroom, taking deep breaths and releasing all that bubbles up with nerves. But no stomach meant no feelings. First time I ever spoke in public with dry hands.

A car approaches: a red hatchback. I glance at Jerry. The fringe of his hair curls up a little, like shiny black spider legs. Looks itchy. It's dark enough now for headlights. Best to keep them on until the turnoff. It's a bit of a gamble. Where there are two moose, there are many.

When I accidentally shoplifted the first time, I realized the possibilities. A pack of gum at the bottom of the basket; I forgot to put it on the counter. I shoved it in my back pocket and left. The gutful version of myself would have gone back, paid, apologized.

I was on a budget. It was hard to go from a solid paycheque to the sixty per cent disability threw at me. And no stomach meant a new approach to eating. Big meals became such a waste; I'd eat three bites and be full. I'd reheat the plate over and over, eating the same supper all night. Drinking plain water made me feel raw and chafed inside. The nutritionist said it wasn't a good idea anyway to fill up on no calories and it was vital I maintain my weight. Thirty-five pounds gone in the first four months. I needed new clothes. I needed to find ways to eat more. I stood in an aisle at Sobeys with a different protein drink in each hand, trying to decide which one to buy, and I just slipped them into my pockets. I paid for my other items: deodorant, raw almonds, yogurt. No one noticed. I waited for those fingers of worry to poke me from inside, but nothing. A couple of ghostly sensations. Nerve endings were cobwebs. I thanked the cashier. She put the change right into my hand.

The first raindrops hit the windshield. We'll be there in five minutes. If it rains all night, it may prove complicated. But I have enough supplies.

At first, the stealing happened in pairs like that. I'd be trying to decide between two types of products: recharge-able batteries, light bulbs, vitamin pills. The thought of returning one—remembering to keep the receipt, driving back to the store, finding a parking spot—shag that. I took them both. Then I always had extra stuff, so I gave it away. Dean caught on pretty fast to what I was doing. He usually came by once a week to play cards, so I'd offer things to him. I'd try to trade it for weed.

Dean knew a guy who ran one of those "outlet" markets supplemented with stolen stuff. He showed me how to make those bags with the foil lining that could fool the scanner. It was great for razor refills. Those things are marked up at least 200 per cent. I'd go to a drugstore and fill the bag when the aisle was empty.

We're getting close. I won't be able to stretch or piss once we turn off the road. Best to pull over for a minute. The grey of the sky deepens in its last attempts at light. Rain spits on the pavement. I relieve myself in the woods and do a few lunges. Jerry's stillness rings with anticipation. I get back in the car.

Where was I? I say. Oh yes. The stealing. It went on for months before I got caught. I was real cocky that day; I left the store and went to another part of the mall to go to the bathroom. Julia was there when I came out of the toilet. I had no idea she was store manager. Waiting with her arms folded. She wasn't a rigid ghost anymore; she was this fierce little woman with a buzz cut and a Walmart jersey.

But I was lucky with her. She pulled out her cellphone to call the cops. And I asked her to let me have a cup of coffee first. That's another thing; I wouldn't be so bold if my stomach was full of fear. We sat in the Tim Hortons and I sipped my double-double slow. Figured I'd talk to her until I got an idea.

I smile at Jerry. It's amazing when you meet someone again, someone you thought you knew, and it turns out you have so much in common. Julia and I are beings once ruled by fear. Mine was cut out while Julia had to chop up her whole life: sneaking belongings out of the house in small batches, squirrelling away money, finding people who could actually help her. That was the hardest, she said. I didn't want my family to have to deal with him. I didn't know where alliances lay. People don't understand. They see a nice house, they see Red Seal trades and three vehicles in the yard. Some even seemed to sympathize when he poisoned her recall; she was up for a contract on the mainland, working with hydraulics. Suddenly she was known as difficult, a complainer. Suddenly former co-workers weren't available to provide a reference. Well, he was upset at the time, they said. You know what Max is like. He can give it, but he can't take it. He's said it himself, he knows he flares up too easy.

But look at you now, I said. Even though it's not your ideal situation, you got promoted. You manage the whole store.

Indeed, Julia said. I have access to all the supplies.

The turnoff is hard to see in the dark. Good thing the

GPS gives us lots of notice. I mute it and turn off the head-lights as we creep up the drive. The silver Dodge Ram is parked in front, just like Julia said it would be. Nasal twangs of new country reverberate from the house. I let the car glide past and park by some trees.

Julia knew where to get the ingredients for thermite. We googled how it worked. There are videos for everything now. And Julia's really quite creative. Max had made a lot of enemies, she said. He'll likely blame his old ex or someone close to her. He still thinks I'm a big dummy, see. He doesn't know what a big dummy can do.

The possibilities are vast, I replied, depending on what's inside it.

The rain ends quickly. When the music stops and the lights go out, I haul Jerry out of the car. Dealing with Jerry is pretty awkward. With everything inside him, he's top-heavy, while his legs swing like a rag doll's. But I get him over the fence. The wet grass softens my footsteps. I lay Jerry on the hood of the Dodge Ram and prop up his back on the windshield. I arrange his nylon legs straight out from his torso. He's weighted at the feet and knees so he won't slip. I apply the lighter fluid in strategic places: the front of his shirt, the top of his camouflage pants. It's important that he doesn't flame up, but that everything simmers enough to get to his innards.

I lay one finger on the tip of Jerry's plastic chin. His synthetic eyes stare back into mine. I light his shirttail and cross the lawn in loping steps. I start the car. Jerry is smoking up. Julia said with Jerry's bum right over the centre of the hood, the thermite will heat up and become molten iron. She said it will pour into the engine block. His head and chest will melt gradually. I don't put on the headlights until I am past the house and speed up on my way to the pavement.

It's quiet back on the bypass road. I don't pass anyone else. It occurs to me that I didn't flash my headlights at that red hatchback after seeing the moose. That would have been the courteous thing to do.

THE LOBSTER

ON THE FIRST DAY OF Christmas vacation, Uncle Walter tells me the only shows he likes are the classics. When he's in the living room, the TV stays on the Retro Channel with its reruns of series like *All in the Family* and *Happy Days*.

Those reality TV shows melt your brain, Gaby, girl, he says. They don't make TV like this anymore.

I hate *The Honeymooners* and *Maude*, Aunt Zoe says. Just Americans yelling at each other.

Personally, I don't mind the Retro Channel—when you're a guest in someone's home, their ways and belongings can be a novelty. But when they announce *This show was filmed before a live studio audience*, all I can think of is how all those people are probably dead now and how it's a no-longer-live audience laughing at Archie and Edith Bunker (also no longer alive). If I was in my own space and still with Julian, he would get what I mean. But I'm only here till Boxing Day so I keep that morbid shit to myself.

Get Walter to tell you the eagle story was Mom's last piece of advice before she left for Jamaica. Back in November, when Julian and I broke up, every conversation she and I had came with suggestions for this visit. Mom has left every Christmas since Dad died, but now with no refunds on the flights home for Julian and me, she feels bad about not being in the province while I'm here. Aunt Zoe's invitation is definitely a pity present: poor Gaby, home from the mainland and alone in St. John's while her ex goes off to Central. So I am prepared with Mom's tidbits: Ask Cousin Melanie about rowing, her team did well in the Regatta. Aunt Zoe is a baking fiend, you can help her out. Melanie's kids are really into Minecraft. Make sure you take it easy. It's a difficult time of year. Hardships shine brighter at Christmas.

Helping Aunt Zoe in the kitchen proves difficult, as there is a gadget and a system for everything. Zesting a lemon doesn't happen with a grater; there's a zester on a hook over the sink. She cooks eggs with the antique egg coddlers on display in the glass cabinet. She has to show me how to use the lemon zester because it's shaped like an angelfish and I can't figure out how to grip it. I've never heard of egg coddling. Sweat perks on her hairline. Now, what did I do with the egg beater? she says. Sorry, Gaby, I get into a real puttering rhythm and lose track. Can't chew gum and walk at the same time, ha-ha.

In the basement, I watch the kids play games. Reese is six and wants me to play Mario Kart but is disappointed when he's way better at it than me. His sister, Sabrina, is nine. We watch cartoons until Sabrina says, There's a boy in my class named Cody. He told everyone he saw his mom give his dad a blow job. Do you know what a blow job is?

I do, I say. But you're too young for me to discuss words like that with you.

I know what it is, Sabrina says. The proper name is fellatio.

What's fell a-sheet-oh? Reese says.

I stare at the door. Any second, an adult member of my extended family will enter to find me discussing oral sex with two children. I have to go to the bathroom, I say.

The spare bedroom is mine for sleeping, but it doubles as an office and Cousin Melanie needs to work from home until Christmas Eve. Her employer runs a chain of luxury hotels and this is a busy season. In the mornings, I try to vacate by nine so she can get in and do her work. She says I can sleep in, it's no big deal, but every morning she's downstairs, dressed and prepared. She wears a lot of fuchsia and plucks her eyebrows into sharp, clean arches. I still dress for the office even when I'm home, she tells me. There are a lot of Skype meetings.

When I ask about these meetings, she discusses certain clients they've accommodated. She drops names I think I'm supposed to know. She asks about my work. As I explain what goes into auditing pension information, she swallows a yawn and how can I blame her, really. She points at the book I'm reading, *Us Conductors*, and I tell her it's a fictional account of a nonfiction character, about the man who invented the theremin. The story follows his journey from Russia to the USA and how he becomes a bit of celebrity, and when he meets the love of his life, suddenly the point of view of the story changes—he starts talking to her as *you* and the reader realizes they aren't really the audience, everything is about this person he can't be with.

Melanie sways in sturdy understanding, like she's withstanding a stiff breeze. Talking to her is like trying to open a pill bottle with one of those tricky childproof caps: push down and turn, spin and click, nothing. Julian would always open those for me.

It must be busy being an executive assistant, I say.

I'm the personal assistant, she says. The executive assistant has to deal with everyone. The PA goes between the CEO and the clients.

Maybe she told me this previously and I forgot. I excuse myself to go to the bathroom.

I take a bathroom break every ninety minutes or so, just to sit on the edge of the tub and not be seen. I flip through Aunt Zoe's collection of *Canadian House and Home* and consider words like palette and aesthetic, phrases like adding pattern and texture, this space features a fresh mix of blue and white. Stuff I would grab onto and play-say, create a special voice for. Like with yesterday's slippery sidewalks: Notice how the pavement surprises the eye with a matte appearance but is actually polished with a delicate layer of ice. Details like this make a memorable impact. I would play the clown with this kind of stuff until Julian said knock it off.

I will remember from now on that Melanie is a PA. That was the abbreviation Julian used when he thought I was being passive aggressive. Why is PA always your knee-jerk reaction? he said when I presented him with the blank Loblaws birthday cake.

It's not PA, I said. I heard you complain to Kevin that I ate the last piece of your promotion cake. So, here you go.

Oh my god, Gaby. If you're so pissed, why don't you tell me?

Why would you say those things if you weren't mad about the cake? You said it, I heard it, and now you've got another cake. I'm trying to fix the situation.

Jesus suffering Christ. Just call me an asshole already.

In Uncle Walter and Aunt Zoe's house, I am smiling and ready to engage. The past three days have been a flow of offerings: tea, chocolates, drinks, observations, and apologies: Oh, you're so quiet. Sorry we're not more entertaining. Carroll O'Connor was a big anti-drug activist. I wish Melanie's kids read more, like you. More snow on the way. Each time I settle down with my book, I wonder how long the stillness will last, like a penned animal bracing itself for the inevitable cage rattle.

I get outside even though, as Melanie says, everything is rotten with ice. I take two strolls a day. I pretend to admire the neighbour's outdoor lights reflecting in the icicles dangling from their roof. Lengthy icicles are a bold finish for window frames and unsightly roof gutters. Paired with a lingering anxiety over possible lack of proper home insulation, it evokes a daring "je ne sais quoi."

The neighbourhood houses are reruns of each other. There are parks nearby. There's a coffee shop on Commonwealth Avenue. I think the area has character, but maybe I'm seeing it with Greater Toronto Area eyes; all the brick houses we looked at, further and deeper into the suburbs. This neighbourhood would score Good Walkability on the Realtor.ca app we used. I don't want to live in a place where we have to drive to walk, I said. We should make that a priority.

We need space for two cars, he said. And a low mortgage.

So, we're going to purchase based on our current commutes? That can change.

Until you find a job you like, what choice do we have?

Julian said he has his own copy of *Us Conductors* and

I can keep this one. And when I was packing, he said I could take whatever I wanted. But I might write him when I'm finished to let him know my impressions. It could be part of a Happy New Year message.

On Tibb's Eve, Uncle Walter drinks Crown Royal and tells the eagle story. I remember Mom saying to bring it up and guilt nudges me for not remembering.

When I was a kid, he says, my dad and I would go duck hunting. We built up an isthmus on the river leading into the bay so we could walk out close to the middle. When the bay and the river froze over, the isthmus made this kind of eddy where the water didn't freeze. It was kind of a barachois, where the salt water meets fresh.

I nod and sip my wine. Isthmus, eddy and barachois. Uncle Walter is the kind of man who takes his knowledge for granted. Melanie likely gets it from him.

One day, it was February, I'm out walking and I see this eagle dive into that patch of water. It flies out with something large in its talons and flies up and up and up . . . and then it drops. Like a propeller.

Uncle Walter twirls his index finger down through the air. So I go over to where it landed, he says. And there's a lobster on the ground. And there's the eagle's body. No head. Completely decapitated.

Uncle Walter slaps the arm rest: What are the chances of that? He munches a Ganong Delecto as a reward.

So the lobster . . . chop-chop?

Yep. Got him in midair.

That's wild, I say.

I tell him he should have bought a lottery ticket that day, Aunt Zoe says.

Melanie rolls her eyes. He tells this story every time he drinks, she says. We hear it a thousand times a Christmas.

So what? Uncle Walter says. It's a good story. I like that lobster. Giving the ol' fuck you to its hunter.

Language, Aunt Zoe says.

Great story, I say. The wine warms my belly and I like that the TV is off and we're talking. It's really poetic, actually, I say.

Animals strike out when they're panicked, Melanie says. Everyone knows that.

The next day is Christmas Eve and Coffee Matters will close early. I have ten pages left in *Us Conductors*. I will walk the neighbourhood and finish the book with a latte.

I catch Melanie's comment as I pull on my boots. It's a quiet aside to Aunt Zoe: House guests are like fish.

Shh, girl, Aunt Zoe says. Be nice.

I know how the saying ends. After three days, they stink. I tighten my laces. You people invited me. I didn't ask for this.

Outside, a neighbour's trash bag is ripped and it looks like something's gotten into it. One can enjoy subtle winter shades on their own or pep them up with splashes of colour. Like a bouquet of intense hues from a torn bag of garbage, frozen to the ground. Someone else's garbage tucked under Melanie's bed would be a lesson in stink. I step around takeout containers and brown lettuce. How can I be that annoying? I'm staying clear of everyone. What a bitch.

It has snowed, but the sidewalks are mostly cleared. The roads are built wide to accommodate multiple vehicle ownership. Julian and I saw communities like this, newly built houses with designated parks. We can't afford it now, he said. Maybe after the starter house. Maybe after kids.

But we've moved so many times, I said. And I loved the bungalow, the one with the finished basement and secluded yard.

We'll have to budget hard to make a down payment, he said. No restaurants for a long time.

The air is calm around the house with the hum of businesses a few streets over. Cousin Melanie had all these things growing up, her own room, a clean house, places to go. Maybe she's never·had to share them. Maybe for her, I am monopolizing the holiday resources, the attention, the space, the Ganong Delectos. People get territorial. Julian got that way with the thermostats: If you want your dream house, put on a sweater. Turn it down and layer up.

I am walking fast. I'll get to Coffee Matters in no time. After I finish the last ten pages of *Us Conductors*, I'll want to dawdle, stay absent longer. Fucking Melanie, fucking extended family, making me toss my time in the trash. When I get near the café, I should see if there's any shops around where I can buy a scented candle or an air freshener. Here you go, Melanie, to mask my house-guest stench. Or I could clean the spare bedroom so it's way better than I found it. They taught us to do that in Girl Guides, I'll say. Make sure you aren't left with my visitor hum.

The sidewalk is covered with thick snow. A stamped line of footprints weaves its way into someone's lawn from the sidewalk. Rather than stick to convention, this winter day isn't afraid to mix it up a little. Here, we've stamped random trails through snowbanks, possibly through old dog shit, for a cohesive, yet unexpected, design. Maybe the municipal workers are disgruntled and gave up the snow clearing. The hell with this, they said. We need a raise.

On Julian's birthday, he wanted a wine and cheese. He picked up good stuff, not the no-name brands and coupon products we'd purchased for months. The price tag on the wine was $66.50. Châteauneuf-du-Pape. I wasn't consulted.

Once all the birthday party guests arrived and I had drunk myself bold, I turned all the thermostats down. I left a folded stack of sweaters on a chair. Put them on if you're cold, I said. We have to keep things tight these days. Kevin's wife shivered in her black mini dress. I handed her a Costco-brand fleece.

The next day, Julian talked continuously while picking up empties. My head throbbed. I grew up in a house where people yelled when they were mad, he said. We got it all out at once. It wasn't a big deal.

I don't want to yell and scream every time I'm frustrated.

All couples need to learn how to disagree. We should know how to do this by now. It always has to be death by a thousand cuts with you.

There is one set of footprints before mine in the park. They leave the walkway and arch around out into the grounds. Snowflakes fall in a hovering, encircling pattern. Disco-ball snow is what Julian called it. I wipe one from my eye. A figure stands about twenty metres away. They have walked out into the clearing. They are just standing there.

I wave. No response. They are dressed all in yellow. I take out my phone like I have many times before in Toronto, pretending I'm texting or talking so I can let the man pass me or be ready to call for help, take a picture. I cannot tell if the person sees me. Maybe they are an apparition. This is the moment I see a ghost; this is when my whole belief system does a nosedive. I wave again. Nothing. Are you okay? I ask. My voice emerges chipped on the edges.

The person's hands are clasped before them, their head raised, looking ahead, not quite at me, but at something beyond. It's a man with a beard. Snow is collecting all over his body. He is doing nothing about it.

A dog barks and I almost fucking die of fright. It bumbles into view, some kind of terrier. It circles the man, sniffs, and lifts its leg. The man is a statue now, a plastic figure. One of the wise men from a nativity scene, stolen and abandoned. Some wise-ass took a wise man.

The owner calls the dog. My legs are triggered back into action. It could be a neighbour of Walter and Zoe. Later, they'll pop in and recognize my coat in the porch, oh, were you out earlier trying to talk to the wise man? Melanie's eyes rolling. People rolling their eyes really is the worst facial expression. It should be illegal.

I make new footprints through the walkway. The dog and its owner move into the grounds. They don't look at me. I am alone here, making a big deal over nothing.

I return to the start of the path and go to the coffee shop. The last ten pages of the novel are perfect. I stare out the window and watch disco-snow dance and imagine theremins playing. Today was the first day I felt anger and fear since I put the book in my bag and left. When Julian became irritated, I was overcome with a wariness, like walking alone through a parking lot, checking the parked cars.

Are the engines running? Can drivers see me? How alone am I? The lobster wasn't brave. It was pulled out of everything it knew. It reacted out of the biggest fear it had ever known.

Back in the house, Melanie's down in the basement with the kids. Uncle Walter pours me a glass of wine. The Retro Channel is on. *All in the Family* was filmed before a live studio audience, the announcer says.

I bet that live studio audience is dead now, I say.

Oh, indeed, Uncle Walter says. A totally dead studio audience.

Shh, you two, Aunt Zoe says. That's so dark.

Uncle Walter slurps his drink. I don't see it like that, he says. I like knowing I'm still alive to do the laughing.

THE MUMMERS PARADE

Sasha

CLYDE SAYS THE PARADE TAKES about an hour from Bishop Feild school around Georgetown to Bannerman Park and back. I can smell my own breath inside the horse-head mask and my hips are sweating under all this padding. But Judith's pink lips shine bright through her face doily and she's so excited to see the other mummer-fied kids her size.

Wow, Mommy, she says. Everyone looks magic!

I could friggin' squish her.

Maybe I should have worn pyjama pants, like Clyde. He jokes his sleeping attire will give away his identity, as in some old hook-up could recognize him. He's probably right. St. John's knows way too much about each other's inside clothes.

Lauren

Extra socks are first on the list of What I've Neglected Today. Already, the pavement cold is seeping into my foot bones. Billy reaches for my hand and slips the flask from his sleeve into mine. That's better.

There must be at least three hundred masked strangers. We are a mass representation of a smaller time, when it was acceptable to grab an opportunity for a little leverage on your neighbour, especially if they were well off. Get a little gawk at their properties and guzzle their winter stores of rum. Because in the haze of alcoholic groupthink, it's their problem if they can't see through your disguise. Surely your own neighbour should be able to recognize the glint in your eye.

But I do love a tradition of skulduggery and numb-skullery, even when it's purely symbolic.

Sasha

The Mummers Parade contains a feeling of some ancient mischief, like if I don't pay attention, Judith might wander off and be replaced with a changeling. Last year she wasn't big enough and the weather was shit. Maybe this can become our tradition, something she can anticipate more than the Santa Claus Parade. We'll say we're avoiding raising another consumer and be right smug about it: Oh, Judith dies for the Mummers Parade. Somehow it's less creepy than a strange man in the chimney.

Bells jangle and people whoop and sing. We wave at photographers and strangers. This is weird and fun, Judith says. I keep my balance with my new long horse neck and head. My legs pump under their saddlebag pillows. It's a pretty good workout, when you think about it.

Lauren

Five minutes into the parade and all I can think of is if Sasha wants to be a good mummer, she needs to suck in that voice. There it is, Sasha's rat-a-tat-tat giggle. My heart turns to eggshell.

There's a mummer behind me who could be her. Sasha's height, in an overstuffed costume with a horse's head. It's been over a dozen years, but I am 95 per cent sure it's her. High stats for me since I'm never 100 per cent sure on anything. Really, no one should ever be 100 per cent sure.

Sasha

My eyes return to the mummer with the lampshade hat and crazy quilt. It's Lauren's quilt with those mint green and fuchsia patches on the back. If I get close, I bet I'll see the cross-stitch sampler her grandmother added, the "Families are Forever" bit.

I kept my hand steady on that patch as I wrapped her up and placed her in the back seat of the taxi. Lauren's back soaked and frozen and on fire. My face wet as we turned onto the parkway. Heat jacked to bust.

She's not on Facebook. I checked back in 2007 or so, when everyone else first joined. For a while, I thought maybe she got married or chose an alias. Then the site stopped letting people do that, so I tried again a couple of years ago. Fucking Scott is on though, with regular posts from his BC life. He has a baby with a striking woman. She is lean and elegant and looks too sophisticated for him. He lost his hair, or enough of it to legitimize the tough-guy, shaved-head thing. I wondered how his profile would make Lauren feel. If she was online. If she looked at it.

Underneath the lampshade, the mummer wears a veil, black or navy blue, a slate of a face. Lauren's blanket and facelessness. I used to worry she'd end up some kind of ghost.

Lauren

Billy holds my arm and laughs at the guy in front. Buddy's putting on a real show. He wears a pink tutu and shakes a tambourine: When I say mummers, you say lawd'in. Mummers!

Lawd'in!

Mummers!

Lawd'in!

No one can tell if you don't sing or yell when your face is covered. No one can tell if you're smiling or your toes are froze or you're half cut at teatime.

If it's Sasha, that's her kid. I spotted her in Sobeys around five years ago, the baby tucked in a carrier on her chest like a rosebud. I hid in the pet supply section, praying she didn't still have Bella and need dog food. Then she didn't enter the aisle and I thought, of course, Bella would be over fifteen now. Bella's probably long gone.

And suddenly I was angry all over again. Fuckin' Sasha, too chicken for a confrontation, taking off in the middle of the night with a note, the most cowardly form of communication or at least it was before we all started texting. *We both know it's not working. It's just easier this way. You already know my concerns.* Couldn't even allow Bella and me a goodbye, like I was too much of a shit show to be around a dog. Getting up that morning, padding around the apartment, seeing all the empty shelves. Listening for the tick of paws on hardwood and then nothing and Sasha, how fucking could you.

Sasha

In Georgetown, people wave from their homes. Clyde and Judith do a little dance in front of Lorraine Maddigan in her doorway. She laughs and pretends she doesn't know who Judith is. It's so friggin' darling.

The mummer who might be Lauren claps and moves slowly. We're about to pass the corner of Mullock and Hayward. If it's her, I wonder if she remembers calling me from that house party: He says he doesn't want to be with me anymore. I can't take it. It hurts so much. And the next day, her bedroom door didn't open. Hard night, hungover, okay. Deciding to make her lunch, laying out the bread and condiments and opening the cutlery drawer and the slot for kitchen knives was empty. When she finally got up to go to the bathroom, I found them in a bird's nest pile under her bed, like she wanted to have a variety of varying length and sharpness, like she was doing a survey.

Judith tucks her hand into mine. She hasn't asked to be carried yet. Maybe we can all get naps this afternoon. This exhaustion didn't exist when it was Lauren, Bella and I in our little Lime Street house. I'd come home tired but be welcomed by them and feel alive all over again. Vitamin L and

B. I thought it would be the same with Judith and Clyde. Instead, it's tired, so many layers and textures and flavours of tired. Always something to be done that isn't done and needs to be done now, can't you see, it's garbage day, we're out of milk, we're out of so many things. No, it is not my turn. Always a pause and reminder to be patient, to wait before speaking. I could let it all out with Lauren and she'd hand me a glass, a candy, a morsel of something. She would make herself so fully a friend of mine.

Lauren

I love the safety in incognito, Billy says. I nod. How many in this parade are taking long looks at former secret spaces? There's the place Scott broke up with me, right out of the blue: I love you, but not as much as I've loved others. So it's not really fair to you. And we were so, so loaded and I was crying and it felt like everything was coming out of me until I could taste nothing but booze and grief. Staggering home in a T-shirt, the winter snow cold enough to burn.

And then Scott came back and everything was apologies and tears. I got out of the Waterford and we pretended everything was okay, like it made us closer. We possessed this new knowledge branded with permanent status: I did something serious and he's taking it seriously. It must be love.

Sasha would have none of it: What is it about this guy? I don't get how he can have this kind of hold on you. This makes me nervous. Me sitting up in bed, shaking my head at her: You don't get it. You wouldn't understand.

I get why she wanted to run away from me. Because you can't just do that and not have everyone know you can do it. And we still know what I did is something I can do. How I hated it. How I hate it.

Sasha

Fucking Scott. Just stay away, I said. Let her get over you. Off to the Waterford he goes, all apologies and caresses. Sasha, how dare you tell the doctors not to let me in? Who actually says the words how dare you?

How are you going to look out for her? I asked him. And he was all, We love each other, we're all each other needs. Then he can't even take Bella out for walk when he knew Lauren was with doctors all day and I had work and class. I've got a lot on my mind, he said as I laid paper towels on the dog shit trail from the kitchen to her bedroom. It's not like the dog is mine.

Maybe it's not her quilt. Maybe my eyeballs are trained to see her in bits of other people. Like the shade she dyed her hair, that birch-bark blond. One of the moms in Judith's class has the same shade, plus Lauren's complexion, like icing sugar on strawberry mousse. She introduced herself, Melissa or Melanie, asked if Judith was in swimming. We talked about the Aquarena and the new community centre in the East End.

Later, I remembered how Lauren would paint a perfect swoop of waterproof black eyeliner on her top eyelids, every day. And that guy, whatshisface, Robert Mahon, we were just getting on the go, he said that eyeliner swoop proved she was *batshit* with her *crazy eyes*. And I agreed and now I resent him and myself, because *batshit* and *crazy* validated dissolving the situation into something I could stomp around with: Well, if Lauren wants to be this weak and clichéd over some asshole, she's not as sharp as I thought she was. I regret that now. But no one ever talked about what it meant to want to kill yourself back then.

Lauren

Billy staggers when we get to Bishop Feild. I thread my arm under his pits. What do you need, b'y, what do you need. We're back now, we can stop. His eyes find mine through our disguises. I'm so froze, girl. Water, please.

The volunteers should have some.

I'll be good here, he says. I'll wait.

Water for Billy. If Sasha's here with her family when I come back, I'll say hello. Ugh no. I'll lift my doily. She's with her kid, she may not want to. But I want to give her that, I don't know, an offering. Here, see. Here I am.

Sasha

Back at Bishop Feild, there's live music and trays of refreshments. The crazy quilt mummer stands alone. It will not hurt to guess. I can even guess she's someone else, someone other than Lauren. Either way, it's an excuse to get up close.

The mummer who could be Lauren freezes as I approach. The lampshade head lowers in fixation, like a bull about to charge. Within three feet, I spot the bristles on his chin through the veil. I keep moving. My heartbeat is a cold trickle in my chest.

Judith pulls my dress. She wants a cookie. Clyde says his feet hurt. Fine then, fine. A cookie, a look around and home, I say.

Judith nods. I love the Mummers Parade, she says. It's the best. Like Halloween and Christmas, all wrapped up together.

GUTLESS BRAVADO, PART TWO

SANDWICHES ARE A JOB TO EAT. So many simultaneous categories of food. Digesting a sandwich makes my post-gastrectomy body feel like Windows 10 with too many applications open.

But the gastro doctor says this is normal. After they removed my stomach, they made a kind of bag from the bottom of my esophagus and the top of my intestine. Gradually, it will stretch and be able to hold more food. Until then, I get full quickly and digestion steals my energy. The doctor said I have to keep challenging myself with more food, more variety. He makes eating sound like preparing for a math exam. But I'm still on disability and have lots of time. Every day I eat a sandwich and a salad, no matter how long it takes. A lettuce leaf is a crumpled sheet of paper, snagged in my core.

Dean picked up a ticket to Dublin on a seat sale and I get to stay in his house while he's gone. I am lucky for homeowner friends like Dean who know I crave solitude. I am lucky to live in this present, when my DNA can be tested for prickish little demise-plotting genes. I am lucky to live in a country where expensive surgical procedures don't bankrupt me. These are things I tell myself. I make my hand write them down. Maybe if I write them down, I'll eventually feel too fulfilled to pour a drink or light up a smoke.

I think when Dean bought the house in Mount Pearl, he believed he was doing what he thought he was supposed to be doing. His permanent job with Schlumberger means good pay and benefits. His Mount Pearl house has a garage and basement, a back deck and a freshly paved driveway, on a freshly paved street. His house sits with a fringe of similar houses with spotless vinyl siding in comfortable colours, diplomatically alike with their allotments of land and sunlight access, in a new housing division named after a local athlete who placed in the Olympics.

But I am five days in and the sterility is fading. Neighbourhood rhythms surface: winter barbeques, shed parties, beers in garages, smokes in driveways. It is a community of drinking buddies and play dates. Women pad across wide streets carrying cellophane-wrapped trays for their book clubs/wine tastings/ladies' nights. Men stand together outside drinking beers, examining each other's parked equipment: trucks, skidoos, campers. The women have arduous, processed hairstyles. The men wear ball caps and moustaches. This is the dream they all wanted, everyone in their own nest. And Dean believed if he made the nest, the woman would come. But it's still no ladybird for Dean.

He hasn't done much decorating. A few family photos: one with Dean in his twenties, his hair long but already thinning. Some Chinese trinkets he picked up on a work trip to Beijing: a leathery map in a frame; a statue of Guan Yu, god of war and business. The kitchen feels unused but ready for action. Cupboards lined with patterned paper, a spotless stove. I have never known Dean to cook. The few dishes I dirty for sandwiches and salads seem odd and sparse in the dishwasher, so I wash them by hand. This limbo kitchen makes me a little sad.

The living room is spacious, with wide windows facing the street. While I digest, I lie on the couch with the side window cracked to let in fresh air and neighbourhood sounds. Dean's coffee table bursts with magazines, mostly *Time* and *Sports Illustrated*. I root through them for something to read and discover a coil-bound three-subject notebook. Dean has filled the first section with hand-drawn graphs. Each graph is six rows of six squares and each square has one or two check marks or an X and he has tabulated a score at the bottom: $10,550. $5,000. $12,750. Some boxes contain dollar amounts in them. I am confused about the game, but it looks familiar.

I am sorry for whatever it is I am doing wrong. This is what the woman from the house on the right says as she crunches her way to her door. The man with her has been talking since they were in the car, the tumble-dry reverberation of his voice at a steady idling of frustration: Every goddamn time we see your friends. Every time.

Then voices of kids outside, the shush of snow pants, one of them singing a jingle from somewhere. Do-DO-do-do, do-DO-do. The *Jeopardy!* theme song. This is what Dean is doing in the notebook; he's keeping score to see how well he does at *Jeopardy!* And this also makes me a little sad. But I check the graphs again. The two checks in each square must mean he got the answer before the contestant rung in. There are lots of double checks. Good job, Dean.

The last subject section in the notebook does not contain *Jeopardy!* scores and after staring at the scrawls for a minute,

I realize it is a journal of sorts. I make a mental note to remember where I found the notebook on the coffee table.

And then I read it. Fuck it, like he wouldn't go through my stuff. The guy found out about my surgery by poking through my papers. What's this? he said, holding up the stool specimen requisition. What do you have to turn in your shit for?

Most of Dean's entries are about women. The first entry is about a woman named Mary: *She's a hot mess that's been reheated too many times.* This makes me laugh because I can hear Dean saying it. Other entries have dates and times and he mentions POF and it takes me a while to realize it stands for Plenty of Fish:

> *Jan. 15th, POF date, Lana, real estate agent, 42. Nice, but no spark. Into running and when I said it was bad for her knees she got a bit uptight.*

> *Feb. 9th. Joyce from across the street had a party. Met Kara there. She lives in the neighbourhood. Very shy with angelic face. Met Shelly too. Cute, blond, big tits. Reads tarot cards. I don't go in for that shit, but I might let her read mine just to see what she says about me.*

> *Feb. 16th. Asked out a missus from POF, Debbie. I'd been talking to her for a week or so. She said no cause it was obvious I was waiting for Valentine's Day to be over. Whatever you say, Missus.*

> *Feb. 25th. Joyce says I should go out with Kara. Says she's a single mom, two kids, she needs to meet more nice guys. I said I wasn't sure about kids, but I thought she was very pretty.*

Feb. 27th. Hooked up with Shelly after 2 weeks of texting.
When I got her bra off, her tits popped out twice as big
as I expected. It was like opening a can of surprise
snakes.

I laugh out loud at that, which sounds weird by itself
in the living room. Maybe the neighbours can hear me.
How aware are they of my presence? I lie and listen. The
voice of the father of the family on the left says, You kids
are ridiculous. You could heat the house with the number
of computer screens on. I shut the window. There is a naked
intimacy in the suburbs that leaves me dark inside. From
now on, I'll close the curtains. I'll park Dean's car in the
garage when I return from errands.

When the sun goes down, I'm idle. Maybe a glass of
wine. Dean told me I could help myself to whatever food
and drink is in the house, but I plan on replacing the bottles
I've gone through. Like everything else, his wine collection
is ready for presentation. Wine is instant warm euphoria
from my mouth right into my bloodstream. I keep the
empties so I can remember the brands and dates I've consumed.

I read more entries as I polish off the Malbec. They
make me feel less sad for Dean—at least he's getting some
action. I wonder when this need will return for myself.
Companionship. A bit of touch. My libido departed along
with my stomach. I don't miss it yet.

March 3rd. Joyce still wants me to ask out Kara. She told
me a story about some asshole who hangs around her.
The guy shows up once or twice a week with groceries
and doesn't leave until she cooks him dinner. He always

comes when he knows she's alone with her kids and can't go anywhere. I told Joyce that sounded really sketchy.

March 4th. Shelly wants to get together again. Her place smells like eggs and patchouli, kind of grosses me out.

March 10th. Bumped into Kara at Sobeys. She had taken a cab there and I offered her a ride home. Back at her place, there was a black car parked in front, and when she saw it she got quiet. I offered to help her take her groceries in, but she grabbed all five bags in a lazy man's load and took off. It's too bad because she's very sweet and we had a nice conversation about travelling in Asia as she lived in Korea for a bit. I like her laugh.

March 13th. Hooked up with Shelly again. The sex was pretty good, but then she wanted to loan me all these books on homeopathy and when I said I didn't believe in it, she got pissed.

I wake up on the couch. I have to stop doing this. Or at least fall asleep on my side, although having no stomach means I don't puke often or very much at once. Maybe I should ask my doctor about the risk of choking on vomit.

If I was more comfortable in the neighbourhood, I'd go for a walk. But I don't like the idea of trotting by people's houses looking into the wide windows into their lives. I don't want to be watched from living rooms and kitchen dinettes. But I want to go out. I'll go to the liquor store and replace the wine I've drunk.

At the NLC, I buy five bottles to replace Dean's and it costs almost a hundred and twenty fucking dollars. No more drinking Dean's wine. I get a box of Pinot Grigio for myself even though white wine fucks me up. I'd better be careful.

When I come out of Sobeys, there is a woman standing by the car. She holds two cloth bags of groceries and makes small nervous steps back and forth. She looks like she wants to smoke. Or I think this because I'm trying not to smoke. She jumps when I remote unlock the car.

Oh. You're not Dean.

No, I'm just using his car. Dean's in Ireland.

Oh yes. He told me that. You're the house-sitter. Sorry. I was waiting for the bus and recognized his car.

Do you want a ride home?

It's okay. She hauls the bags up and winces slightly. Well, if you don't mind. The bus is taking forever.

It's no problem.

And I'm Kara.

Hi.

Kara gnaws her cuticles for most of the drive. She asks a lot of questions and nibbles while I talk. Most of her questions are about Dean: How long have I known him, how did we meet, how do I like the house, what was he like when he was younger? I mention the picture of him with his long hair and she giggles and she really is cute. When she notices the box of wine, she says it's her favourite. I like the cheap stuff, she says. Then she immediately apologizes and I laugh and tell her the cheap stuff is great. She tells me where her house is and when we get close to her place, she says, Oh fuck.

What's wrong?

Nothing, she says. Some company I'd rather not have.

A black Pontiac Sunfire is parked in front of her house. The snow on the lawn has thawed in patches and is peppered with kids' toys. Someone is sitting in the car; I can see the outline of a ball cap and the crook of an elbow on the window's edge. I pull over and Kara thanks me quick and scurries up the walk with her cloth bags. The Sunfire driver doesn't move.

I'm right in the mood to act like a brat. I could stroll up to the car, talk at him like a nosey neighbour. I loop around, re-enter the street, and park a few houses from Kara's. The Sunfire driver is out of the car now, crossing the lawn. He's gangly and walks cocky, wide steps with his hands in his pockets. I can't see his face, just a Bulls ball cap. Jeans and a jean jacket. What's that called? The Canadian tuxedo. A white-haired woman stands in front of him, shaking her head. She holds up her hands and he sidesteps around her. She yells at his back, We don't need this. He walks into the house and shuts the door. I use my phone to take a photo of his licence plate. Not that I know what to do with it, but I feel like his presence should be recorded.

Instead of going home, I stop at the McDonald's. It takes forever to eat a hamburger, but I figure I can take small bites while I wait. I park across the street and a few doors down from Kara's house. Dean's car is one of those silver Hyundais everyone has. Hopefully I'm not too conspicuous.

The sun is down when he leaves Kara's. His shoulders are stiff in his jean jacket and he makes a point of stomping the purple My Little Pony castle on his way up the walk, which makes me laugh. I want to be a nuisance to him real bad. I've probably been too bored lately. I want to find out where he lives. Maybe some kind of prank is in order: a bag of flaming dog shit, random cash-on-delivery orders. Maybe I just need to follow him, something might come to mind like it did with Max. I set up my phone on the dashboard. Filming him is a good idea if he has a tricky route.

I try to keep a car or two between us. He enters the Tim Hortons drive-through on Merchant Drive and I wait in the parking lot for him. But when he indicates to go left, he turns right instead. Bastard. Then a couple more tricks like that, signalling to turn into Smitty's, but going straight, then left instead of right on Old Placentia Road.

He starts speeding up on Southlands Boulevard and I don't want to follow him till the end cause there's nothing really down there. But he takes the exit onto the highway towards St. John's. If he goes into town, I'll probably lose him. He might drive around all night. He might lead me to a dead end and confront me. He might keep a weapon in his car. He speeds up and I do too. At least he can't do a U-turn on the divided highway. I'll turn off at Kilbride if he goes past.

The Sunfire does at least a hundred on the ramp and doesn't slow for the yield/merge sign. He flies along the shoulder of the highway. There is another vehicle, a blue Volvo, in the right lane. The Sunfire speeds by, passing on the right. The Volvo swerves into the left lane too fast. It tips into the barrier between the divided highways and rolls, once, twice, once more. The Sunfire doesn't stop, its red back lights like cat eyes shrinking. I pull over. The Volvo has landed right side up, right before the opposite highway. I get my phone. Stop goddamn filming. 911 ready to press. The driver's door opens and a man steps out. His face is shock white, but he stands straight and unharmed. He takes three precise steps and regards his car, his own hands. There are no other passengers. An oncoming car on the other side slows and stops. People come towards him. You okay? You okay, buddy? I put Dean's car back in drive and pull back onto the road.

Back in Dean's area, music vibrates from the neighbours' house. Vehicles line the street, gleaming with industry. The roads here are wide and accommodating. I imagine they planned to contrast with the narrow pathways downtown. I fiddle with the keys and let the voices bounce around me. Does Dean receive invitations to local get-togethers? Did he get the code to click open the cliques? He's made the investment. He should be part of this world.

Inside, I pop the box of wine in the fridge. My guts contain discomfort from the hamburger. I chew gum to get things moving inside me, grinding the gears for intestinal momentum. Christ, eating is so much effort, I have to practise for it. But if it's one thing that makes life easier in the long run, it's worth it.

The Sunfire is back at Kara's two days later. I borrow Julia's car to use to wait for him. When he's inside, I leave the note under his windshield wiper. Just one sheet of paper with a still from the little film I made that shows the Sunfire slipping past the blue Volvo. One sentence: *Stay away or this goes to the cops.*

I do a little drive-by every day before Dean comes back. Six days, no sign. I vacuum and clean the bathrooms before his flight comes in. I leave the rest of the box of wine in the fridge. Not all ladies like the pricey stuff, I'll tell him. He should drink it with someone he likes.

BRADLEY AND MOLLY

MOLLY HATED HOW EVERYONE LUMPED her with Bradley. It's only geography and population, she wanted to say. Geography meaning Man's Harbour and population meaning seventy-seven. Bradley was the only person in Man's Harbour her own age, in her grade. That meant they took the bus to school together every day, they were in the same classes, and they attended the same Sunday mass. The school covered all the kids from all the surrounding communities, but in Man's Harbour, it was just her and Bradley.

Molly's house sat at the end of Man's Harbour Road and she should have been the first person picked up on the school bus. But Bradley got on the bus on its way to her, even though it would pass his house again on its return. Always the only one on the bus when Molly got on, sixth seat from the front with his slow-blinking eyes and hair parted scissor-sharp on the left, where his mother combed it. Bradley first thing with a question about math homework or their English assignment: Molly, you get page twenty-two done? And she wordlessly passed her notebook to him. But he'd have more questions anyway: How'd you get that answer? I didn't understand the ending to that story.

Whenever there was an event like a sock hop or a party, the phone rang and there was Bradley's hollow timbre: Molly, are you going? Can I get a ride, please? And her parents said absolutely, lots of room, this is what neighbours do, and she wasn't allowed to say no. Bradley's mother was so grateful. With Bradley's father always on the road, she said, it's such a blessing to have good neighbours. She sent Bradley over on the weekends with fresh eggs and home-made bread to thank them. Bradley, wandering into Molly's house, planting himself on the living room couch: Whatcha watching? And Molly wanting to leave the room and her parents saying, be polite to your guest now. Bradley in her house, Bradley on the bus, Bradley on the phone. She and Bradley, getting out of the truck together. Here they come, Bradley and Molly.

In junior high, there was air cadets and baseball games. Bradley joining up too, needing to be picked up, needing a way home. Unlike school, where the teachers would give her sister or Bradley's sister homework to take home if they were sick, the coaches and cadet leaders would give her messages to pass on to Bradley, as if she was his keeper, as if telephones didn't exist.

Then senior high, and Molly overhearing some of the boys list off the single girls in school in a teasing way, provoking someone to ask out someone, and the surprise in Jeremy Collier's voice: Molly's single? I thought she was with that Bradley dope. Getting on the school bus and little Patsy Billings in grade five showing Molly her new binder with her list of senior high couples doodled on it: Tracey + Colin, TLA. Shelly n' Todd. Bradley + Molly forever!

Why'd you write that? Molly asked. We're not together.

And Patsy's sad eyes: Did you guys break up?

Bradley was ever-present, insisting his part. The occasions when Molly's parents were out of town and she and her sister threw a party and Bradley always managing to find out about it on the day of, even though she did her best not to discuss it on the bus or in class. Right after supper, Bradley on the telephone: Molly, you having a party tonight? Can I come, please? And she'd sigh and say yes, come after ten o'clock, but sure enough, there he'd be, fumbling up the driveway at eight, the first person to arrive. I was bored so I thought I'd come down. Drinking his grape Crush while she and her sister put beer in the fridge. Sitting up straight at the dining table so he's the first goddamn person anyone sees when they enter the house. I'm not going to drink till I'm legal, Bradley said over his pop. Goody for you, Molly said. I bet that makes your mother very happy.

Meanwhile, there were other things that only she seemed to notice. Sitting next to Bradley in the cab of the truck, tolerating the quiver of his knees and elbows. Realizing he was staring at her and when she met his eyes, his gaze slithering down to the bulge in his gym pants. His little half smile. Catching him staring at her chest when she got on the bus. She glared back ferociously, his innocent blink in reply and continuing to gaze at her tits until she sat down. The way he always managed to forget if she or her sister were in the bathroom at her house, the way he tried the door before knocking. Goosing her from behind in gym class and pretending it was an accident. I was just trying to get the basketball, he said and that smile again, but now directed at the other boys. His shoulders jiggling with secret laughter, as if she was his, due to time and proximity, as if he'd earned a right to do that to her.

Molly hid from him when she got the chance. Saturday morning television and there's Bradley, over-combed and bear-marching up the driveway, Molly scrambling to get the TV off, ducking behind the couch with her sister while he knocked on the door. Hullo? Anyone home? Catching a glimpse of him and his mother carrying bags of school supplies through the food court in the Valley Mall; she stayed in the gift shop, reading birthday cards until she was sure they were gone.

Now it's grade twelve and spring and less than three months left to sweet freedom. She had preliminary acceptance for both MUN and Dalhousie. Bradley applied for trade schools, the military, Fisher Tech. Soon there would be a fresh start and new places. But it would be nice to get with Jeremy Collier before everyone disappeared with summer jobs and vacations. Jeremy Collier, not the most handsome, but magnetic and clever. His laugh resonated in the hallways and made her smile in knee-jerk empathy. He walked with comfortable confidence and she liked the way he moved his hands when he spoke, not huge gestures, but with precision, to strengthen points. He used people's names when he talked to them. When Jeremy talked to her, she felt known.

The Colliers' house was two communities over in St. Victor's and Jeremy's parents gave him permission to throw the end-of-year party. Molly had never been inside the house, but she was told the Colliers had a Jacuzzi and a backyard surrounded by trees with no neighbours close by who could complain about noise. There were four bedrooms and a basement with a pool table. Most of the grade twelves said they were going; a few said no way, like Mark Stead, who said Jeremy was a snot, but everybody knew Mark was just pissed because he didn't have enough credits to graduate. Molly thought about the Jacuzzi and her bare legs next to Jeremy's. She thought about four bedrooms. She thought about the logic of losing her virginity before university.

Molly, you going to Jeremy's party? Bradley next to her in the hallway. His mouth left open after his slack pronunciation of party. *Par-tah.*

Nope.

Oh. I was hoping to get a ride.

No one's going to that party.

Sounds like almost everyone is.

Nope. Molly's eye caught on the yellow Xeroxed sign on the bulletin board: *Last School Dance of the Year.* She pointed to it.

Everyone's going to the dance. No one's going to Jeremy's.

Really? Bradley gaped at the poster. H'okay then. Can I get a ride?

Sure.

On the evening of the last day of school, Molly got permission to take the truck. Bradley called twice: first to ask when she's going to the dance, second to say he'll be waiting by the end of his driveway. She saw him combing his part as she got close.

Look at this, Bradley said. He opened his coat and pulled out a paper bag. One large Wildberry cooler.

I took it from Mom. That's why I didn't want you to pull into the house.

Livin' on the edge, Bradley my son.

There were only a few cars in the rec centre parking lot. Molly recognized some of the grade ten students standing around the entrance, sullen and bored. Patsy Billings and some of the grade six girls stood by the corner of the building. Finished grade six, really. Exercising their big-girl rights to be there. Bradley got out of the truck and stood with the door open.

Hardly anyone here.

Yep. Anyway, Bradley, I gotta run an errand.

Where ya goin?

Bradley, I don't have to tell you where I'm going.

Are you coming back? You're coming back, right?

Why?

Well . . . Bradley fidgeted with the edge of the truck door. I thought you were going to the dance. And I need a way back.

You said you wanted a ride here, not a ride back.

No, I asked for a ride.

If you wanted a ride back, you should have been specific.

That's not fair.

Well, that's life, Bradley. Molly reached for the door handle. Have fun.

In the rear-view mirror, Bradley stood with his shoulders slumped. Pity twanged her heart and she resented him for it.

There were so many people at Jeremy Collier's house that parked vehicles spilled out of the driveway and lined the side of the road. Inside, she and Christa Healey sat on the living room floor drinking and playing caps until she gained enough nerve to approach Jeremy and ask about his summer plans. When he took her outside to show her the frame for the boat he was building with his dad, they kissed and eventually moved inside, up to his room. Molly didn't lose her virginity, but they tried oral sex a little bit and she decided that's pretty good for the last day of school. Maybe other things would progress with Jeremy over the summer. He said he'd call her.

In the morning, her parents were at the dining room table with pale faces and twitching hands.

When did you see Bradley last?

About nine o'clock at the dance, she said. Why?

The cops took him away first thing this morning, Molly's mom said. We're not sure why.

Well, there are already a number of stories going around, Molly's father said. It's best not to listen to them. The truth will come out.

Those stories are garbage, Molly's mother said. We know the boy, we've known him his whole life. There's no way he could have done any of those things.

The stories varied in detail and enthusiasm: Bradley got young Patsy Billings drunk off wine coolers. The two of them in the woods. No, it was in one of the dressing rooms in the rec centre. No, it was Bradley and Patsy behind the rec centre, kissing, him leading her off by the hand. Patsy coming home with dirt on her skin under her clothes. Bradley had blood on his fingers. Patsy, not even twelve years old, really. She skipped grade two. No, she's thirteen. No, she's eleven. And no one has laid eyes on Bradley. Mark Stead says he's seen him. Everyone knows Mark Stead is full of shit. Bradley's mother has him hid with relatives in Gander. No, he's in juvey. He's too old for juvey. In jail then.

In mid-August, Bradley's mother showed up at the door, eyes pink with fear. Please Molly, she said. There's been a full investigation. The Billingses are out for blood. The lawyer says a character reference would help. Anything would help. You know Bradley, you two are like cousins. You're a good writer. A letter, please. A letter saying how you know Bradley couldn't do something like this.

She'll help, Molly's mother said. Of course she'll help.

Bradley's mother left the address of the lawyer. Molly's mother put paper in the printer by the computer. You're a good friend, she said. I'm proud of you.

Molly stared at the computer screen. She knew more about Bradley than anyone. She'd seen him every day for over twelve years. She should have an idea what he's capable and incapable of.

Molly's mother kissed her on the forehead when she passed her the envelope, sealed and addressed to the lawyer. I'm glad you did this for him before you're off to Halifax next week, she said. Molly hugged her mom. I have to get ready, she said. Going to Jeremy's place.

In the truck, Molly tossed her purse on the empty seat beside her. She rolled down the window and let the late summer breeze comb through her hair. Tonight would be the night with Jeremy. This weekend she'd pack for school.

If she managed it right, she'd answer the phone when the lawyer called. He'd say, there must be some mistake. All you sent was a blank sheet of paper. And before she hung up, she'd make sure to say, I'm very sorry. You seem to have the wrong number.

COLLEEN'S BIRTHDAY

ANNIE RANTS AND ROLLS. Her hand-eye coordination has always impressed me. Almost ten years of semi-regular pot smoking and it still takes all my silent concentration to roll a single loosely uniform joint. But Annie does it with instinctual grace.

The problem is, there are more women than men in this town. Even the skeetiest guy with homemade tattoos and saggy-ass jeans can get a nice girl—nice girls—'cause there are so many of them. They does what they likes.

Do you think Colleen will want to go out later?

Probably. Annie licks the sticky stripe and smooths the thin white line. She'll want to dance. And that's another thing. Since when does not dancing prove your manhood? You go out and the women dance while the men hold up the walls. Like it's a spectator sport.

Waiting for the ones they like to get drunk enough, I say.

Waiting for us. They can do that here, they can do as little as possible.

Who do you think will be at the party?

Definitely her work friends. And Kelly and Ian. And her cousins. Sean and Carl and the fat one.

I nod. Just hearing his name feels like one of those air dancers has taken up in my belly, those "fly guy" tubes with dangly arms used for advertising that stand up in the wind. The tiny one in my gut inflates and waves at me. Sean Sean Sean.

There is a cough and a shuffle in the kitchen. Annie's grandmother is up and moving around. Hey, Nan. You want anything? Annie places the CD with its pile of weed under the coffee table in one practised movement.

No, getting a cup of tea. Is that Robin with you?

Yes, it's me. Hi Lorraine. I get up to say hello. Lorraine sleeps most hours of the day and gets up after dark to prowl around; she makes soup, she listens to late night CBC radio. She lives the life of a cat. She sits at the head of the wooden table in her long flesh-coloured housecoat. Annie calls it her peach sheath.

Flick that over, would you? Lorraine gestures to the can of Belvedere tobacco on the kitchen counter. I place it next to her and she opens her slider for rolling cigarettes. Where are you two heading out to tonight? She wedges small clumps of tobacco into the crevice.

Colleen's birthday.

Ah, the fair Colleen. Lorraine grins. Her teeth are ridged with yellow. The peach sheath brings out all her shades of nicotine. The grey in her hair has an amber tint, and so do her long fingers with their pointed red tips. Even the whites of her eyes aren't pure; their edges look jaundiced, matching the cracks in the kitchen walls. If you could get a block of cancer, like it was soapstone and carve a person out of it, that's what Lorraine looks like. Although Lorraine is likely to be one of those people who lives off smokes and Cheez

Whiz until they're a hundred and twenty years old.

We're going to head out now, Nan, Annie says. She waves a joint at me behind Lorraine's back.

Take a few of these before you go. Lorraine presses the top of the slider down and snaps it back and forth, like an old credit card machine. She nods to the Tupperware container on the table full of rows of prepared cigarettes. I take two and thank her. Really, I only like a smoke when I'm drinking, and even then I like the light stuff. Lorraine's smokes tear my throat out.

Outside, the weather has gone from crisp to bitter. It will take about ten minutes to get to Colleen's with a stop for beer. Annie walks with little brisk steps like she's chugging on wheels. Take Todd for example, she says. Colleen thinks he's a catch. If we lived in a different city, there's no way that guy would be a catch. Ten years I've known him and he has the exact same haircut. Short on the sides, brushed back. Annie draws Todd's haircut in the air with two fingers, an invisible rectangle. She exhales hard and her breath clouds up in the cold air, erasing the idea of Todd's dumb haircut. She buries her nose in the top of her scarf. She's trying to grow out her bangs and they drape over her left eye, the right eye glares out. Fuckin' freezing out.

I pull out the invitation when we're in the convenience store. Colleen likes to go all out with things; she went to the trouble to make paper invitations and lick a stamp for every guest. What do you think "Universal Holiday" Birthday party means? I duck into the back fridge and hook my fingers into a box of beer.

As long as I don't have to dress up to go to someone's house, I don't give a shit, Annie says. Friggin' theme parties.

Too many people's birthdays involve a shopping spree. I don't want to buy a new outfit for someone's birthday. This shit gets expensive.

We leave the store and trudge up Merrymeeting Road. I try to ignore the oscillating energy in my belly. Anticipa-Sean. I've bumped into him a few times over the past couple of months. The last time was two weeks ago at a party on Bonaventure Avenue. Everyone had congregated in the kitchen even though it was a big, sprawling house. More people kept showing up and it got louder and warmer. I ducked into the dining room to escape the din. Snacks were laid out on the dining room table, chips and a veggie tray. There was a lazy Susan in the middle of the table with bowls of candy. I wasn't really hungry, but I wanted an excuse to be by myself for a minute, so I was nibbling.

Sean came in and grabbed some chips, started slowly turning the lazy Susan. This could get dangerous, he said. Spin it too fast, disaster. Skittles everywhere.

Waste the rainbow.

Good one. Sean gestured to the lazy Susan. What are these things called, anyway?

It's a lazy Susan.

Why is it called that? Do you know?

Probably named after someone named Susan.

Huh. Maybe it was her job to pass stuff around the dinner table. Sean popped a Smartie in his mouth and crunched it. He looked at me with his head tilted. His eyes and hair are the same shade of earthy brown; it has a dis-orienting effect, like suddenly seeing the boat in one of those 3-D pictures.

Yeah, and she invented this, I said. She thought, wow,

everyone's going to think I'm so creative. But everyone was like, look what Susan made 'cause she couldn't be bothered to pass the plates around. I gave the disk a push around with one finger.

Fuckin' lazy ol' Susan, Sean said. He grabbed a couple of Reese's Pieces as they glided by. These are my favourite.

These are mine, I said, plucking up a Smartie. The bowl sailed on towards him.

I said goodbye before I left and he left his hand on my arm in what I hope was a lingering way. I cursed myself the whole way home. Why didn't you ask for his number? Why didn't you suggest he call you? Why didn't you do something flirty and cute? Fuckin' stupid ol' Robin.

Since then, I've been seeing him everywhere. A stranger in front of me in line turns and for a second, he's Sean: the way he moves his head, the cascade of his cheekbone. The shape of Sean's shoulders appears in another person's jacket, shifting and shrugging as they pass me on the sidewalk. Each time, the realization that it's not him is a little falling, like the way Lorraine smokes her cigarettes; she lets the ashes build and never taps them until finally they flake off into a little grey pile. Oh. It's not him. And then Colleen's invitation in the mail with the time and the date and the building tingle of certainty.

As Annie and I approach Colleen's house, the party theme is made clear. There are Christmas lights in the window and a jack-o'-lantern on the porch step. I notice some jelly beans stashed on a corner shelf while I take off my boots. There's a chocolate bunny peering out of a closet door. Where did she get Easter shit in November? She must have stored it away.

Colleen bounds out wearing a cone-shaped birthday hat and a Canadian flag wrapped around her like a toga, Christmas garland around her neck. Come in, friends! The living room is decorated with strings of hearts, shamrocks, red Chinese signs and a Christmas tree. There is a menorah on the table next to her birthday cake. The cake is decorated with cinnamon hearts, mini eggs, candy canes. There are maple-leaf-shaped shortbread cookies, bowls of Halloween candy—that would be on sale this time of year. Run-DMC's "Christmas in Hollis" is playing. It's too early for Christmas music, says Annie. I can't deal. She picks up the beer and heads to the kitchen. I follow her.

Sean leans on the counter next to the sink, talking to Todd of The Bad Haircut. Annie opens the fridge and crouches down. The waistline of her jeans stretches and her shirt rides up, exposing a wide sheath of flesh to the top of her bum. She doesn't seem to notice. She shoves jars and condiments out of the way and starts piling our beer in.

I take one and twist it open. The beer foams up and over the top. I clamp my mouth over it and lunge over to the sink. Beer drips down the bottle and over my chin. Sean looks around and hands me a dish towel. Don't you hate it when that happens? he says. I blush. He continues talking to Todd. I wipe off my hands, then the drips on the floor. The original plan was to just walk up and say hi. Present myself, basically. Now it feels like an interruption. The air dancer deflates and bends in half.

Christ, Q-tip Head is already here, Annie says. She rolls her eyes towards Todd. She opens her beer. No foam. She walks out of the kitchen. I follow. I take big sips from my beer. The quicker the bottle is empty, the sooner I'll have an excuse to go back to the kitchen.

In the living room, Michael Jackson's "Thriller" is playing. Colleen and Kelly are doing the zombie dance moves. I smile. Must look like I'm having fun. I wonder if he's seeing anyone. I wish I could relax. The screen door whines, there's a clatter in the porch. Three girls in tall boots with long, straightened hair. I've never seen any of them before. I wonder if Sean knows them.

Annie is talking to Brett and they want to go out for a smoke. They get their things together. I wish there was just one bar where you could smoke, Brett says. I agree with the non-smoking rules, but they could leave one place. One bar where you could smoke, a little sanctuary.

You should start it.

We should open it together. Brett and Anne's Cigarette Plan.

You should open a bar and call it "Secret Fags." Everyone would think it was a gay bar, but it would actually be for illegal smoking. Fags like cigarette fags, get it. Annie jostles Brett with her elbow. He purses his lips at her in fake offence. Maybe not fake offence.

Coming? Annie looks at me. I glance back towards the kitchen. One of the straightened-hair girls hugs Sean in greeting.

Sure, I say.

You can smoke in the basement, Colleen says. We're going down for a draw now the once. She twirls so that the flag flaps out around her.

Even better, says Brett.

In the basement, Annie sparks up a joint and Todd, Sean, Kelly and the straightened-hair hugger come down.

Oh, great minds, says Todd and pulls out a joint of his own.

Colleen takes one from her cigarette pack as well. My friend Joy gave me this yesterday. Todd lights his and the nine of us stand in a circle passing his and Annie's around.

Sean stands next to me and when he passes me the joint, our eyes meet and the dimple in his right cheek twitches. He has amazing dimples. The smile hasn't happened and yet there are dimples. They are as much a part of his face as his nose and eyebrows. Everyone laughs and talks, a magic circle.

Upstairs, *Jesus Christ Superstar* is playing. Sean frowns. Oh, for Easter, he says.

I can't think of any non-religious Easter songs, I say. Except "Here Comes Peter Cottontail."

I don't think I know that one.

Sure you do.

I don't think so. Sing a bit of it.

You know that song.

Give us a few bars. Maybe it will spark my memory.

Yeah, I think you can remember without my musical help. I laugh. My face heats up.

No, it would really assist me. How does it start? Sean's eyes are all twinkly. Another joint comes by. I take a puff and get a flake of weed in my mouth. I turn away from him to remove it.

Is there tobacco in this? Colleen waves Annie's joint at her.

Yep, that's how I roll.

I'm off the smokes. I'll spark this one up. Colleen lights her own joint and takes a puff. She passes it to Todd.

The reaction starts with Colleen: a look of horror, then

realization. She lunges for Todd, who is exhaling and handing the joint to Annie. Stop, stop! Colleen says.

Todd has the same reaction. Exhaling as Annie inhales. Laced! Todd says. Don't do it! Annie lets out a stream of smoke from her lips. Fuck! The air is tinged with the scent of something harsh, like burning plastic.

Oh shit, there's coke or something in that. Colleen takes the joint from Annie and puts it out.

Where did you get it?

Joy gave it to me, Colleen says. She said it was special. I just figured it was hydro. Colleen sways back and forth. Whoo. Special. Oh, fuck you, Joy.

Maybe it's speed. Todd runs his hand through the top of his hair, warping the smooth helmet. He exhales slowly. Okay. This is my night now.

Just try to enjoy it, man, says Sean. Nothing you can do about it now.

Annie clasps the back of her neck and stares at the basement floor. Robin. Could you come here please? I go to her side. She doesn't look at me, continues staring at the floor. I need. To get the fuck. Out of here.

Oh Christ, Todd says. Don't have a panic attack. If you have a panic attack, it might have some kind of trickle-down effect. I do not want to have a fucking panic attack.

Do you want me to take you home? I say to Annie. Come on, let's sit down. I take her over to a couch by the wall. She sits and leans forward, hugging herself.

No. Can't go home. Can't be around the old woman right now. Annie passes her hands over her face, the back of her neck. I don't mean here. I mean this place. This country.

Do it then. Leave if you want. No one is stopping you.

Todd rocks back and forth on his heels.

You know fuck-all. She glares at him. He rolls his eyes and jerks his head away.

Annie rubs her hands over her face. I wonder what she needs. Water? A cigarette? The straightened-hair girl stands next to Sean, looking concerned. They talk to each other with their heads close.

I wonder if this is how it feels when you have a break-down, Annie says. Can people actually sense it when they lose their minds? She starts to sway in little jumps. I don't know what to do. I rub her back. I produce a cigarette. I light it for her, she puffs.

Last week, she says, I thought Nan had died. I hadn't heard her stir all day. I looked in on her. She looked dead. She was just lying there in her peach sheath. I thought, she can't be buried in that. What outfit should I pick out for her? She hasn't bought any new clothes in years. I don't know what fits her. And then she moved. Annie inhales and lets out a long stream of smoke. I felt this kind of disappoint-ment. Like I was only one number away from the bingo jack-pot. Fucking horrible.

I say nothing. What to say. I like Lorraine, but our affec-tion is a cup of tea, an idle chat. The woman is work, the kind that gets into your joints. She's an ancient factory of bad habits and worse advice. It's natural to feel like that sometimes, I say.

To want her to die? Annie's voice goes up. Only an asshole would say that. Are you trying to say you're an asshole, Robin? Her eyes bore into me, her hair sticks out where she's mauled it.

No, that's not what I mean, I say. I love Lorraine. But

it's just been you and her for a long time. It's hard. Sean and straightened-hair girl stare at me from across the room. Todd talks away to them without noticing us.

Why don't we get some fresh air? I say.

Colleen hears this and gives a little hop. Yes! I want to go on the swings, she says. The swings! I have swings in my backyard. She moves towards the back door of the basement. Someone get my coat? Get our coats!

Annie's lips quiver slightly. Will you push me on the swing? Will you give me a push, Robin?

Of course I will.

Not too much. I don't want to go too high.

We bundle up. Kelly pushes Colleen and I push Annie. They babble on and on. Once in a while, I look up and see the glowing light of the basement window. I can see the tops of their heads, Todd, straightened-hair girl and Sean, still talking together. It is like looking at coins at the bottom of a well. Wishes once made. I tuck my hands into the sleeves of my coat to warm them and push Annie's back.

When the taxis show up, I help Annie get in. She wants to go to my place. She has stopped talking about her Nan, stopped talking altogether. Colleen hugs me. You're awesome, she says. Her eyes shine in the cold night air. I hug her back. The house behind her is dark inside, but the Christmas lights are still on. Someone has kicked in the face of the jack-o'-lantern.

Another cab pulls up. Todd and straightened-hair girl are waiting for it. Sean comes out carrying their coats. A candy cane dangles from his mouth. He helps her into her coat. The air dancer lies flat. Can't even sigh. He takes the candy cane out of his mouth and looks over at me. He waves a trick-or-treat sized box of Smarties. Here, it's the last one. Sean says. He passes it to me. Be careful opening it, you never know what people put in these things. I say thank you and get into the cab. I don't look at them as we pull out.

In the cab, Annie leans on me. I love you. You're a good friend. I squeeze her hand. Don't fall asleep, I say. My back feels stiff from pushing the swing.

I take the tiny box of Smarties from my pocket. It's already been opened. Inside, there is a slip of paper with the candy. Seven digits and a note: *Don't be lazy, Susan. Call me.*

GUTLESS BRAVADO, PART THREE

AT JULIA'S THIS TIME. I continue my practice of sprawling out on the couch after eating and sometimes I end up in a three-hour nap. But no matter what, I wake up at the crepuscular times: dusk or dawn.

Julia's couch is burgundy and reminds me of a thick slice of organ meat, like liver or tongue. From its living room location, I watch the wedge of sky between the curtain rod and the window frame. Sometimes, the sky appears brown before it makes its decision to go bright or dark and I think about other animals that become active in these transitions: moose, bats, birds, and fish. Bugs rise out of slumber to orbit puddles and ponds. Crepuscular is one of those words that feel good in your mouth, like a quality baguette and sharp cheese. Although it's still hard to eat bread. Gluten in general is difficult.

Julia got a machinist apprenticeship out west, so I get another free place to stay. It reassures her to have a presence in her house: lights and movement and a regular gutting of the mailbox. And I feed her cat and keep things less dusty. Once my weight goes back up and stays stable for a couple of months, I can look at getting work. For now,

I take supplements and short walks. I drink herbal tea and eat slowly. I watch crap TV shows. Recovery takes resigned boredom. At least the cat is content. I'm a warm mattress and source of scraps.

Julia has no backyard or deck, but there's a public green space behind her house, a small parking area edged by a lawn. It's poorly maintained. The lawn slopes down and ends at a fence lined with clusters of used coffee cups and empty cigarette packs. There is a park bench with an overflowing bucket of cigarette butts. There is one garbage can, usually packed with dog poop bags. But there are trees, and they are all tall and leafy and calming.

Sheila, the neighbour on the right, likes to smoke her joints on the park bench and complain about city council. She has skinny arms and legs that project off her barrel belly and big boobs. She dyes her short hair a strawberry blond verging on brassy and she dies for a tanning bed. She is overall compact and kind of orange, a nectarine of a woman. If I see her outside, I might join her with one of my own joints. It's good for me to talk to people.

Sheila says she leaves weekly messages about the state of the green space on the 311 service. Empty the garbage, mow the grass, would it kill them to plant a few flowers? Can we get a cleanup crew for the spring litter? Nothing happens. It's so over-unionized down at City Hall, Sheila says, that everyone has to wait for the person assigned to each individual job to do it, even though you could get the whole place cleaned up in less than a day. We smoke our joints and shake our heads. What a bunch.

I get the idea when I see the push-mower on Kijiji. No one can complain about the grass being cut late or early if there's no noise. It would give me something to do when I wake up at dawn. I could mow the grass, put in some plants. I like the idea of people waking up and finding things transformed, like Christmas morning or controlled demolition. One day the grass will be cut, the next a row of pansies. Would anyone ask questions? Would they assume the City did it? Maybe the neighbours would joke about a magic gardener elf.

Dean told me when he planted trees up in northern BC, they would trim their shovel blades on the sides for digging and flipping the soil quickly. Dean also says he knows a guy who works at the botanical gardens who has piles of hostas he can't use. There is space for at least thirty or forty hostas down the slope and along the fence, if I clean up the garbage. Julia has about four snow shovels in her basement and I take the rustiest one to get cut down. I get gardening gloves, two bags of Miracle-Gro planting soil. The push-mower is really cheap.

I wake up just after six o'clock in the evening. The shadows lengthen outside. My belly feels tight with the pasta I had for supper. I turn on the TV to distract myself. The NTV news anchor says a coyote has been spotted downtown. There is a cellphone video of it, lanky and grey-brown. It trots casually down King's Road and sniffs around the ice cream store.

When I go outside for a toke with Sheila, she says she's keeping her cat inside from now on. That's what they go for, she says. Her sister in Alberta told her coyotes killed a whole colony of feral cats in her community. Lived off them for months. Sheila licks her fingertip and lays it on the canoeing ember of her joint.

Weird that it's by itself, I say. Maybe its pack was killed off.

Too bad it's not out in Airport Heights, she says. It might do something about the rat problem.

On a Tuesday evening, I make a spinach salad, but can only get half of it down. I'm so tired afterwards, I drop off on the couch with my arms folded behind my head and they lose circulation and my brain thinks it's armless and screams itself awake. I have to bring my arms down slowly; they are empty and aching. When they thaw out, I take up my newly sharpened shovel for this night's plantings. There is only one light post in the space. I figure I can pick up the litter and get the bottom of the slope done tonight without being noticed. The shovel goes in quickly and I get a nice rhythm going, plunge, dig, drop, pat. The sod separates like tangled hair. It's quiet enough in the green space to focus on the ripping sounds, the cool air on my arms, the scent of uncovered earth and moisture.

I don't see the coyote until I'm finished. It creeps by the side of the fence. Its face is grey-brown and mottled and its eyes are yellow. It freezes when it sees me looking, then takes two steps and slinks away. I follow it from a distance. It disappears in the alley across the street and slips under a house. There's a for sale sign in front and all the windows are dark and musty. I peek around the space where it went under the house—it looks like an unfinished basement. Probably makes a nice burrow.

When I go to bed, I think about the coyote. People walk dogs in the green space all the time. There are cats about.

Compost piles in backyards, early morning garbage. Coyotes are scavengers. There's an elementary school nearby. How many daycare centres are around, formal establishments and private ones, run out of people's homes? There's a dance school down the street. There's a rotation of sex workers standing at the bottom of Long's Hill every night, all of them thin and tired looking.

Dominion has Purina on for half price. I get a big sack and bring over a few handfuls. I leave a little pile just inside the space between the boards. What am I thinking? Curiosity with elements of greed and boredom. I don't want to tame the coyote, but I want its presence. I want it to mistrust everyone but me. I'll be the only one it allows within a six-foot radius and it will follow me from a distance. I'll reward it with scraps. Because of me, it won't bother local cats and small dogs. Our relationship will have a greater benefit for the community and help the animal itself—if it's well fed and non-destructive, there is less chance it will become a target of knee-jerk panic and trophy hunters. I know I am rationalizing this, but I also know when it comes to the morality of it, I really don't care that much.

Every night, I leave small piles of the dry dog food by the basement entrance and at the edge of the fence. In the daytime, I check the piles. They are always gone, but I don't know if it's the coyote or dogs. On the fifth night, I see the coyote a second time. It is early dawn and the light is turning mauve. As I place a handful of dog food on the ground, I see eyes shining about twenty feet away. It sits on its haunches, watching me. It doesn't move as I straighten up, but when I take a small step closer, it hops to its feet, ready to flee. I turn and walk away, hoping to give off signals of peace and trust. I wish I'd had a good look at it. I wonder if it has gained weight.

Sheila doesn't mention the changes to the green space, but she points out a knapsack left by the park bench. Probably someone stopped for a smoke and forgot it, I say. Oh no, she says. This has been gutted. It's the third bag she's found this year. Thieves break into cars by the Masonic Temple and go through what they find here. She opens the knapsack; there are bound manuals inside. Somebody's school notes. Shitty for a student to lose all their notes.

The police should put up a security camera here, I say. Cops are worse than city council, Sheila says. They don't investigate car break-ins. Even though, I guarantee, it's the same group of skeets every night. I don't understand the police. It's like if they fix the problem, it will raise the bar and they'll be expected to actually do things.

I spot the thief that night. I am crouched by the back fence, low to the soil, pushing a hosta into the ground with my fingertips. The thief wears a jacket and cargo pants that look grey in the darkness. His head is shaved and his pale face is creased and sunken from a life of chemicals. He carries two backpacks. I keep my breath light and maintain my pose; I'm just doing some gardening. It would be counter-productive to make me an issue.

The thief lays the backpacks on the park bench. He yanks out papers and books and lets them slide to the ground. He takes something small and white from a side pocket, an iPhone maybe. He finds some change at the bottom and stuffs it all into his jacket pocket. It's casual now when he walks away.

I rub soil between my fingers and wonder about his potential for aggression. How far will he go to get what he needs? Breaking into cars is pretty easy, really. Like Sheila says, the cops shrug it off. I could do it too, if I wanted. People park overnight on downtown streets, show up hung-over on Sunday mornings to get their vehicles. How much can you really get from the average car? I'd have to know what to look for and be quick with tools; how fast could I remove a car stereo? I'd need to be able to jiggle a door handle with nonchalance, bust a windshield into blue bits with one bang. Sounds like a lot of effort for little payoff. Better to leave it for the desperate.

It's after four on a Saturday morning when I see the thief and his girlfriend get in a fight. I am taking a break with a joint on the bench. I have a clear view of the street through the lane leading out and I see her pass. She walks with arms folded, taking furious scissor steps. She has bright blond hair with roots so dark they make a bullseye of the top of her head as she concentrates on the ground. Wait, he calls. Stop. She doesn't stop, but waves back one outstretched hand, middle finger up. He follows her, moving in a slow, ex-aggerated swagger, pausing to glance up at the darkened windows of Julia's neighbours. He passes my view and half a minute later, I hear their voices ping off the pavement, like small yapping dogs. C'mon. Fuck you. Don't talk to me. C'mon, Lily.

On Monday afternoon, Sheila comes over to tell me the house across the street from hers was broken into, right in the middle of the day. The owner was in the backyard setting up for a barbeque and the front door was unlocked for his expected guests. The thief or thieves walked right in and took the laptop off the kitchen table. When is Julia coming back? she asks me. Thursday, I say. She's lucky she has you, Sheila says. Obviously some arsehole is around, looking for vulnerable spots. She gives me a hard look. She's probably seen me outside at night.

I have three nights to finish up the green space. The grass is mowed and a row of hostas line the back fence where the lawn slopes down a bit. There's a bare patch of dirt behind the park bench, and I have time to put in a news-paper garden bed there, some flowers, a little surprise for the eyes. I pick up a bag of mulch and the flyers from Julia's recycling bin. I eat an exhausting meal of steak and broccoli which renders me fetal on the burgundy couch, balled up like a cyst on a piece of kidney.

On the last night, I put the finishing touches on the flower bed. It's a neat rectangle surrounded by beach rocks. Marigolds peek up from the mulch. I pat down the sides with the edge of my shovel. I open the side door and put in the unused flyers and I see the girl, Lily, standing on the other side of the street. She stares at her phone, texting. I can't see her expression, but there's something about her shoulders that suggests the verge of tears. I pretend I'm examining the shovel for cleanliness or something while keeping my eyes on her. She is a stereotype of vulnerable. Maybe she's not okay. Maybe I should call someone.

There is a clicking sound around the corner, where Sheila's front door is. I pull the hood of my sweatshirt up over my head and walk out to take a look. The thief is turning the knob on Sheila's door and opening it, his jagged profile leaning into the line of darkness between the door and the frame.

What are you doing, I say.

Jesus, he says.

He jumps back from the door. He glares across the street at Lily. She was supposed to be watching out. I'm going into my house, he says.

That's not your house.

It isn't? He leans back and looks up at the windows. Oh, you're right, it's not. My bad.

I think you better get out of here, I say.

The thief points at the shovel in my hand. What are you? he says. The midnight gardener?

It's way past midnight.

Lily crosses over to us. Jordan, she says. Let's get out of here. He winces and looks at her: Holy fuck, girl. You are such an idiot.

Let's go, please, she says. She passes her hand through her two-toned hair. She is trying not to look at me.

What do you do with stupid girls? Jordan the Thief says to me. You look like you're ready to bury them.

Come on, Jordan, for fuck sakes, she says.

She pulls on his sleeve. Stop saying my fucking name, he says. He pushes her away. She falls down hard on her butt. Owowowow. Jesus Christ, he says. Useless. He stomps his foot close to her, making her scooch away.

You shouldn't do that.

You need to mind your own business, Gardener, he says. He stamps at Lily once more and I step forward.

You're making her scared.

I think I should make you scared, he says. His pupils are dilated in the dim light like glass buttons in his white face.

What scares you? he says. He reaches out two fingers to poke me in the belly, right where my incision scar meets my navel.

I bring the shovel down in front of me to shield myself as his hand comes forward. But the reflex is much faster than I imagine. There is a clipping sound and a flash of red and two splats on the sidewalk. Jordan the Thief wails. I look down and there are the fingertips of his index and middle fingers, two white and red blobs on the pavement. The physics is really quite astounding; of course the shovel would be extra sharp, cut down as it is.

Lily says, Oh my god oh my god oh my god. Jordan clutches his bleeding hand, moaning and panting. I dash into the green space, down the slope, by the fence. I can't have them see me go into Julia's house. Jordan and Lily's voices are urgent, but getting distant. I sneak up behind the park bench. I can see their crouched backs retreating down the street, she is helping him walk. How many witnesses are there? I should call the cops. I should save the fingertips. I'll go to the house, grab a tea towel and ice.

A low, greyish shape emerges from the shadows close to where Lily was standing. The coyote trots across the street. It gobbles up Jordan's fingertips in two quick chomps and keeps moving. When I reach Julia's door, it is already gone.

Inside, I check all the locks twice and sit on the couch with the curtains drawn. Julia's cat purrs in my lap. I listen and wait. It's easy to hold still with a cat on you. I try not to flinch with sounds of oncoming vehicles, maybe it's Jordan coming back, maybe one of his friends. But no one stops.

When the light between the curtain and window begins its browning into mauve, I lie down. Julia herself will be home in the afternoon, in a few hours. After I sleep, I'll make sure the place is clean for her. I'll call my sister, tell her I'll be over by supper. Next week, I may start looking at job listings. It's probably about time I did. All this gardening and fresh air—perhaps I am stronger than I thought.

LOSING MARSHA ZANE

THREE DAYS AFTER MOM'S DIAGNOSIS, Brenda comes up with Family Game Night. She brings it up as we're cleaning the house for Mom's return, watering plants, wiping down shelves. She's out of the hospital Friday, Brenda says. We can do it Sunday nights. Charlene and I agree. Now is the time. We will be more family than ever before.

What kind of board games does everyone have? Brenda asks. Charlene, you have Trouble, right? David, what do you have?

I don't think I own any, I say.

David doesn't do games, remember? Charlene says. He calls them bored games.

I was joking, I say. And we only played them when the power went out.

Whatever, Brenda says. There's no point in negativity.

Afterwards, in the car, Charlene shakes her head. For Brenda, anything that isn't 100 per cent positive is negative, she says. Like she can keep Mom alive through stubborn enthusiasm.

On Sunday, I conduct an honest search for a contribution, but all I find are playing cards with naked men on them, a stocking stuffer from Roger last Christmas. If the kids weren't present, I think Mom would get a kick out of them. I bring chips instead.

For the first game night, we play Monopoly. Brenda's twin boys are on their best behaviour and rub the dice between their palms with the same solemn motion. If it wasn't for Charlene going to the bathroom every few minutes to blow her nose, the atmosphere would be serene. Sorry, Charlene says. I have a cold. She presses down her grief with steady breaths. I am so glad I smoked up before I came over.

Mom is benevolent in her chair. Charlene took her to get her hair done and it is composed in smooth walnut curls. She wears the maroon sweater-tunic I gave her last Christmas, the one she admired in the shop but wouldn't buy for herself. A nice departure from her regular wardrobe of elastic-waist jeans and fleece tops. Or, most distressing to me, one of Dad's old shirts he left behind. You know, Mom, the shop is full of great men's shirts, I once told her. Oh no, she said. Those won't be broken in.

I didn't expect her to look so good. If you weren't aware malignant tumours were burrowing into the tissues around her heart and liver, you'd think she just got back from a cruise. Marsha Zane, you're looking good, might be the words of a casual acquaintance or a Facebook comment. Looking younger every day, Marsha.

I roll the dice and move the silver shoe to Community Chest. Roger told me when his father was sick, the waiting point happened fast. Suddenly he was skeletal. There had to be an oxygen tank in reach all the time. I'm sure he would have gone in for assisted suicide if it was an option, Roger said. I pass go and collect two hundred dollars. What will Mom want when the time comes?

After the game, the boys hug Mom with dutiful affection. Charlene shoves on her coat and exits to cry in peace.

I'll call in the morning, Mom, Brenda says. David, you want a ride home?

David, why don't you stay a while? Mom says. She licks her finger and runs it along the bottom of the chip bowl for crumbs.

So, you'll take a taxi? Brenda says. I have to get the kids to bed.

I have cash for a cab if you need it, Mom says.

I bet Brenda's wheels are churning. Aw, luh, Mommy's got money for no-car, baby-boy David. They all take debit now, I say. I'll put the kettle on.

Brenda says something soft before the door shuts, something like call if you need anything. Mom doesn't answer. Goddamn it. Whatever she's doing, she'd better be diplomatic and do it with all of us. All I need is for her to establish regular tête-à-têtes with me and leave Brenda and Charlene feeling denied.

I'm going to have a sherry, Mom says. Want one?

Sure.

She selects two tiny glasses from the hutch. These belonged to your great-grandmother, she says. Do you think you'd like to have them?

Mom, don't worry about that.

No no, the three of you should decide what you want. Make lists. Avoid a fight later.

The glasses are like tiny tulips. Perhaps she thinks I'll

get more use out of them than Brenda with the kids, or Charlene, who keeps moving. She sets the glasses down and fetches her sherry.

Roger said his father went through a phase of giving away his belongings. And later, he started sitting everyone down to give them advice. Save at least ten per cent of your salary. Stay connected with who you are. And as he got worse, he wanted to make apologies, amends. I'm sorry you never got to know your grandmother. I'm sorry I didn't teach you Japanese. Maybe it was fear, Roger said. Or we weren't as receptive to his advice as he wanted us to be and he regretted his approach. All his old rigid edges began fencing him in at once.

I don't think Mom owes me any apologies. I know I am one of Dad's reasons for leaving. Sometimes, I suspect she's secretly grateful.

She pours the sherry. I'm not really a sherry or port drinker, I say.

Well, I want you to have them. Maybe you'll grow to enjoy it. Maybe some of your friends do already.

She has never said *boyfriends* to me. Dad once slurred, Which one will you be, the girlfriend or the boyfriend, and Mom lost her tolerance: Don't speak that way to my son. That's right, he said, he's *your* son. Finally, I said, givin' up the lease.

Mom holds the cup with her pinky extended. The sherry glasses are designed for primness. She takes a tiny sip, like a bee. Did you smoke marijuana today? she asks.

Oh, Jesus. I had a little earlier, I say.

I keep reading how it can be good for pain relief. Especially with cancer patients.

Yes. It's one of the reasons it's legal now.

She regards the sherry glass. It's like a doll's toy in her hand. I was thinking maybe it would be good to try it, she says. Before I get to that point. Of too much pain, I mean.

It might help, yes.

Do you have any on you?

Yes.

She folds her hands in her lap. Well then.

I go to my coat and remove my Pax and the baggie. I feel her eyes on me. Yes, I am the son with drugs in his pocket. Ten years ago, she'd have flushed it in a storm of tears and fear. There'd have been threats to call the RNC.

Do you roll it in a cigarette? she says. That always seemed tricky to me.

I have a vaporizer.

I turn it on and pass it to her. The lights circulate on the front to show it's warming up, I say. She smooths it in her palm. It looks like an Apple product, she says. How much did it cost you?

Um, two hundred and seventy-five dollars.

Her eyebrows make their leap of judgment: That's quite an investment.

Well, I tried one at a party and liked it. When the light turns green, it's ready.

She takes a slow inhale from the lip. Thank fuck she doesn't cough. What a nightmare if she convulsed, spat blood.

It's like roasting an herb, she says.

It is. Much smoother than a joint or bong.

I wouldn't know.

She takes another hit. Should I stop her? Hey, Mom,

you're a lightweight.

I can see how people enjoy this, she says. Especially the ill. It's boring being sick. She exhales a thin line of smoke. Look, she says. I'm a dragon.

We'll start calling you Puff.

She giggles and settles back in the couch, two-fisted with her sherry and the Pax. I enjoyed the game tonight, she says. I never think about playing board games like that. Your father was never interested. It was just poker with his buddies. And wives weren't permitted.

'Cause he knew you'd win.

She gets out the cards. We play blackjack. She giggles every time she says, Hit me.

I'm having such a nice time, she says. She takes a puff and eyes me: David. What other drugs have you done?

I've experimented.

I thought so. It was something I worried about with you. Especially when your father left. I was scared you'd wash yourself away.

Wash yourself? Like I should clean myself somehow? There was acid before pot, actually, I say. Acid, pot, mushrooms, ecstasy, speed, Special K, and um, coke. But all experimental. Once or twice each.

Oh my. Well, I'm glad it was just a couple of times. Especially the cocaine.

I nod. I can't tell her coke is what happened to Roger and me, first our fun centre, then his crutch. Mom, I say, if you like the pot, I'll leave you some.

I wouldn't know what to do with it.

I'll leave the vaporizer. I'll show you how to refill it.

She lies on the couch and watches while I pop off the bottom and show her the roasted bits. My goodness, she says. It really is an appetite enhancer. I could eat more chips.

Do it, I say. Why not?

I almost say, what do you have to lose? I go to the kitchen and track down a bag of Party Mix. I pour it in a bowl and wipe my eyes before bringing it out. I don't want to ruin her stone.

The stereo in the cab plays "All We Are" by Kim Mitchell on the way down Newfoundland Drive. All we are wishing for is a nice few months. This will be my life now, biting back tears over songs I don't even like. We can do nothing with our old lists of If Onlies: if only she'd abandoned her Protestant ideas of goodness, if only she'd allowed herself more pleasure, if only she hadn't given up things like driving. Her email to all three of us: *I do not wish to drive anymore. It is too stressful these days and I do not require much more than a weekly trip to Sobeys and to church. There is also the upkeep of a car and insurance which I can do without. I hope you will not mind giving your old mum a ride here and there. xo*

Charlene wanted her to embrace being single. She emailed links to singles-only resorts and dating sites. The men my age who become single go out with forty-year-olds, Mom said. And if they've never married, there's a reason why.

Why is it all or nothing with her? Charlene said later. I just want her to get laid.

She considers herself so undeserving, she's become an enemy of fun, Brenda said. Spend a little money on yourself.

Go down south or something. This martyr shit.

I don't think she's a martyr, I said. I think she's afraid.

Oh, she's totally afraid. That's what happens when you turn fifty and make the executive decision to be old.

Back home, I give myself over to a long, hard cry. Gotta get it out when I can. Here we go, new routine: work, family duties, purging weep. I will not call Roger and ask, was it like this for you? Did all your family silences seem extra quiet? I plug in my phone and leave it. I don't check any of his profiles.

On Tuesday, Mom calls. I think it needs to be recharged, she says. And . . . do you have any more? I put some pot in a baggie and fish out some ancient brownies from the freezer. If she prefers them, I'll email Roger for that cannabutter recipe. Email, that is all.

At her house, she examines the baggie in her hands, pinching the dried buds and sniffing. It's kind of like pot-pourri.

I can see that.

When you tried . . . hallucinogens, which was your favourite?

Um, I like—I liked mushrooms.

Did you pick them yourself? Back when we had the cabin in Avondale, a bunch of college students showed up one day. They asked if they could go on our property to look for herbs. Al said they were looking for mushrooms.

I didn't pick them myself, no.

I see. Why did you like them?

They made me feel euphoric.

Interesting. I thought I was euphoric when I smoked marijuana, but from what I read on the internet, I'm just very relaxed. And there are different types of euphoria.

She traces the green light on the Pax with her index finger. Your father tried acid once, back when we first started dating, she says. We were at a party with his friends. Boy, was I mad at him. I kept saying, Why did you do this? This isn't good for you. And he kept saying, I'm sorry, and laughing. The angrier I got, the harder he laughed. Afterwards, he said he had genuinely felt sorry, but there was something about the way my face contorted that he found hilarious. I never understood his reaction.

She takes a slow drag and exhales. So the mushrooms, she says, they didn't make you sick?

No. Maybe a slight tummy ache when they were kicking in.

I'm scared when I go on the strong pain meds, it will interfere with eating. I know fentanyl does. And oxycodone.

She looks down at her lap. If I wanted to try something like mushrooms, she says, I'd have to do it now.

Do you want to try something like that?

Well, why don't you get some and I'll consider it.

It's hardest to avoid crying during the more monotonous chores, like folding sweaters or unpacking merchandise. In the shop, I stretch to reach a box of neckties and Mom's whimper exits my mouth, the one she makes when she lifts heavy things: the end of the couch, bags of groceries, me as a child. I lock myself in one of the change rooms and bite down on a wad of paper towels. I do not contact Roger. When I calm down, I call Charlene and tell her about Mom's hallucinogen curiosity.

Are you going to do them with her? she says.

No. I don't think that's a good idea.

Psychedelics shouldn't be done solo the first time.

She doesn't seem interested in doing them with anyone.

Because she has no idea. What if she gets in a dark place? Oh god, she could get really freaked out by herself.

I don't know. But you know, she's a big girl.

Is she? When Gerald's mother died, Mom was so kind to him. I remember he said, She lived a long life, she was eighty-seven, and Mom said, Doesn't matter. When it's your mother, she might as well be sixteen. God. It hurts so much, David. It physically hurts.

It does. I think she should just be happy now.

I think she should do what she wants. I just wish she wasn't so fucking alone.

Roger says meet at The Duke. He enters in his deliberate manner of straight paces to the bar without looking at anyone. He likes to plow a path of confidence in public places. I once joked he walked with the show-offiness of a much shorter man. He didn't like that one bit. From my seat, the thinning patch at the back of his head is visible and gives me some relief.

He plants down with two beer and two shots of Jäeger: Good to see you, Davey. We clink and drink. To your mom, he says. I'm so sorry.

Thank you.

How much time does she have? He sips his beer and winces. Never mind. We don't have to talk about it.

Could be three months, could be a year.

Jesus. You talk to your dad?

He knows. He's in Florida until May.

Fuck sakes.

I know.

How are you holding up?

I shrug. My eyes meet his and regret it immediately. All day I conjured up shitty Roger memories: those times he left in the middle of the night because he was *hungry* and went out for *food*. The text messages to the dealer: *if u bring it 2 the house & leave it under sink, you get another $50.* But now he is all earthy-eyed comfort. And the new beard is kind of cheesy, but it works, goddamn it.

He pushes over a small paper bag. I made chocolate peanut butter balls with them, he says. I think Marsha will like that.

That's great, thanks.

How is her emotional state?

The same. Infuriatingly the same. My sisters are stressed trying to please her, which Charlene gave up years ago. If she's not going to say what she wants, I'm not going to guess.

Friggin' mothers.

It's the first time in ages she's asked for something directly. Well, mostly directly.

I'm surprised she's never tried them before. You know, being a baby boomer and everything.

He signals the waitress for another round. So. I'm kind of wondering something, he says. Don't answer if you don't want to.

Shoot.

Why didn't you introduce me?

I never introduced anyone.

Okay.

And I was never sure if you were serious. She's pretty serious. But I should have. It would have been nice for you to know each other.

You talk like she's already gone.

I don't know how receptive she is to meeting new people.

I understand.

The waitress sets down two beer and two more shots. He asks about the shop. He compliments my new brogues before calling me a fucking dandy. I compliment his new beard before calling him a fucking hipster.

Then my voice cracks on the word *cancer* and his hand is on mine. I fight the urge to interweave my fingers with his. Charlene is worried about the shrooms, I say.

She doesn't have a friend to join her?

Her friends are mostly from church and high school.

Not really the tripping-out kind. Or maybe they are? What do I know?

Even if they are, I can't see her asking.

What about you?

I'm scared I'd get upset and ruin it for her.

Yeah. Oh, shit, that would be bad. It really is something you want a companion for.

He strokes the top of my knuckle. I want to close my eyes. I can be an option, he says. If you want. I mean, if she wants. You can just say I'm your friend.

He lifts his hand to sip his beer and I am immediately forsaken. I wouldn't say that, I say. I'd say who you are.

And then I want it, I want her to know one of my boyfriends. The boyfriend, even if he's not anymore. I'll ask, I say. The alcohol buzzes in my flesh. I want to move my chair next to his so I can talk into his neck. God, I say. I'm stressing out so much.

It can't be helped.

I'll see if she's up for it. And if not, I want you to meet her anyway.

It would be an honour.

We order another round. I remember how sometimes, when he got on a bender, he'd get maudlin about his father. Don't let me cry about Chichi, he'd say. We must follow the No Drinking and Talking about Dead People Rule. This also will be me. I'll move on, get through the days, get into normal till grief rears up when I'm trying to have a good time. It will be another thing Roger and I will have in common.

I can see the Virgin Mary, Mom says. She points to the glass door connecting the kitchen to the deck. Those smudges are her veil and hands.

Roger blinks. I see it, he says. She's praying.

I pour more wine. Mom made beef and mushroom stroganoff—her little joke. He answered her questions. Yes, he's done mushrooms many times. No, he's never known anyone to get brain damage. Usually he likes to do them outside. Maybe we could go out on the deck, she said. It will be chilly tonight, I said. Bundle up, kids.

Who's she praying for, Roger?

Well, you need it most. But I'm the bigger fuck-up.

We both deserve it then.

We both deserve it then, Roger says. Oh Marsha, you're so sombre. You sound like a prophet.

Maybe I am. I could start now. Go into the prophesizing business.

I bet you'd make a profit.

Roger had seconds and asked questions. Why never before, Marsha? Were you ever curious?

No, not at all, Mom said. I thought drugs were for damaged people.

And you never saw yourself that way?

No. I always prided myself as being comfortable in my own skin.

My fist clenched under the table. It was Dad who wasn't comfortable, I wanted to say. My skin fits fine.

I asked David about what he's tried, she said. And he mentioned cocaine. I was surprised.

Well, Marsha, Roger said. Since we're being honest, it was a problem for me. Scratch that. It is a problem for me.

Isn't it disgusting, though? Putting something in your nose?

It's the immediacy of it. Inhale and there you are, on that level. And it felt bad. I mean, the shame comes in the long term. But in that moment, it's doing something just for badness, you know what I mean?

Lately, Mom says, I think if Al and I had done more— had let ourselves go a bit when we were together, it would have been different. If we'd really travelled. Had experiences.

At least he'd have different memories of me. I wouldn't be his old ball and chain. I'd be his partner. Real partnership is rare. We never had that, Al and I.

Roger winked at me. We used to joke about the word partner and its not-so-gay-in-your-faceness. Friends are friends and pals are pals, but partners? Those people fuck.

But here we are, he said. And we're gonna do some shrooms. So, being comfortable in your own skin isn't your thing now?

How can it be? she said. Would I like to escape my reality for a bit? Yes, I would.

We need music, Roger says. He bustles out for the iPod dock. Mom's eyes are fixed on the setting sun. She is wrapped in layers of blankets and clothes topped with a purple pashmina, which gives her a kind of regal air. I remember Charlene bringing it back from her trip to Europe.

How are you, Mom?

The colours are fabulous, she says. I should enjoy sunsets like this all the time. She reaches for the joint in the ashtray.

Well, within limits, I say. I mean, it's still cold even though the days are longer.

She turns to me. Eyebrow crease set on scold. Don't take this the wrong way, dear, she says, but I can do whatever I want.

I laugh. She stares at me. Her weight loss has intensified her cheekbones and she affects almost old Hollywood glamour. Yes, I say. Yes, you can.

Roger appears with the iPod dock. Okay, requests? I bet

you're a Fleetwood Mac girl.

Stevie Nicks, Mom says. "Rooms on Fire."

I fall asleep on the couch to the rattle of their delirium. Roger wakes me at dawn. We go to the spare bedroom. He slides under my arms and sleeps. Mom remains outside, layered in warm protection, watching the sunrise.

Mom's schedule fills up. Sundays are Family Game Night, Mondays with Roger and me, Movie Tuesdays with Charlene. Brenda brings her to the twins' events. Every day she has a tea or a meal or a time.

Bits and pieces I've given her over the years emerge: a cashmere wrap, the Labradorite pendant. Things she once declared *too good to use*. She pours wine into her Waterford crystal goblets. I know Brenda wants these, she says. And I should be careful. But I've hardly ever used them and they're so lovely.

She wears lipstick and dark tops. She doesn't brush out her curls and Roger compliments her on her hair and she giggles like a teenager. The house is tidy when we visit as a family. But if it's just Roger and me, she leaves bits around, baggies and papers. We wipe the ashtrays and tabletops when we leave. She asks us to show her how to clear her browser history. Brenda might be alarmed about her research on microdosing. Charlene would feel left out.

She's doing so well, Charlene says. She's really loosened up.

Is she though? Brenda says. I was over the other day and

she was completely exhausted. Super moody.

Who's negative now?

Well, she definitely wasn't herself last week. She'd been all excited about seeing those Irish tenors at Holy Heart, so I got tickets. I reminded her twice during the week and she was keen to go. Then I call to say I'm coming to get her and she says not to bother. I asked if she's okay and she goes, I'm perfect. Then I say, well, Jim has the boys, I'll come over anyway, and she goes, No thanks, dear.

So? She's allowed to be a jerk once in a while.

When Brenda leaves, Charlene gets antsy. You should tell her about the pot. Mom probably doesn't want her to know, but she's getting the wrong idea.

Maybe she just didn't feel like Irish tenors.

If Brenda finds out, she'll be offended about not being told. And she'll blame Mom's behaviour on it anyway.

Well, it's Mom's choice to tell her.

Fine, David, be a chickenshit.

I'm not stepping on anyone's toes. You tell if it's so important.

On Sunday, Brenda's boys want to play Trouble, but Mom says the popping sound of the dice in the plastic globe gives her a headache. Charlene deals cards for a game of Knock.

So, the doctor says it hasn't spread, Mom says. She arranges the cards in her hand. No tumour growth. Everything seems to be hanging tight.

Oh, Mom. Oh, thank god.

Mom, that's fantastic.

How do you feel?

I feel great.

We need to celebrate, Brenda says. She goes to the kitchen. There's some wine around here somewhere. Here. She hoists up a bottle of Cabernet Sauvignon. Mom, where are the glasses?

There are lots of glasses in there.

No, the crystal ones.

Hmmm? Mom stares at the cards in her hand.

The crystal goblets, where are they?

Oh, I sold them.

What? They were Waterford crystal. They cost $170 a pair online.

Well, I got a good price for them, then.

Why did you sell them? Brenda says. If you need money, why not ask us?

I don't need money. If I feel like selling something to simplify my life, I shouldn't have to discuss it. Pour the wine. Use the mugs even. Who cares?

I can't believe you'd do that without me.

I got a temporary clean bill of health. I got a few more months. And I'm doing whatever I want, Mom says. She places her cards down. And I hate this game. It reminds me of your father and his douchebag friends.

Later, after Brenda sucks her teeth at Mom's d-word drop and Roger changes the subject to what everyone is watching on Netflix, I remember Dad and his smokes. I was nine and he had quit, or so he said. I was using the bathroom sink to make a magic potion of shampoo and Pepto Bismol and whatever might make bubbles. The Alka Seltzer tablets would make a satisfying pop and fizz. Inside the box was the open pack of Du Maurier. And later, Dad and Mom's argument, ricocheting off the kitchen walls.

Mom's medicines stare back at me from the bathroom cabinet. Above them, Oil of Olay, a peach-tinted lip gloss, a bottle of Shalimar. A box of shower caps. I've never known her to use one. I've never seen one drying in the shower.

The cap is pale pink and transparent. Two white babies rest inside, little pebbles. The plastic wrap on the powder bound tight into balls.

I take deep breaths before I check the wastebasket. Empty cellophane wrap. Bloody tissue. She went to the bathroom twice during supper and once before.

Roger's hand jerks the stick shift. She was adamant about trying it. I got some and left it with her.

You're an idiot.

Listen, she knows it's an issue for me and she didn't want you to know. I think she put it as, David didn't tell me when he was doing whatever he wanted, so why should I?

You should have told me.

She said she deserves to feel good in whatever way she can. I'm just trying to make everyone happy. And I help her. I make sure she doesn't drink too much when she's high. A girl her age, her condition, she doesn't have the liver function.

We don't speak, and when I get out he doesn't come with me. I call Mom to tell her I'm coming over tomorrow. Yep, yep, yep, she says. It's all good. I think about the ways she sat down tonight, like she didn't want to, like she wanted to strut around the room. Charlene's attempts at conversation. Hey Mom, you see that article about literacy levels, you hear that Gerald's daughter is pregnant, you see the forecast? Mom nodding. Pretending not to hear. Shuffling the cards without dealing.

The next day, she asks if I have pot. When I say no, she sighs and smokes her own anyway. When I ask about the coke, she shrugs. I don't think you should be worrying about me, she says. You have *your* whole life.

I used to think if someone knew you worried about them, they'd understand that concern meant love, she says. That maybe there was a reason for concern. But why worry about me now?

Mom, we can't help but worry. And you're not acting like yourself.

You try being yourself when you're full of cancer. Good luck not wanting other feelings to consume you for a bit.

She starts rolling a joint. Her fingers aren't proficient, but she's committed. At least I'm not going around with prescriptions at every pharmacy between here and Whitbourne, she says. Charlene should watch that. Her and her Ativan.

I text Roger: *We need to talk about what we're going to do about my mother.* When he arrives, I yell at him. I tell him to find a way to fix things.

But it isn't me, Davey, Roger says. It's her. I don't think she's addicted to anything. But she doesn't want to stop.

You're a shit.

But she lied to me. She told me the doctor said she only has a month left. So I figured it wouldn't hurt to help her.

And it didn't seem like . . . like it would be a problem for long? She wanted me to believe that. And I told her I can't. And she said fine, give me your source.

Did you give it to her?

Yes. But he's over in Torbay.

He tries to hold my gaze, but I'm too furious. And I'm not taking her, he says. So she's shit out of luck. She's not addicted anyway, Davey. She just likes it.

I take deep breaths. She doesn't drive and she's lost her enabler. Unless she gets cabs. Unless the guy will deal with her alone.

We make a plan. Roger will talk to her while I clean the place. I'll dump what she has. We'll talk about how well she's been doing heath-wise. We'll talk about conflicts between her medications and recreational drugs. We'll talk about breaking the law. And if she's difficult, we'll tell Brenda. She loves us, she'll listen to us. When we tell Mom she's hurting us, she'll stop.

Okay, Davey, Roger says. We'll fix it.

At the house, the door is locked. My key doesn't work. I knock on the window while Roger calls out. All lights are off. Maybe she's with Brenda, I say. Maybe she had an appointment.

We turn at the sound of an engine. The Corolla lights up and moves. And there she is, Marsha Zane, behind the wheel. Her hands clamped on at 10 and 2. Her curls casting a wild silhouette in the dying sun. Her eyes meet mine and she raises her index finger off the steering wheel in the most nonchalant of gestures.

THE NEAL CONTINUUM

NEAL WARREN KEEPS ONE INSPIRATIONAL quote stuck to the fridge: *Life is like riding a bicycle. To keep your balance, you must keep moving.* Albert Einstein.

Neal has not checked if this quote was actually coined by Albert Einstein, and the fact that he doesn't care about its accuracy reflects how he has established Balance in his life. Some people would care and believe he should care. But Neal keeps himself busy and thus avoids contact with those kinds of people.

Routine is the most important factor in keeping busy. Five days a week, he rises at four a.m. to go to the bakery. Most recipes are his versions and he doesn't have to think about them. Tuesdays: Rosemary Garlic Potato Focaccia. Wednesdays: Molasses and Ginger Marble. Thursdays: Multigrain Date. Fridays: Cheese Baguettes. Saturday: Classic Dinner Rolls. Sundays and Mondays off. Sifting, mixing, kneading, cleaning—calming, predictable work. Too busy for much more than a quick conversation with Sophia or Ryan. Sophia talks about what she did on the weekend and what she'll do the coming weekend. Ryan obsesses about his record collection. Neal nods here and there without prompting anyone for more info.

Afterwards, it's deliveries to coffee shops and convenience stores. When he gets into a rhythm, he's home by 8:45 a.m. with a third cup of coffee, savouring the pleasure of being flour-dusty and done, a morning spent with few words and full hands, oven heat exuding from his skin. He watches the start of rush-hour traffic from his front window. See ya, suckers.

But sometimes there are variations, like special orders of Saturday's rolls for group lunches and suppers; soup and rolls are easy to distribute. Usually it's fine, but last week, the rolls were for a baby shower at a legion hall. Neal entered the main room in error—made sense at the time, that's where the platters of cookies and dessert squares were laid out. But he was chased off by the grandmother-to-be. She half-ran towards him, all determined swishes of electric polyester, her head compact with white curls: No men! No men allowed! He did an about-turn, balancing the trays. A nearby table exploded with old-lady laughter, bouncing off the legion walls like a chorus of rusty sirens: What a sin for you, Marion. Was it really that funny? He left the rolls in the kitchen next to some Styrofoam plates.

On the return drive, he fought to keep his mind in order. These gender-segregated events, planned to a T, an opportunity to serve themselves and not men, their laughter so shrill, silly, and desperate. No booze, no drugs, just stuffing their mouths with sweets all day in safe, ritual indulgences.

This kind of thinking always stirs a dark disgust in his core, something leftover from junior high, the fierce, unnameable resentment towards female teachers close to retirement, like Mrs. Metcalf, the English teacher, and Sister Sheila, for religion. Doling out punishments if he didn't look and listen to what they were doing, the creak of their voices and flash of dusty rose bra straps as they aged before his eyes.

But what was worse, certain classmates, like Blair Ingram, with his over-combed black hair and huge Adam's apple that wiggled suggestively when he spoke. People like Blair enjoyed using Neal's full name as a command: Kneel, Warren! And then a bent knee in the back of his own knee so he couldn't help but crumple forward. Or someone standing over him with raised, demanding arms: Kneel, Warren! Always the pause. Yes, you recognize how a grammatical pause gives new meaning. Good job, asshole.

Blair called Mrs. Metcalf and Sister Sheila dried-up cunts and sloppy old sluts and wrote nasty things about them on the bathroom walls. Once, Neal told him, as quietly and directly as felt safe, that he should knock it off. Blair's shiny Adam's apple all up in Neal's face. Fuck off, Warren, it said. You fucking homo.

When Neal returned home after the baby shower, he reorganized the Tupperware drawer and the dry goods cupboard. He aligned can labels until the darkness faded into Balanced grey. On Sunday, he woke early and drove to the old apple orchard in Torbay. He filled three Sobeys bags with apples and as he rinsed and dried them, he felt confidence restore itself with the sight of their firm green skin. Such great candidates for chutney and applesauce.

This labour of obtaining his own food is part of Balance but involves connections with the right people. There is Neal's neighbour, Richard, who enjoys anything homemade and will trade for it: some moose meat, the occasional cod, some homegrown pot. There is walking Mrs. Freeman's dog in exchange for fresh chicken eggs. There are people who like his baked goods and know where the best chanterelle locations are or grow their own vegetables or snare rabbits. Knowing he can forage nutrients by his own hands and cashless barter is soothing. He can survive without being shaped to fit some consumerist box. He can distance himself from the pressure to be impressive on paper. He can rest easy in the knowledge he is capable and resourceful and not some worry or project or obligation.

But all interactions require management. Neal maintains a few batches of homebrew and wine for when he's invited to house parties. Richard has a shed full of tools which Neal is welcome to borrow, so he makes sure to show thanks with a few bottles. But, with this much booze around, plus pot and the small collection of pills from East End Mark, one needs control. Pre-Balance, before the accident, involved too many benders and frustration. Meeting a girl in a bar and trying to get her in bed by nodding and expressing concern with eye contact and buying drinks. And late, unsatisfying nights, occasionally with someone only tolerable because they had cocaine. And hangovers, and gritty feelings sparkling like new asphalt in the bright sunshine.

And even with control, things happen. Neal recently brought over blueberry jam to Richard's and was asked to stay. They smoked up to Grateful Dead records. Which started fine, but then the combination of Richard's baritone voice and grey beard and the Grateful Dead lyrics with their undertones of hippy-dippy melancholy—*come on all you pretty women with your hair hanging down*—made Neal crave other focus. He got way too high and paced his house for hours, shaking out thoughts of mistakes with women and the accident last year: the black Pontiac Sunfire sliding into view on the right, his hands on the steering wheel jerking the Volvo into the left lane, the slow-slow-fast spin towards the opposite ditch. And falling and turning and falling and turning. Except, in his dreams, the calmness doesn't fill him as it did that night, when the car stopped rolling and he realized he was unharmed and, in that moment, accepted death without fear. Instead, he opens his mouth and a thousand sounds escape and he wakes glazed in hot panic.

The next time Richard pulls out the pot, he'll make sure he has an excuse to leave early. Gotta work tomorrow. Gotta wicked headache.

It is Tuesday. Neal is dropping off an order of focaccia to Fixed downtown. Which wouldn't be so bad, but the café doesn't have a back entrance and he has to wait at the counter. The place is all trendy aqua and wood panelling. The patrons are the kind who wear winter hats all year long and speak with an affected fry like their sinuses are congested with apathy. Everyone's faces are in their phones. Neal wonders what today's generation will be like as old people. Backs stooped from hand-held devices, Alzheimer's patients picking up small things and making texting gestures. *My son never retweets me, WTF?* Fights erupting in retirement homes when Nickelback is played or someone denies the value of craft beer.

As he waits for the bearded barista to sign the invoice,

he spots Jenny Tilley. She sits near the window with a book. Jenny always enjoyed cafés like this, places where she can sit and read intellectual-looking things. She also enjoyed Instagramming random, boring items: her five-dollar latte, her new shoes. Adding a filter to a photo of clouds to *make them more vibrant*. Seeing her reassures him it wouldn't have worked out. He is glad to see her here and not in a place where this reassurance may not come so easily.

It was in a coffee shop like this that he told her to go fill her boots. Their table had an uneven leg. A man and woman sat at the next table and the woman talked and the man nodded without looking up from his phone. But nothing she said was that interesting: I'm dreading having Sunday blues tomorrow. Cindy says she's joining the roller derby.

So, Jenny said. We've been together a couple of months now.

Six weeks, Neal said.

Okay. And I'm not really sure what's going on. But I got asked out by someone.

Yeah?

Yeah. I wasn't sure what to say. I mean, I don't know if you want to be exclusive or not.

By all means, say yes, Neal said. He took a swig of his coffee. It burned the top of his mouth. He wished it was something stronger. He should have made it Irish.

Really?

Yeah. Fill yer boots.

Jenny stared at him. There was a little leaf pattern on her latte foam. The woman at the next table looked at her fingers: My lips taste like hand sanitizer.

They finished their beverages. Jenny left right away.

Later, he learned it was Shane Summers who asked her out. Shithead Shane fucking Summers, bass player and downtown douche, always getting laid even though he never has money and still wears those low-crotch, saggy jeans that look like sweaters worn as pants. For months, Neal left rooms Shane entered, once walking out of a show when he realized Shane was playing with the main act.

Neal senses movement from Jenny. He prepares to be friendly, but neutral.

Hey Neal, Jenny says. She still wears her hair long to her shoulders, straight and marshy brown. She has new glasses with black, squarish frames.

How you doin', Jenny?

Pretty good these days. Finished my thesis.

That's great. Finally put that bastard to bed.

You still at the bakery?

Yeah, just dropped these off.

He gestures to his tray of wrapped focaccia loaves. She leans over them. They smell amazing, she says. I'm getting one. Her head hovers under his nose and her hair exudes something tingly warm, like cloves or allspice. Her hair smelled like that back then too, in bed, spilling over his collarbone as she leaned over him.

Don't bother buying one, he says. I'll get you one from the car. No charge.

Really?

Yeah, I'm just doing deliveries.

My lucky day.

She follows him to the car talking the whole time: Her master's advisor is recommending her thesis on local sustainable agriculture for some lofty-sounding publication, she's planting sunflowers in her backyard to try and remove the lead from the soil. He nods and nods and when he turns to her from the trunk of the car, she peers at him over her trendy glasses.

So, how are you, Neal? I never see you around anymore.

Best kind. Keeping busy.

I sent you an email. When I heard about the car accident.

Yes, I got it. Sorry I didn't write back.

Did they ever find who ran you off the road?

Nope. Some random asshole. This city is full of bad drivers.

He puts a loaf in an empty Sobeys bag and hands it to her: We make this kind every Tuesday. So you know.

Thanks so much. You should come over some time. My boyfriend Paul and I live on Young Street.

Oh yeah? Paul, huh?

Yeah, we just moved in together.

Didn't work out with Shane, I guess.

He says this with a little laugh which is supposed to be light, but comes out like a cough. Jenny stares at him.

Shane? Shane who?

Shane Summers. You know, he asked you out.

Oh that. Jesus. I never went out with him. She crosses her arms at him: Where'd you hear that?

Well. You said, back then, someone asked you out.

Oh yeah, he asked me out, but I wasn't interested.

Oh.

Yeah, I guess when I brought it up, I basically wanted to know if things were getting serious. She shrugs. The Sobeys bag bounces lightly on her thigh.

Oh.

Everything is timing, I suppose. You seeing anyone now?

No.

You should come over some time. Paul and I throw the occasional dinner party. My god, the food you make? You'd be the potluck star. You on Facebook?

No.

Well, I still have your email. I'll drop you a line.

Okay.

Or you know, write me sometime. Don't be a stranger.

Sure. Will do.

Talk to you later.

Neal gets in the car. In the rear-view mirror, Jenny unlocks her bike and brings it to the street. She mounts and is instantly full of grace and speed. She pedals off standing over the seat, the silhouette of her ass shifting side to side. He remembers how, when she would get on top of him, she would rise up on the balls of her feet to slide up and down, her ass cheeks slapping his thighs. He closes his eyes and lowers his forehead on the top of the steering wheel.

Going out for one drink is fine and the house doesn't hold enough distractions. He changes his shirt and places three five-dollar bills in his front jeans pocket. It's a Tuesday, there won't be much on. Some places promise live music every night, but it usually translates to one guy with a guitar who knows the full repertoire of Tom Petty.

The Rose is empty except for two people at the VLTs and the regular bartender, Gary Something. Neal knew his surname a long time ago. He orders a Guinness. Stout is something he's never tried to make, so it's a treat. Plus, it's easy to sip slowly and The Rose has a good draft pour. When he and Jenny were together, she liked Guinness too, said it was full of iron. She insisted it tasted different when she was in Dublin; she drank it every night there and never got a hangover. Because of the iron and fish oil and stuff, she said.

Why is he thinking about her? It lasted maybe six weeks. It was before the accident even. She talked too much, her friends even more, stupid topics—reality TV and Etsy and who was at what show downtown over the weekend. Jenny, so smart and educated, embroiled in insipid conversations about cake decorating and award shows.

But she was funny. She got what she called overpackaging rage and broke brand-new things trying to release them from what she called their finicky-ass-plastic-bullshit casings. Wrestling with a package of scissors in her tiny hands: Fuck this irony, throwing it across the table. She admired Neal's tactile patience, his ability to tie proper knots, the details he put on loaves of bread and pastries. Her legs, so skinny with knobby knees, but holding up that lovely, round bum. How she tanned dark that summer so her hazel eyes stood out like new pennies.

Whadderyaat, buddy?

Shane Fucking Summers is at Neal's elbow. Since Neal last saw him, he's grown his hair long and acquired a squirrelly moustache. He punches Neal's shoulder: Dude, I haven't seen you in ages. How've you been?

Keeping busy. Baking and making stuff.

Busy, huh? You were always like that. Shane presses his hands together and wiggles them back and forth: Forever on the move. Like a shark.

That's me.

Check this out, man.

Shane opens his wallet and slides out a photograph of a baby in a pink onesie. Black ringlets encircle her head and her chin shines with drool. Shane taps the photo: This is what I've been busy making.

Neal holds it and nods. Shane could have wiped the youngster's face before taking the photo. Beautiful, he says.

Her name is Nevaeh. Know what that means?

Sounds Gaelic.

It's heaven spelled backwards. And she's made my life heaven, man. I was against it at first, you know. Me and her mom were just hooking up and she got pregnant. My first impulse was to have nothing to do with it. But we're a family now.

Congrats, Neal says. If Nevaeh is heaven backwards, wouldn't that translate as the opposite of heaven? But Shane's eyes are extra shiny and it makes him somewhat tolerable.

What about you, man? You with anyone?

Nope.

Neal sips his pint and realizes it is half gone. Since Shane appeared, he's taken big gulps. This guy's presence makes him drink faster so he can leave the bar and go home. Shane Summers, making people drink, making people pregnant. Making people break up with their girlfriends when they don't want to.

A stream of people enters the bar. They wear matching T-shirts, white with the German flag. Some have their legs tied together three-legged-race style.

Must be a pub crawl, Shane says.

MUN German society, Gary the bartender says. They

order the same shirts every year.

Let me get the next one, Shane says.

No, I should go.

Dude, I never see you. Gary's already pouring it up.

The students surround them now. They are impossibly young. Does Gary bother to ID? One of them jostles Neal's arm and the photo of Nevaeh flutters to the floor. He retrieves it and when he sits back up, the fresh pint is ready.

Cheers, man, Shane says.

He grins. Neal glimpses the bottom row of his teeth under his hipster 'stache. Like road pylons. How has this clown managed to get so much tail? Neal clinks his pint glass against Shane's bottle: Cheers.

The bed is hard and cold. Neal shifts and his face peels off the sheet like a sticker. Something is different. He opens his eyes. The bed is made of white square tiles. Above his head is the base of a toilet. What the fuck.

Neal sits up. He is on a bathroom floor. Someone has covered him with a grey army blanket. His mouth tastes like metal.

He rubs his face. There is a patch of some kind of grit on his left cheek. He rubs his hand on his jeans. His jeans are caked with dried mud. He stands. Dirt falls off him in flakes. His hands are filthy. He goes to the mirror over the sink. Streaks of mud line his face. There is a cut on his chin. Blood on his shirt and what looks like puke. Holy fuck.

The bathroom is familiar. A plaque over the towel rack. Royal Canadian Legion Regional Darts, 2013. Richard Puddicombe. Richard's house. Did he see Richard yesterday?

Was he at the bar?

Downstairs, Richard butters toast at the kitchen table. He sees Neal, purses his lips and gives a low whistle.

How you doing, soldier? Richard says. Breakfast?

The smell of scrambled eggs buckles Neal's stomach. No thanks, he says. What happened?

You were in the alley off McMurdo's Lane. Gus and I came out of The Duke and he goes, Look at that poor fucker. And there you were on the ground. You were the poor fucker.

On the ground?

Yeah, we brought you here. Your legs didn't work. We kept you from falling down, but it looks like you were falling down all night. Richard points to Neal's mud-caked jeans.

I don't remember anything.

Some bender you were on.

I had two pints, I think.

You had more than that.

That's all I remember.

C'mon, b'y. It's okay, we all tie one on once in a while.

I don't remember finishing the second pint.

Maybe you got date-rape drugged or something. Richard laughs and chomps into his toast.

Neal regards his right hand. The fingernails are edged in black. Maybe.

Richards slurps his tea. What kind of bars are you hanging out in? he says. He smiles so hard tea dribbles down his chin.

I was at The Rose, Neal says. He pats his pockets. Keys are still there. No wallet. But he didn't bring his wallet; he brought fifteen dollars in cash. He checks. Cash is gone.

But the first pint was eight dollars anyway.

You want to clean up? Richard says. Take a shower if you want.

No, I need to get home and call work.

You sure you don't want something to eat?

I don't think I can eat anything.

Well, hope nobody dosed you. Fucking epidemic. Oil money has ruined this town. All these girls getting roofied. Why would anyone want to fuck a woman when she's passed out? Necrophilia.

Richard chuckles and munches into a piece of toast. Neal eyes the crumbs dusting Richard's bearded chin. He could reach out slow—ya got something right there, Richard—and clout him good on the lips. Hard enough to send him backwards. Let him fall on the floor like a fat, smug, grey fish.

Outside, the sun pounds him. His legs sweat in his stiff, filth-caked jeans. Three teenage boys with backwards ball caps and skateboards move out of the way as he passes them. Pig-Pen's off to see Charlie Brown, one says. They explode with laughter. He keeps going.

Back home, Neal undresses in front of the bathroom mirror. There are brown smudges on his underwear and streaks on his thighs, three long ones, like fingers. His fingers? Fuck. Maybe he should go to the cops. If he's going to the cops, he should take pictures. He opens his flip phone and snaps a photo of his thighs. What could this prove? These could be anyone's thighs.

He examines his face and head. His cropped hair is

matted behind his ears. He didn't think it could collect so much dirt at its short length. The filth on his face makes his eyes greyer than usual. Pig-Pen indeed. Is he really going to take pictures of his smeared body with his pants down? Will they need to see his dick too? He pulls back the elastic on his underwear and looks. The fabric is clean inside. Nothing in his pubic hair. He cups his balls. Nothing there. Nothing on the shaft or foreskin. Oh good, no dick tampering happened. Jesus Christ.

Make a decision. The police station means questions and tests. Questions like what are his habits and does he drink often or do drugs. Tests like inspections and swabs. It will be a long day. He won't be able to shower until later. And if he hasn't been drugged? Don't drink so much, Buddy.

And if he's been drugged, the cops will go to The Rose and question Gary. Ask about security cameras. Most bars have security cameras, yes? And fucking Shane, they'd have questions for him. What are Gary and Shane like, really?

The blur of students, their matching clothes. There were girls with them. Maybe this was someone's dirty little plan. Maybe he did someone a favour, some girl who might have been harmed. But fuckers like that carry more than one dose. They'd be slick about it. They stay sober while others drink, wait for opportunity—someone makes a joke and everyone turns and laughs or the band starts playing and everyone looks to the stage or someone puts their glass down while they're in the bathroom.

The phone squishes out of his sweaty hand and clatters onto the floor. He has to remove this slime of fear and shame and strange interference. This is his decision.

In the shower, he blasts hot water and frisks the soap into a thick, coating lather. His fingers discover collections of dried crud in his right ear, left armpit, ass crack and behind his knees. He lathers and rinses three times. He lists what he'll do when he's clean: call the bakery, tell Sophia he had food poisoning, sorry Sophie, sorry. Put on soft clean clothes, order a pizza. Watch movies he's seen before—distractions without surprises. Go to sleep, sleep as much as possible. Maybe take something to knock him out. What if it messes with something leftover in his blood? Jesus.

He leaves the shower and wraps up in a towel. He sits on the toilet and focuses on the word breathe. Breathe for Balance, breathe. When his breathing is regular, he notices the shower is still running. He listens to the constant fuzz of water, keeping on without him.

Sophia says, Oh no, with high raw concern and he says, It's okay. Then he says one of his friends brought him soup and painkillers and she doesn't have to come over. When he hangs up, he is relieved but also maybe he should have said yes to soup and ginger ale and kindness.

When the pizza arrives, he puts on Star Wars. He has all day to watch the original trilogy. He dozes off at the start of *Empire Strikes Back* and wakes to a pounding at the door. Jenny Tilley is on his step.

So. You are home.

Hey, Jenny. Um, sorry, I wasn't expecting anyone.

I guess you didn't read my emails. I tried calling you, but your number's different now.

Yeah, haven't been on the computer.

Yeah, well. She purses her lips. Christ, Neal. You were out of your mind last night.

Yeah, I know.

I wrote to see how you were and you didn't respond. I needed to see if you were okay.

Sorry. Didn't mean to make you worry.

She stares up at him, biting her lip. Can I use your bathroom? I forgot to pee when I decided to come over.

Sure.

In the living room, she eyes the sweaty pizza box and Gatorade.

Want some pizza?

No thanks.

She perches on the edge of the couch so her knees don't touch the blanket. Paul and I were out for dinner and we saw you on Water Street with Shane, she says. You were babbling. Shane was holding you up. I told him to get you a cab. When I texted him later, he said you told him to fuck off and ran away.

Oh, Neal says. Of course, she has Shane's number.

Yeah. I think he could have tried a bit harder. But he was pretty drunk himself.

She draws her legs in, like she's trying not to put too much of herself on the couch. They had sex on that couch once, him sitting, her straddling. She said it was her favourite way because she could stick her tits in his face and he said it was his favourite too.

A good friend of mine had her drink drugged a couple of weeks ago, she says. She was messed up, like you. We had to carry her home. She's going back and forth with the cops and the bar now. I just—I'm really scared for my friends these days.

Something clusters and rises in Neal's throat. He should

tell her to leave, go on home to your boyfriend, whatshisname, Peter or Paul. Her eyes are dark and gentle behind her square lenses. I think that's what happened to me, he says.

Jenny is on his computer. Search results for Men being roofied and Men on date rape drugs bring up mostly blog posts and forums: *How can I tell if I've been roofied? What to do if you see someone drug a woman's drink. Symptoms of date rape drugs.* She reads the list: Drunkenness, confusion, nausea, passing out, memory loss. There's an article that focuses on rich guys in New York City getting roofied and having their Rolexes and credit cards stolen.

I had less than ten dollars on me.

Have you thought of going to the police? she says. Might not be too late to do a blood test. Not that it's what you should do. No pressure.

I know.

Although, if you were a woman, I'd encourage you to come forward. And there would be an investigation.

No doubt.

It's not a women's issue, you know that, right? I mean, this happens to everyone. There's not a lot online 'cause men don't come forward. But if men did, it'd be a social issue, not a women's issue.

Yeah, I see that.

Like the Question of the Day that radio station did: What should women do to protect themselves against date-rape drugs? Why not say, what should we all do? It's infuriating.

He nods. He kind of remembers the news item. More of Richard complaining about how people pick at the question's wording rather than answer it. He might have agreed at the time.

I'm so sorry, Neal.

It's okay.

No. It's horrible this happened to you.

Well, it should never happen to anyone.

See, that's what I mean. You get it. You're a good guy.

Her phone jingles. It's Paul, she says. I gotta make a move. She stands an arm's length away. He could touch her. In a neutral way, hand on her shoulder.

My number's on your desk. Call if you need anything. She hugs him, a quick squeeze. I'll email you tomorrow.

And she's gone. He sits in his computer chair. It's still warm from her presence.

At bedtime, Neal takes one of East End Mark's Ambien. He needs sleep, but lying around all day means it will take time for his body to get tired. And there will be thoughts. Tonight, a sleeping aid, tomorrow, back to Balance.

The pill is a good idea because his mind starts up immediately. Someone else out there joins the Getting Away With It Club. People run you off the road or poison you, leave you to die in the street as they go home and watch TV and masturbate over their mischievousness. He remembers his sister on the phone after the accident: So, the cops can't find the driver? She paused, getting her words ready like she was preparing to spit. It's just, I don't know. This town ain't that small. Are you sure you were straight that night?

And then his voice on pins: Why would I fake it? You know what, Carla? Go fuck yourself. He hung up. The residual anger bubbles, but the pill kicks in and everything is warm and dull.

The next morning at the bakery, he gets right on the dough maker. He makes extra and bakes a large batch of cinnamon buns, makes cream cheese icing with a zap of orange zest. He gives some to Sophia and Ryan and there are still a dozen left over. An offering to Jenny wouldn't be out of line. For her and Whatshisnuts. She's been kind while he's been a zero-communication goof. Giving back is good for Balance.

Jenny's place is a narrow downtown house painted apple green. You're so thoughtful, she says at the door. Come in. Paul's at work. I'll make tea.

They sit in her small kitchen. An herb garden flourishes on the windowsill, the refrigerator door explodes with colourful magnets.

I bought a coffee this morning, she says. They left it on the counter so I could add sugar or whatever. I thought, who's to stop someone from putting something in that? Like that Detroit girl who died when her Mountain Dew was drugged.

I never think about stuff like that.

The RCMP did a drug presentation at Paul's work last year. The cop said people will just drop something in your drink for shits and giggles.

Of course she told Paul. He was there when Neal was messed up on Water Street. He met Jenny's boyfriend and doesn't remember. Nice first impression, Warren.

How do you think they do it? she says.

A bowl of candy sits on the table, retro stuff, probably from the overpriced kitsch store on Water Street. He unwraps a package of Rockets and takes out one sugar pill: How would you slip this into a drink?

Try to drop one in my tea, she says.

There's something on your shirt, Neal says. He reaches across the table and points at her collar. One pill falls from his palm into her tea with a plop.

Real subtle, she says. Let me try. Hey, what's that? She points behind him. He glances back quickly.

Did you do it?

Yup.

Wow. You're smooth.

They make a game of it, divvying up the candy. Jenny wins, 7-4, undetected. He is about to challenge her to a rematch when Paul arrives. He is tall, dark, and business casual. Great hair. They shake hands and there is a spark of recognition in Paul's eyes: Yeah, nice to meet you. Neal's face flushes: Well, I better be moving on. Enjoy the cinnamon buns. He takes a slurp of his cold tea. Ugh, the Rockets. He keeps it in his mouth until he's outside and spits it on the sidewalk.

He takes another Ambien that night. He doesn't expect to dream, but one lingers when he rattles awake with the four a.m. alarm. In the dream, he stands at the counter in Fixed. There is a shelf lined with things he needs: keys, phone, a pile of coins. He reaches and small white pills rain from his sleeves. They plop into a row of prepared lattes set up below on the counter. Someone screams. He looks to the window.

The black Pontiac Sunfire is parked outside.

On Friday, it's Cheese Baguettes. Ryan rants about how he was a member of some vinyl collectors' group on Facebook, but the administrator asked him to leave because of his comments. Thin-skinned pussies, he says. It's everyone's business to get offended these days.

Maybe, Sophia says, if you didn't refer to people as pussies, they wouldn't ask you to leave. They are still arguing when Neal goes to make deliveries. Why do they have to fill the bakery with drama? Everyone is an asshole.

Traffic is backed up on Military Road and he finds himself gazing into car windows. Drivers, passengers. How many are thieves? How many are violent? Maybe the person who drugged him is there, some upstanding citizen who gets their dark jollies on the weekends. Someone cuts him off at the Basilica intersection. He flips them off.

At home, he thaws Richard's moose meat and opens a bottle of wine. Just for today. He can take the edge off and still have Balance. The red is quite good and he chills a bottle of white for later. He should see how it aged, how it tastes cold. He'll allow himself some alcoholic euphoria. Things will be fine again soon.

He pours a glass and checks his email. One new message from Jenny:

Hey all. I've officially completed my master's degree!
Please join me at The Martini Bar tomorrow night for
celebratory beverages. Can't wait to see you!

Xoxo

Jenny

She's a friend now. He should also be a friend and go to her important things. And maybe, someday, who knows. She hasn't been with Paul long. Who knows what will happen? He'll go, have a couple of drinks and leave early. He'll congratulate her. They'll hug.

On Saturday, Neal drinks some homebrew to warm up for socializing. He drinks one before supper, then two more, but instead of mellowing, he finds himself staring out the window at passing cars and faces. He is glad he doesn't live in a larger city, no views of skyscrapers and teeming humanity. Before he leaves, he pops one of East End Mark's Percocets and takes along another for later.

When he arrives at The Martini Bar, he's buzzed enough that it doesn't bug him that Shane Summers is there. He stands by Paul, showing him what Neal assumes is Nevaeh's photo. For a new dad, he goes out often. He probably brags about changing diapers when he's only done it twice.

Shane claps him on the shoulder. Neal, buddy, how's it going? he says. Sure did tie one on the other night.

Something like that, Neal says.

Yeah, little Jen Tilley was worried about you. She's a good egg like that, eh Paul?

Shane clicks his glass against Paul's. Paul gives a benevolent nod. He wears a button-up shirt with a neat blue tie. He's a classy motherfucker.

You guys know each other? Shane says. Paul do you know . . . KNEEL, Warren!

Oh wow, that didn't occur to me, Paul says. He high-fives Shane. Neal stares at Paul's tie. He could yank down it real hard. Imagine, Paul's face gasping open like a drowning fish.

Kneel, oh baker of the sweetest breads! Shane raises his arms above Neal.

I don't think so, Neal says.

No, do it, humour me for a second.

Humour yourself.

No, I'm going to knight you, Shane says. He makes gestures with an imaginary sword.

Getting a drink.

Neal pushes past them to the bar. He glimpses his reflection as he waits for his pint. Face stony, eyes like piss holes in the snow. C'mon, Warren, compose yourself. Jenny's not even here yet and you have to look like an ol' sport. He glances back. Shane does some kind of staggering walk. Paul laughs.

There is no one else around who Neal knows. When his pint is ready, Shane waves him back over. He goes to them and lays his pint down. Maybe he should take another Perk.

Anyone call you that before? Shane says. I just thought of it.

In high school, yeah.

Oh man, I remember this guy back in Gonzaga. Rick Bentley, Shane says. We used to call him Dick Bent. And then some chick said he actually had a crooked dick. Poor fucker never lived it down.

There was a Jack Hoff in my sister's class, Paul said.

Oh man. That's child abuse.

Neal shoves his hands into his jacket pockets. There is something small and tubular at the bottom. A row of wrapped Rocket candy from Jenny's. He loosens the cellophane with his fingertips and a single, smooth tablet is there.

If it was a real pill, how easy would it be to dose one of them? Would they notice? It might be nice to know that they're as dull and vulnerable as he is.

Here's the girl of the hour, Shane says. The bar rings in enthusiasm as Jenny enters. Shane and Paul step forward. Neal's pint is next to Shane's. He reaches over Shane's glass and the single candy pill falls into the brown stout. The slightest of ripples. His fingers find his own glass and he brings it to his lips. The carbonation has settled nicely now. He allows himself a long, indulgent sip.

What did you just do?

A short woman with cropped dark hair is up in his face. Her chin juts out. Breath is gin and something sticky sweet, like pineapple. Behind her is a shaggy-haired person in a black hoodie. The face is gaunt and smooth.

Nothing, Neal says.

We saw you put something in that drink.

The woman pitches her voice so people turn around and stare. Jenny is in mid-hug with Shane and they both look over.

I didn't do anything.

Here, the woman holds up Shane's pint. This fucking guy dropped something in this drink.

Warren's my buddy, Shane says. He wouldn't do that.

It's just candy, Neal says.

It looked like a pill, the hoodie person says.

Yeah, a candy pill.

Why would you put candy in Shane's drink? Paul says. Jenny is by him now, biting her lip.

I was just fucking around, he says. It's only candy.

Prove it, the woman says. Empty your pockets.

Look, Neal says. He pulls out the open packet of Rockets. Candy, see?

Now the other pockets.

Neal swallows hard. This isn't fair. He pulls out his wallet, keys, phone. The pill canister of Percocet.

What are these? the woman says. She brandishes the Percocet for the bar to witness. There is a deep collective inhale and murmurs.

Those are mine.

Yeah? Yours for what? the woman says. Destroying people's lives? I'm so sick of the goddamn dirtbags in this town.

They're Perks. They're mine.

The hoodie person steps forward. Neal is suddenly reminded of an old cartoon, a wizard about to demand the answer to a riddle. Their voice is low and even. Listen, they say, we saw you put a pill in someone's drink. We see you have pills. You can say they're for you, but we don't know that. You can say they're Percocet, but we don't know that either. The person's eyes are hard and calm. They aren't fucking around.

Neal, is this for real? Paul says.

Everyone in the bar is watching. Angry mouths. Jenny's face is open and scared. Neal takes his wallet, phone and keys from the table. Casual, now. Hot and damp all over.

Take a look at Shane's drink, he says. It's just a bit of extra sugar.

But why would you do that? Shane says.

What odds? Neal says. His voice is high and unpractised. There's nothing in that drink to hurt you.

Maybe not this time, the woman says. Maybe we caught you rehearsing.

Someone call the cops, someone says.

Neal walks to the door. Get back here, the woman yells. A bouncer, tall and solid, comes around the bar. Neal runs out. The air is cold and stabs into his cheeks and neck. Voices, more yelling: Get that fucker! His boots smack the sidewalk. Clusters of people smoking outside the bar turn and stare. More yelling. Footsteps.

Neal makes it to Water Street and runs as hard as he can. How long has it been since he ran? How long has it been since he's been chased? Games of tag, games of softball. Run, Warren, run.

At the courthouse, he allows himself a look back. He's alone. He slows and his stomach lurches. He spits up. Half the bar knows him. Would they send the cops to his house?

He'll go to Richard's. Say there's a problem in his house, plumbing issues. He'll go home now, grab a few things. A cab appears and actually stops when he waves, a blessed, glowing, empty cab.

He takes long, steady breaths. Thighs on fire. Tomorrow, he'll email Jenny, give an excuse and an apology. Blame the booze and pills. He'll think of something to say to Shane the next time he sees him. He'll stay occupied and try not to shrivel up every time he thinks of what a goddamn idiot he is. His sister was right about him being fucked up. He is fucked up and should talk to somebody, see a doctor. If he wants Balance, he must be able to ask for help.

In the house, he fills a knapsack with T-shirts, socks and underwear. When he calls, Richard says no problem. I'll see you soon, Neal says. My phone is about to die.

He opens the door. The short-haired woman and the hoodie person are there.

No one would tell us your last name, the woman says. But I remembered someone yelling Neal Warren. Canada411.ca and boom, there you are.

What do you want?

I don't want much, the hoodie person says. But Julia here dealt with people like you before. She's at the point she can't try to forget it anymore.

Her eyes are beer-bottle brown and the bags underneath them hold all the sad feelings in the world. She holds something hard and metal that moves too fast to recognize, and when it hits Neal's head the pain is white and shining.

As Neal falls, he realizes he is without fear. Julia mouths things at him, her arm raised. Once again, he thinks, I am a target for strangers. But I am a stranger too, to them. They are strangers who believe I am bad and they stop bad strangers.

Good for them.

He might die now. Or he might lie here and recover. And if he recovers, he will find Balance again. He closes his eyes against the figures above him. When he finds Balance again, it will be with healthy ways, ways that involve people. He'll eat right, get some therapy. He'll go out in the world. And when he's ready, he'll call old friends, invite them over. With the food he makes, he could have a spectacular dinner party.

HANDS IN POCKETS

YOU ARE AT THE AIRPORT TOO EARLY. You know this, but at home you couldn't stop clock-watching and checking your passport in your carry-on. Might as well get here and stop thinking about getting here. In the check-in lineup, you ensure there are no coins in your pockets or obvious metal distractions. You are ready.

You get your boarding pass and check your suitcase and there is over ninety minutes until boarding. This will be your day: travel limbo and overpriced airport food, four-dollar bottles of water. You tuck your boarding pass into your passport and reach into your carry-on to check it once on the way to the bathroom and once again when you take a seat in the lounge area; your fingertips recognize the slim vinyl cover, the strip of cardboard, there it is, still there. Sean would call you antsy—he did call you antsy, the time on the ferry to Saint Pierre and you kept sliding your hand into your purse. He said what do you think they're going to do if your passport is gone? Make you swim back to Fortune? And then he was the one who let his passport expire.

There are two men sitting across from you. One is a cop and the other wears pale blue pants with a matching shirt.

They are handcuffed together. You notice other passengers noticing them, eyeing the handcuffed connection between the two men and the chain linking the prisoner's feet. A guy with dark-framed glasses and a beard and an iPhone stares hard at them and texts. Maybe he's tweeting about them. Maybe a complaint about tax dollars spent paying for prisoner travel. Maybe a joke about carry-on luggage.

You take out your own phone. There is a text from Sean: *Have a good flight. Love ya.* When you left, he was still in bed and he sat up to kiss you goodbye. His hair was stuck up on the pillow side of his head and he still smelled a little rummy. He didn't notice that you were leaving early, but you had the sense that he was waiting for you to leave. Last night, the both of you went for drinks with Todd and Cheryl and when Todd said, Too bad you're not going too, buddy, Sean gave this resigned sigh and you wanted to flip over the table. At home afterwards, you said to him, So now you're going to act like you want to come and he said, Why are you keeping score of my reactions.

The prisoner is falling asleep. His mouth hangs crumpled and open, like a cardboard box that's been stepped on. You can't tell if his eyelids are completely closed and suddenly you are overly present; there are no other people around you; if his eyes open, you will be where he will look. You hold your phone like you're going to call someone and move to the hallway. There is a bench close to the gates and you sit down, holding your phone like you're speaking into it. No one is watching you. Put your phone away. You are ridiculous.

A line of people waits to go into security. You watch a man and woman hug and kiss goodbye. She touches his face;

he has the appropriate amount of handsome scruff and her hair is tousled in a way that looks like she just crawled off him. The man goes inside and then waves and mouths things at the woman from the other side of the glass. She gestures and mouths things back. You watch them and it reminds you of a story you heard about a couple, both deaf, but they had a hearing daughter. When she was a toddler, she threw silent temper tantrums, fake wailing in grocery stores, her hovering parents trying to calm her, index fingers shh-signalling on their lips.

It was Sean who told you that story; the deaf couple were related to his college roommate. Both of them deaf since birth, but only the woman knew proper sign language; the man used his own system of gestures and pantomimes. Sean said they would come in to take his roommate out for lunch and invite him along. He said when they disagreed, they would reach out and clasp each other's hands to stop their words, physically interrupting each other. The last time Sean told that story, he said, Those people could really communicate, and you thought there was a pointed tone in his voice, a bit of stank on *those people.*

You watch a slender woman with blond hair join the security queue. She wears a white fleece jacket, expensive-looking yoga pants, and flip-flops. You should have done that, dressed in things that are soft but look clean and crisp. At least you could have worn shoes that don't lace up. And you could have brought a hat, something to hide the travel-frazzled hair that manifests from recycled air and removable headrests. These things and something to remove the layer of anxiety and public germs. A couple of moist towelettes in your bag wouldn't have been so hard.

Or you could decide not to care. You could get drunk on the plane. Or start drinking now, go into the airport restaurant, shoot shit with the bartender. You could pretend to be an American tourist on your way home. You could order something you never normally drink: a Harvey Wallbanger, a vodka gimlet. But would it relax you or lead you to do something stupid: forget your phone on the bar, walk away without your Visa card. You reach in your carry-on to touch your passport and your fingers swim through the empty expanse of your bag and your heart jumps to its feet but there it is, your passport just shifted deeper in the pocket when you sat down, relax, you foolish thing.

You check the time. In ten minutes, you'll go through security. You'll let yourself sink into a seat by the gate and put in your earbuds. Then it's just waiting to be told what to do. When the plane lands and you reclaim your luggage, you will change up some cash and put a small amount in your fake wallet, in case you get mugged. You will put a larger amount in your travel belt and later you will hide some in the secret pocket in the lining of your suitcase. You will go out for supper. You will avoid the questions that floated into orbit when Sean said he has too much work and getting his passport renewed is too much frigging around. But what will you do? What will you do if you meet someone? Someone who might pay compliments, which Sean says is a shallow practice. Someone who doesn't wait for you to initiate. Someone who might make you feel fresh and novel for a little while. Your passport and boarding pass sit in the carry-on, waiting to be touched.

APARTMENT 312

ONCE VALERIE HAS OPENED UP the housing co-op office, she compiles her lists. Today she needs to post tenant reminders: please submit tax forms for rent subsidies, annual fees are due May 1, please don't leave your clothes unattended in the laundry room. Brian has assigned a bunch of penny-pinching tasks: inventory the office supplies, send warning letters for overdue parking passes, make a sign encouraging everyone in the office to reuse paper if one side is blank. She writes these out in columns in her Day-Timer. And when it occurs to her, she adds to the collection of boy names she is putting together for her pregnant cousin. She adds only names she feels possess a certain kind of masculine grandeur: Desmond. Edmund. Sinclair.

Gary raps on her desk with one knuckle. Want to see something effed up?

I haven't even had my coffee yet, she says.

It's not like Gary to be in the office this early, or at all. Usually, he is found in motion around the building or with the other maintenance guys, smoking by the parking garage exit, tool-belted and dusty.

It's just upstairs, he says. It's really effed up. I kind of need an opinion on what to do about it.

Okay, she says.

She follows the wrinkled back of his navy coveralls up the stairwell. They seem too big for him. Gary is the co-worker who encourages everyone to throw in for lottery tickets when it gets over ten million. Every Friday, he emails corny jokes to the staff list. Stuff like two silkworms had a race. They ended up in a tie. The Friday Funny from Gary. When he kids around with Valerie, she makes a point to shake her shoulders a little when she laughs so she appears more amused than she really is. Gary and his childish-look-ing overalls and nuisance of wavy hair.

He unlocks the door to apartment 312. She knows by the number that this is Sidney's apartment. Sidney Makse, long-time tenant and board member. Every month when he hands her his rent cheque it always feels grubby, like his pockets are damp inside. He usually offers up something like, I was considering withholding rent until the building puts more salt on the steps. Or, Something has to be done about the condoms lying around the back exit. Doesn't Brian know the hookers on Jarvis Street bring men back there? She makes sure to answer, Please bring it up at the next board meeting. She often sees him at the Golden Griddle on Carlton Street, eating alone, pouring syrup on breakfast sausages, his bald head glazed with moisture.

Sidney gave us permission to come in, Gary says. We need to fix the bathroom sink. But I don't know what to do about this.

He holds the door for her. Sidney's apartment is packed with newspapers. They stand in pillars; the shortest ones come up to Valerie's waist, some reach the ceiling. A narrow path weaves through with detours to the bedroom, the bathroom, the kitchen. The apartment is heavy with the slightly sweet funk of old paper and she is reminded of being in a library. Then she thinks of silverfish and crosses her arms to make herself smaller.

What do I do? Gary says.

Well, he has to clean this up.

He was here this morning. I said, You got a lot of papers, Sid. He goes, Yes, but I only keep the ones with a story I want to remember.

It's a fire hazard.

The neighbours have been complaining about mice. There must be nests in here.

I'd say.

One of the piles could be a mouse high-rise. What do I do? Sidney's on the board.

Then he knows better.

Does he?

Gary runs a hand through his hair. He holds out his arms, palms out in presentation. I don't want to shame the guy, he says. But this kind of stuff—this is what sadness looks like to me.

Valerie regards Gary's raw concern. His saggy coveralls. She has never noticed until now that his eyes are bright blue, robin's egg blue. And even with his hair in its confused state, she can see it's good hair, thick and healthy. Gary might be quite handsome, she thinks, and flushes at herself. She and Gary, alone in Sidney Makse's mouse hole.

What should I do, Valerie?

We'll think of something.

That evening, she indulges in her ritual. It happens about twice a week, usually a Monday or Tuesday, when Friday is an ocean away. On these days, she takes the College streetcar home and gets off in Little Italy. Her favourite is Magnolia Deli near Palmerston Avenue. It sells olives stuffed with whole garlic cloves, soft Italian mozzarella, artichoke dip, fresh baguettes. She'll get whatever she feels like, maybe some goose liver pâté, a wedge of brie, smoked salmon. Once home, she prepares her white ceramic tray with little velvety dollops and chunks of everything. She opens a bottle of Shiraz or Malbec and fills a long-stemmed glass. She favours old movies: *Breakfast at Tiffany's*, *Some Like It Hot*. Sometimes she puts on her YouTube playlist: footage of singers like Ella Fitzgerald, Billie Holiday, the classy ones with good posture and clean lines.

When she finishes eating, she tops up her glass and produces the silver mirror and tweezers from the drawer in the bottom of her coffee table. She usually sits with her leg propped in her lap and starts on the middle of her calf where the skin is less taut. She plucks the hairs from her legs, careful to start at the root of each, clearing patches at a time. She still shaves them every Friday, but by Monday, there's enough growth to get a grip.

It is a ritual that usually comes to mind after lunch and gives her wheels all afternoon: alone time with luxury food and wine, a beauty regime at a snail's pace. Regarding the hairs clenched in the tweezers gives her a buttery, soothing level of comfort. She taps out the hairs on the mirror; these are wiped off with a tissue before bed. Sometimes, she plucks a hair out so cleanly, it takes the dead skin around the follicle with it and these ones are so satisfying that they come to mind as she lies in bed. Got that one. Got that one good.

This evening though, she thinks about when she and Gary stepped back into the hallway and he locked apartment 312 and they didn't say anything in the stairwell, but he thanked her at the office door and she asked him if he wanted coffee, even though she tries not to do that, be a coffee-getting receptionist for male colleagues. And he said, No, I'm a tea drinker and she said, Oh, I forgot and he thanked her again and she didn't see him for the rest of the day. She should think of something to say to him tomorrow.

The next day, Brian wants her to take coins from petty cash and check every vending machine in the building. Note the ones that don't work or are out of soda. Note the kind of soda that is sold out. We make money on these things and the guy who does the refills isn't reliable. If the machines don't work, that's lost money. Brian is a cheap bastard.

Valerie starts at the top floor and works her way down, trying to keep the canvas bag of cold soda cans from bouncing off her leg. She encounters Gary changing a light bulb on the fifth floor and opens the bag of cans to him. He takes a grape Crush and says, You're the best, Val. Then he asks her about Sidney's apartment and she says she'll draft a letter to him about it, she'll be kind. In fact, she'll bring it to Gary to see what he thinks.

I'll say it again, he says. You're the best.

As she walks away, she realizes she is grinning to herself. But she hates being called Val. And grape Crush is sickening.

That night, she eats marinated artichoke hearts and goat cheese on focaccia and clears off a two-inch strip of stubble from her ankle to her kneecap. She makes jot notes for Sidney's letter. Mention safety and health concerns: fire hazards, pests. Give him the option to organize and store some of the papers somewhere else. Say for the good of the building.

In the office, Gary points out a newspaper article to her. They figured out the DNA code of the woolly mammoth, he says.

Really? she says. Maybe they'll clone one.

They could. Maybe they could genetically modify them to make them small. Sell them as pets.

You want a miniature mammoth?

Sure.

You could call it Oxymoron.

Huh?

Nothing. Never mind.

Oh. Like military intelligence, he says. He laughs and something unhinges just between her rib cage and lungs. That's pretty good, Val, he says. He lays the paper on her desk. His hands look callused, but the fingernails are clean and maintained and she imagines the weight of his hand, like a warm, smooth beach rock in her palm. He taps the cover photo of the mammoth.

I bet Sidney's keeping this one, he says.

From then on, it is established. When Gary is around, Valerie's mind is a murmuration of competing feelings and ideas. He brings Geraldine, the accountant, a box of macaroons for her fiftieth birthday; he's kind. He teases Kathy, the bookkeeper, about the pink streaks in her hair; he's a hick. Or maybe he's flirting with Kathy. Maybe Kathy is interesting-looking and Valerie is only business pretty with her black dress pants and jewel-toned tops. She starts wearing earrings and decides not to straighten her hair so often. In the staff room, he asks about the leftover antipasto she's eating. It looks delicious, he says. But when she admits that these kinds of things are her favourite foods, he says, watch out, that stuff'll give you gout. And one day, during her break, she witnesses him pry open a can of kippers over the sink, drain off the brine, squirt yellow mustard over the contents and eat it straight from the can with a fork. At home, she clears most of the hair from her left leg below the knee so that she hardly has anything to shave come the weekend. She wonders if she actually likes Gary or if this is just something she has concocted, to make work more interesting, to make her be on time in the morning.

She prints off a draft of Sidney's letter and brings it to Gary. The main paragraph is brief, but hopefully effective and gentle: *It has been brought to our attention that you are keeping a large amount of newspapers in your apartment. Although we respect that this is your private collection, we have concerns about possible fire hazards and health risks posed by such a vast amount of newspaper. We understand that organizing and storing this collection is no easy task, so we would like to offer you assistance in sorting and storing said newspapers.*

Brian doesn't know about it, Valerie says. I thought you and I could help Sidney out. You know, maybe get some boxes and file folders and get him going with it.

Her face heats up, but Gary nods. Good idea, he says. You're a good person, Val. She puts the letter in the internal mail on Friday. Over the weekend, she imagines herself and Gary in Sidney's apartment, bound together by this task that will be awkward and monotonous, but a unique shared experience for the two of them. She'll know then whether this is a real crush or just a distraction.

On Monday, there is a cold disquiet in the building. At her desk, a Post-it from Brian: *See me as soon as you arrive.*

In Brian's office, Gary is already seated. The edges of his hair look dark and damp and he does not look up as she sits down.

There was an incident on the third floor last night, Brian says. Residents called security, said there was a yell and loud noises from Sidney Makse's apartment. Turns out he had towers of newspapers in there. He must have been trying to move one. They toppled over and trapped him underneath.

Is he okay?

He had a bad heart. The struggle to dig himself out triggered a heart attack. He was dead when the paramedics arrived.

Oh my god. Her hand smears over her mouth. Gary does not look up.

Yes. It's terrible, Brian says. He holds up Valerie's letter. Did you send this?

Yes. I thought it would help him.

If there is a health risk in one of the apartments, management has to be informed.

I'm sorry, Valerie says. I was just trying to help him.

Oh, it's not your fault. Gary and I have already determined that maintenance shouldn't have asked you to get involved this way.

But we didn't want to embarrass him.

I understand. But there are existing procedures for these types of situations.

But we were acting on it.

Maintenance is aware—should be aware—of how to handle things like this.

Gary is gone. She goes to the parking garage exit and asks the maintenance guys if anyone has talked to him. Brian likes to be Mr. Cool, Mr. I'm One of the Guys, Hugo says. That's until he gets a chance to make an example of you.

Brian the tyrant, Vlad says. Bri-rant.

I imagine Gary's lying low for a while, Hugo says.

Valerie thanks them and politely refuses Vlad's offer of a cigarette. As she walks away, she thinks that maybe she should have told them to tell Gary she said hi. But maybe that's dumb right now.

Weeks pass. Maintenance gives Sidney's apartment a fresh coat of paint and it is rented out to a couple working at Ryerson. *NOW Magazine* does a piece on a new bedbug scare in Toronto. There is so much coming and going in the building, so many students and temporary tenants; she hopes bedbugs do not become something she has to deal with. One of the security guards gets fired for stealing a box of toilet paper from the supply closet; she has to type up his dismissal letter. She tries not to think of Sidney's last moments, the newspaper stacks tumbling, domino-style, an avalanche tumbling around him, the mildewed stories he wanted to keep becoming a swamp, becoming quicksand, sticking to his wet, panicking face.

She looks up Gary's home number in the employee records. She calls with the intention of hanging up when he answers, after she hears his voice. What will she do if he reacts with embarrassment instead of pleasure? But the number is disconnected and this also feels awful. She wants to ask around if anyone has talked to Gary, do they know where he is now, did he get a new job, but doesn't know what she would do with this information. Maybe say sorry one more time. She finds herself looking at strangers in the subway, scanning faces on the platform as the train pulls away.

One day, she sees him. He is also waiting for the Bloor subway on the westbound platform. His hair is shoved to one side in a kind of part. She has never seen him in real clothes before. She confirms that Gary, in his pilly sweater and faded jeans, is handsome. He is definitely handsome.

She will approach him now. She will approach him and speak. She will put her hand on his shoulder. She will say words like so good to see you and you look good and I'm so sorry and let's go, let's get coffee, no tea, he likes tea. She will tell him she remembers that he likes tea. She will go to work on Monday. She'll use her break time to update her résumé. She steps towards him and opens one hand in greeting.

GUTLESS BRAVADO, PART FOUR

JULIA NEEDS TO FEEL READY. She's home now and between jobs. She's letting me stay with her. She sleeps on the top floor and keeps a rope by her bed with climbing knots spaced out on it. She carries things: a Swiss army knife, brass knuckles she made in the machinist shop. I wonder if she is like this because of Max or if it's always been part of her personality. Or it's a phase. She was scared for a long time and now she craves control. But living together is nice. She likes to cook and doesn't mind my bit of clutter.

She also wants to be on the go all the time. You've been cooped up too long, she says. C'mon, we goes. She likes happy hours and live music shows where we dance in front of the stage like sweaty marionettes. But her guard never goes down. Do you know the US military issue safety warnings when their soldiers are here? she says. George Street is asshole territory. There is a fresh ferocity about her since she returned from Fort Mac. I want a fuck-it list instead of a bucket list, she says. I want to throw a drink in someone's face. Flip over a table. When she talks like this, I imagine her eyes changing like the cat's when it wants to pounce: all pupil, no iris.

Being her going-out pal wouldn't be an issue if I wasn't a lightweight. The way alcohol plays with my new insides makes me nervous. It sneaks up on me and by the time I notice, I'm past the giving-a-fuck line. And I like it too much. I have to pace myself. Beer is easier to sip than mixed drinks or wine. Julia took me to a barbeque at her old journey-person's place. I awoke the next morning curled up in the middle of the floor, alone. You were petting the cat and passed out, she said. You gotta slow down on the wine. You're like the desert needs the rain with that shit. Then she says she envies me: I'd love to be a cheap drunk. I'd just buy really high-quality stuff. Two glasses of good wine instead of cheap beer. But I don't believe her. She'd still drink all night.

Tonight, she wants to go to this place with a martini special. I should learn to make a few of those, she says. We could have a cocktail night or something. She skips out the door but gets dark and glowery as we pass a guy waiting for the bus. His T-shirt says *Violence isn't the answer, but it's always an option*. Gross, Julia hisses. Then the guy falls into a coughing fit and hacks up on the sidewalk. Good, she says. I look over at her. She winks at me.

We get our drinks and a table. I score a pint glass of water to go with my beer. Julia's eyes skim the bar, pausing on individuals. I know she is checking for familiarity, for Max or one of his friends. The crease between her eyes makes me want to tuck her into me. I could cuddle the worry out of her. It's okay, girl, you have friends. You are loved.

Julia gets the two-for-one lychee martinis. The fruit at the bottom of the glasses look like soft little brains.

It's so nice to have a couple of girly drinks without hearing about it, she says. Jesus, working with men. They can't leave anything alone. I hope I don't get recalled soon.

I nod and sip my beer. The bar is busy. Conversations buzz around us: She's neat and twenty-three from the front and a forty-seven-year-old woman from behind, a man at the next table says to his friend. It's hot.

Julia blinks hard and continues: Up in the camps, it's all about how difficult women are to work with, she says. Always drama or some problem when women are involved. Which I think is true, but only in comparison to men. Men just conform.

I mean, it's not like I want things to be completely open, the woman behind me says. But, like, I think you should, you know, be allowed a few nights a year to do what you want. Three nights. No, four.

Up in camp there's no smoking most places, so they chew tobacco, Julia says. Fuckin' Tim Hortons cups all over the cafeteria full of brown spit. Disgusting. Lots of guys complainin' about it. And then I bring it up and I'm a bitch. But the cafeteria is where we eat. This is public hygiene.

These fries are right moreish, one of the guys says. You sound like my Nan, the other one replies.

And then the prick with the laptop, Julia says. She sips her second martini. Thinks it's funny to show hard-core porn at lunchtime. Him and about six others, sitting around, eatin' chili, watching Redtube or whatever. Not one complaint. And they start giving me these looks, like they could tell it bugged me and they were daring me to say something. Because if there's a complaint, it's got to be one of the girls, right? Never mind that one on one, guys tell me how they don't understand why anyone would want to see porn in the workplace. Why would I want to get hard when I'm trying to focus, they say. But no one speaks up. Together, they are gutless. The cowardice of the Y chromosome. The Roman Catholic Church. The military. All these accusations of harassment and racism aimed at police departments all over North America. They all knew and didn't speak up. Groupthink at its finest. That's what happens when it's men together in groups for a long time. They sync up and become the same guy.

She glances at the men next to us. Both stare into their phones. It turns my stomach, she says. How about you?

Last I heard, my stomach is in a lab somewhere.

Smartass.

Could be rotating on a spit for better observation.

Three guys stand by a table close to the bar. Two of them look around, their gazes do jumping jacks around the room. The other looks morose and stares at his pint.

I'm so tired of being scared, Julia says. I thought it would subside. It never leaves.

I won't let anyone hurt you.

I mean, what if Max walked in, right now? He could. This fucking town loves to show you the mistakes you've made.

Warren! One of the guys standing is yelling. His hands straight up in the air. The morose guy looks even sadder. Moroser.

Look at me, look at me, Julia says. Clowns.

A girl walks in and there is a big response from people by the bar. A cluster moves in to greet her. The morose guy reaches for his drink. Something falls from his hand, a distinct splash into the pint glass next to his.

Are you seeing this?

Julia's already on her feet. I'm coming, I say. She is in front of Morose Guy. What did you just do? she says.

Nothing.

Julia's voice gets loud: We saw you put something in that drink.

People stop and stare. A hot patch surfaces on the back of my neck. This guy could get angry.

It's just candy, Morose Guy says.

It looked like a pill.

Yeah, a candy pill.

Why would you put candy in Shane's drink? someone asks.

I was just fucking around. It's only candy.

Prove it, Julia says. Empty your pockets.

And then the guy does. Like Julia and I actually possess authority. He shows us a package of those Halloween candies, the kind in a stack that look like little pills.

Now the other pockets, Julia says. And he keeps going. And he has a pill jar. Julia holds it up for everyone to see and starts yelling. I shake my head at her. She'll get her fingerprints on it.

They're Perks, he says. They're mine.

I want everyone to calm down and also to show him that this is serious. He needs to know we have to call the cops. I can do this, lean in and smile and feel peaceful inside. But Julia is on fire: Maybe we caught you practising for later. Goddamn dirtbag.

When I take my phone out, he bolts for the door. Julia yells for someone to stop him. People hold their drinks close and stare at his back.

Let's get him, Julia says.

We can't chase him.

Her eyes are black with rage and excitement. Besides, I say. What will we do if we catch him? The bar is calling the cops.

If it's candy, can they do anything?

If it's candy, who cares?

No, it's more than that. He called him Neal, didn't he? The guy with the spiked drink called him Neal.

Okay, so the cops will get Neal.

And he yelled Warren at him, before. She taps her phone.

What do you want to do? I say this as neutrally as I can. I make sure to say what do you want, not what will you do.

Hold on. Here. Neal Warren. Pennywell Road. Let them call the cops. We should pay a visit.

We don't know what he's like.

You didn't know what that guy in Mount Pearl was like and you still followed him around.

On the trudge up to Pennywell Road, I try to buy time. I complain about my energy and take small steps: We should leave this for the RNC, Jules. He could have anything in his house, Jules. She steady strides the whole time. I gotta say something to him, she says.

Neal Warren's house is tidy with white clapboard. The guy's lawn is immaculate.

Okay, what do you want to do? I say.

Keep him there. Scare him so he stays.

We should call the cops and say he's here.

Yep. She takes out her phone. I've got the number ready. I want to show him that we'll call if he doesn't talk to us.

Neal Warren is pasty and damp. What do you want? he

says. He takes a small step back. He's holding his knapsack high on his back like he could swing it.

Julia reaches into her pocket. She's going to show him her phone, show him we want to talk or else.

When her hand emerges, I see the brass knuckles have her machinist skill all over them, heavy and effective. She hits him hard and fast and he's down.

What are you doing?!

She hits him again, twice, really fast. Stop it. I step in front of her. Are you okay, Neal? Can you hear me?

Fucking fucker, you're a rapist fucker, Julia says.

Stop, he's bleeding.

She straightens up and stares at her homemade weapon. She stoops and wipes it on Neal's shirt. Her hand shakes as she slips it back into her pocket.

Fuck, Jules. We have to get him to a hospital.

We have to get out of here, now. She grabs my hand. C'mon. We are charging back up the path, we're on the sidewalk. She takes wide paces. This is what we're going to do, she says. We go straight back downtown, back to that bar. Not the front door, up through the basement bar. We go in that way, get a drink and act like we never left. We get a bit loud. Make sure we're seen. We've been gone less than an hour. If we get on like we're drunk, we can say we were drinking on the street all night.

We need to call an ambulance for him.

If I call, it'll be traceable. If the bar really called the cops, they'll be by anyway.

We're half trotting down the hill now. Every step is a relief. I stare at a convenience store. We could check in there for a phone.

We're almost there. We can call in the bar.

The bar below has a side door and no one seems to notice when we duck in. I'll get drinks, Julia says. I duck into the bathroom and call 911 in one of the stalls. I tell the dispatcher I heard sounds and he says they'll send a car around. I hang up before he can ask any more questions.

Julia has a tall stemmed glass of white wine for me. It courses through me right away and I make sure I sing too loud to the music. I bump into wait staff collecting bottles. Julia does a little dance.

We need to burn our clothes tomorrow, Julia says close to my ear. She hands me another wine. We'll do it early. It's all good. No one knows about us.

I watch her as she sways to the music. It's getting hard to keep my eyes open. I hope they get to him in time, I say.

Julia's face swims in mine. Maybe we should get you home, she says. She tries to meet my eyes. What do you mean in time? she asks.

I want to lie down, I say. My stomach hurts.

I wake on the organ meat couch. There is a pounding in my head. There is a pounding at the door. A warning knock, hard with authority. My phone is on the coffee table. The screen is open to recent calls.

And I know Julia is gone. I know without looking what the brassy lump under my shoulder is, the cold shape of Julia's fear and the fresh notches in Neal Warren's face. The cat is a soft motor in the crook of my knee. I wonder who will take care of her now.

SEVENTEEN MINUTES

THE NURSE SAYS TO PUT on two hospital gowns: one like a coat, the other like a backwards coat, on top. Thoroughly gowned. But no bra.

Okay, Faye. Have you had any surgeries?

No.

Implants or piercings?

No.

Tattoos?

Um, I got a cover-up last week. Should I show her? She might get a kick out of it.

A new tattoo might get warm, but it should be okay. Diabetes?

No.

She says I will get an injection, some kind of ink the machine can detect. It might make me feel cold. Or I'll taste it in the back of my throat, like garlic. Does the elastic in my hair have any metal? No, none of that. She leaves me alone so I can double-bag myself in the gowns.

There's a camera in the dressing room for people who are at risk of collapsing. I am to pull the curtain while I get changed, then pull it back. What if I forget? Who is watching?

189

Maybe the last person to see my healthy breasts. If my breasts aren't healthy. Sean saw them this morning, but he doesn't know any of this. The doctor says I'm young for this and it's all unlikely. But just to play it safe.

I layer up and stuff my things into the bag they give me. I can take it with me into the room. The nurse is waiting outside, perusing a clipboard. Her hair is dark and straight and cut in a tidy bob that cups her face in smooth arches. She leads the way to the MRI room; her scrubs are lavender. How many occupations are there where the uniform is soft pants? How easy do blood stains come out? I threw out a pair of pyjama pants last month because they were stained from irregular periods and spilled coffee. Maybe scrubs are unstainable. Maybe you don't need to scrub scrubs.

The machine is a clean white hole, ceramic or plastic. It makes me think of ovens: old-fashioned wood-burning ovens for pizza and artisan food. The kind that inspired Hansel and Gretel: the kind that can fit a whole witch. The nurse passes me earplugs, the orange sponge nugget kind.

Can I listen to my iPod inside? I ask.

No.

My mother could. They let her choose a CD and they played music inside.

Where was this, at the Janeway? They do that for the kids there.

No, it was in Ontario.

Oh no, we don't have that here.

I take off the backwards gown and lie down on my belly so my breasts dangle down between the slats. I am slid into the white hole. How does Gretel get away? She tells the witch she doesn't know how to get in the oven. Show me, show me how to get in. The door slams, the witch howls. The candy house is free for the taking. The nurse says it will take seventeen minutes.

Inside, it's like a washing machine: sloshes, long blaring beeps. More annoying than alarming. Like on Saturday—I set off the car alarm when we were leaving to meet Sean's work friends. I scrambled to figure out how to stop it. You pressed the wrong button on the key chain, Sean said. He pulled it from my hand, pressed the red button. The alarm stopped. Faye, you should learn the difference. What if you were attacked? Knowing to press the alarm could save you.

I know which one, I said. I was just trying to lock the car.

The MRI makes blurry beeps that sound like a finger jiggling lips. I keep my eyes closed. I told myself I would look, check the lighting, see what I could see. But looking might make me move. I keep my eyes closed.

Before we left on Saturday, I put on the new red shirt. It looked raspberry in the store, but in the bedroom mirror it had orange tones. It's so hard to find a good red shirt. This one has wrap-around: sheaths of fabric crossing over the chest. Mom would call it a boob shirt. She would say something like, that's quite the boob shirt you have on. But I figured why not show them off a little. I asked Sean how I looked. I did this even though Sean has recently decided against giving compliments. People depend on compliments too much, he said. They shouldn't rely on others to feel good about themselves.

I don't think you've thought that through, I said.

Everyone likes to be noticed—I know you enjoy being complimented. I did not say I suspect this decision is based on his mood shifting. And that I doubt it's a belief he would state widely, to a questioning audience.

How do I look? I said.

You look fine, he said.

In the car, I asked if he was still annoyed about the tattoo. It's fine, he said. And then, What's done is done.

The removal of the old one would have been more expensive and painful, I said. At least it's not an old, faded tattoo anymore. He shrugged and nodded at the same time. The next time he's in a mood, it will become a thing. I know it.

The beeps go long and high. The emergency signal is a squeeze ball that has been placed in my palm. It reminds me of the cartoon perfume bottle depicted on a poster in the waiting room: No Scented Products Please. A cartoon nose running away from a cartoon perfume bottle, the old-fashioned kind with the squeeze ball applicator. I can't smell anything inside the machine.

We met Sean's work friends for martinis. It was Vivian in Payroll's birthday. The bar had a menu with seventy-five different types of martinis. There were six women around the table; each held a glass of something colourful. They all wore black or black and white. Vivian's cocktail dress was black lace. Even Sean was all in black, with white Velcro sneakers. I didn't know there was a black-and-white plan. The urge to explain was overwhelming, like looking for a place to spit. No one told me there was a theme.

Why don't I take a picture of all of you? I said. Phones were passed to me. I took a couple with each, vertical, horizontal.

You know, Sean said, the great thing about digital cameras and the internet is that you can take one picture and send it to everyone. The ladies laughed and play-swatted at him.

Sean's our big brother at work, Vivian said.

I hope he doesn't rip the heads off your Barbies, I said. That's what my big brother did.

I mean more like he has to put up with our conversations, she said. He must complain about being henpecked.

Later, Vivian and a girl in a dress with black and white vertical pinstripes danced. Vivian two-stepped, but pinstriped girl worked her hips so that the stripes curved and flexed like radiation waves.

The noises change to hissing. A cord rests against my arm. Imagine if it moved. Don't think about the cord moving. Like the snake woman we met in Canadian Tire. Sean and I were looking for supplies for the rolling blackouts. We bumped into her and she wore an off-shoulder black T-shirt and I could tell her nipple was pierced. She said the rolling blackouts had been brutal. She had to take all the snakes to bed with her. It was exhausting, trying to get some sleep with them squirming all over her. Cold blooded, right? They need the heat and there was none.

When we were walking away through the hunting supplies aisle, Sean told me she runs a pet rescue for reptiles.

And when we were in the car, that they used to fuck, a few years ago. An arrangement, not a dating thing.

The nurse's voice enters to tell me the IV is pouring the fluid into me, the detectable ink. What would that be like, snakes warming themselves on me? Their flesh smooth on mine. They flick their tongues out in order to smell, don't they? Being tasted constantly by their tiny tongues. Insanity forming. What do they sound like when they breathe normally? They wouldn't hiss all the time. Just silent, slowly squirming creatures, with tongues like rapid feathers.

The nurse says, Squeeze the emergency ball if you feel pain. I feel my arm get cold, but that's all. It's like I can feel how wet my blood is inside my arm.

Outside the bar, Vivian leaned against the wall. The rain poured off the awning and made a fringe around us as we smoked. She was really high. She said, When I was a kid, I wanted to go swimming in the rain. I wanted to see the ripples the drops made from underneath and find out if the sound of rain entering the water was like rain on a roof. The best form of white noise—makes you feel safe from the elements. Rain through the water might be white noise for mermaids.

She rotated her shoulders against the wall to face me. You're beautiful, Faye. You're the kind of beautiful that everyone can see but you. Which makes you even more beautiful. A pure beauty that doesn't recognize itself.

She hooked two fingers into my cleavage. My shirt was

wide open. How long had it been like that? Look at the rack on you, she said. She wiggled the tips of her fingers. I stepped back. She laughed. On the way back into the bar, she looked at Sean and said, You don't know what you've got.

I keep my eyes closed. The MRI ejects me slowly, like an old VCR. The nurse unhooks the IV and I put my finger on the cotton swab on the hole. I can go change back into my clothes now. Back in the change room, I hook my bra and read the notifications. They are all printed on coloured A4 paper: PLEASE NOTIFY TECHNOLOGIST IF YOU ARE WEARING AN INSULIN PUMP. PLEASE HAVE YOUR MCP CARD READY.

It occurs to me that my new tattoo did not get hot. If there is something wrong and I have to get my breasts removed, maybe I will get some kind of tattoos where they used to be. Someone on Facebook shared a video of that, a woman who got tattoos on her post-mastectomy chest. I could get a floral pattern. An underwater scene. I could just pick out a wallpaper design, fuck it. I wonder if the snake woman has tattoos. I think she must have. Maybe this is why Sean doesn't like them.

The exit corridor leads past the line of people waiting. Wheelchairs and oxygen tanks. Healthy next to sick. I pass all of them and follow the arrows out, the floor tiles like a path of white stones.

MINDFULL (A NOVELLA)

PART ONE

Monday

MOST COMMUTERS WEAR DARK FABRICS, so the girl in the puffy turquoise jacket stands out to me. Her hair is peroxide-copper blond. Scorched in a desire for brightness. Who can blame her?

She wipes her eyes. I follow her gaze to something scrawled by the subway map. Another swastika. Her eyes shine with tears. I fish a tissue from my purse. I am grateful to myself for carrying tissues. I pass it to her subtly. Her eyes flash, defensive, then appreciative. She mouths *thank you* as she dabs her eyes. A yin-yang sign is tattooed on her wrist.

Nice tat, I say.

It's old. Past life.

Always something good in the bad.

She presses the tissue to her eyes. I resist the urge to rub her shoulder. Velma says watch that; not everyone is reassured by touch. Be hands-on without being hands on.

I step back and replace my earbuds. Murray Dove's

podcast enters my mind like a warm tonic: *They say we're in The Dimming. But that doesn't mean it's the dark ages yet. Even in dimming, light exists. Notice light, notice colour.*

At St. George station, I shuffle off the train with everyone else. The crowd is automated by glum routine, economic need. I love feeling how I am one of them, yet brimming with potential. I am Sandra Rebecca Somers, Housing Outreach Worker, Future Life Coach and Agent of Positivity. I am both part of the world and remaking it.

Out on the street, the protesters' signs at Queen's Park are silhouetted in the morning light: NO INTERNMENT CAMPS FOR REFUGEES. NO RACIST POLICIES. FUCK BREXIT. FUCK PRESIDENT SWEENEY. CANADA IS FOR EVERYONE.

From a distance, I spot the girl with the copper-blond hair. She climbs on the roof of a parked car and unzips her jacket. The explosives on her chest are a screaming shade of orange. She gives the Nazi salute before she detonates.

They can't even blow themselves up right, Velma says. A shrapnel bomb? Idiots.

The overcrowding at Toronto General and Mount Sinai means St. Jude's gets the overflow, so fewer shelter beds for the homeless. Velma's curly black hair halos around her bandana. Her pupils constantly move, dark and urgent.

We carry blankets into the meeting room. The Jewish Community Centre, the Muslim Association, and the Salvation Army all donated supplies.

It's wonderful how people pull together, I say.

Why is this fucking door still broken? Velma says. She kicks the doorstop to wedge it in.

In the cafeteria, my co-workers are tending, healing, compiling. Cliff writes on a clipboard, Janelle bandages a child's foot. We are cogs in the wheel of kindness. It's like Fred Rogers said: In times of adversity, look for the helpers.

The JCC said thirty cots, Velma says. There's only seventeen here. Why announce you're sending thirty and give us half? Now we have to ask again and hope someone's reading these tweets.

I'll retweet it, Velma.

You're a big help.

The cops are here to talk to Sandra, Cliff says.

I thought you already made a statement, Velma says.

The cops are young, white, and male. They ask the same questions as the earlier officer except she was nice and let me cry a little. I repeat my previous answers: I noticed the woman on the subway, I dove for cover when she pulled the cord. But they want more: where am I from, who are my parents, where did I go to school.

Velma is pissed when I tell her. They're creating profiles, she says. Like they don't know who's responsible. She yanks fitted sheets over cots, I follow with blankets.

How many letters did I write? she says. The mayor. The premier. Why are cops watching the centre? I record them with my phone. Idle police watching the homeless. Fifteen letters before I got a response.

But you got through it, I say. I bet it made you stronger.

Sandra, we need to put top sheets on before blankets. The blankets are trouble to wash. We can't afford another bedbug outbreak.

I'm sorry. I'll fix it.

Velma sits on a cot. Her forehead shines with sweat. And I know I got through it, she says. Honestly, Sandra, it's okay to acknowledge something sucks, you know.

I untuck the blankets so as not to disturb her fitted sheets. I will not cry.

Your intentions are good, she says. But everyone needs empathy. Especially now.

But I am empathetic. I feel for everyone.

Do you? Because empathy means you relate. And this situation? It's awful. Just be understanding. You don't always have to be Positive Sandwich Sandra.

What?

Velma's face freezes. I mean, you don't have to be on all the time. She stands up and pats my arm. Here, she says, I'll help you.

I unfold the next sheet. I try not to think of Cliff and Janelle last week, when I told them about the new panini place on the corner. You must really like sandwiches, Cliff said and then jerked, like Janelle had kicked him under the table.

We learned about the Positive Sandwich Approach in a Professional Development session last year. The bread symbolizes positive feedback while the innards are constructive criticism. Velma hung the diagram poster in the staff room. There were a few jokes about bologna sandwiches.

I will not be concerned about a nickname. Although maybe not a nickname if it isn't said to your face. I will not consider who coined it, although it's probably Janelle, with her terms for everything: basic, fierce, a player. Janelle with eyes permanently set on roll, like some snot-nosed teen drama character with her fake-fur iPhone case and cracking, smacking gum mouth.

But everyone has their own path. I remind myself of this during the walk home. The police closed the subway, and in order to stay alert I shouldn't listen to Murray Dove or anything else. My feet hurt, but the air is cool. It's a nice night, even though I still smell burning plastic.

Tuesday

I should get up now if I want to do my twenty-minute meditation. But everything feels heavy. Maybe I should call in sick, a mental health day. MHDs are important.

No, Velma needs assistance, and if I stay home I'll think about Positive Sandwich Sandra, imagining myself as some ridiculous mascot, like the Phillie Phanatic, clunking about on the outskirts while the team sweats it out.

What if it's gone beyond St. Jude's? Most staff are on social media and many, I've noticed, are friends with each other and not me, though I would never push a co-worker to connect that way, to each their comfort zone. But what if it's an in-joke, like one of those memes I don't understand, something tossed around in cliques. *#positivesandwichsandra #sosickofsandwiches*

I grab my phone to search. There are three new Twitter notifications.

@MurrayDove liked your retweet.

@MurrayDove retweeted your retweet.

1 unread message from @MurrayDove.

Holy goddess. Murray Dove's retweet includes his own words: *During these #dimtimes, ppl like @SandraRS and*

@StJudesOutreach are the light. Makes me so happy. #positivity
#brightenthedimming.

I stare at his Twitter avatar, his mane of curls, his open arms ready to receive, to give. My hand shakes so hard, I have to tap twice to pull up his DM.

> *Dear Sandra,*
> *Just wanted to shine a little light into your day. Running*
> *Murray Dove Inc. keeps me busy, but I try to keep track of*
> *devoted subscribers, such as you. It fills me with joy to see*
> *people putting positive thinking to good use, especially in*
> *these trying situations. Thank you, Sandra.*
> *Blessings,*
> *Murray Dove*

Deep breaths into my belly. My hands shake as I press reply:

> *Hello Murray!*
> *This message is exactly what I need this morning. It's*
> *like you know me! Thank you so much for everything you*
> *do. Would love to meet you someday—any upcoming*
> *public speaking events?* ☺
> *All the blessings, xo.*
> *Sandra*

I sing in the shower, dance-dress for work, practically skip to the subway. But once on the train, second-guessing sets in. Murray has discussed second-guessing in his podcast, how it signals lack of self-faith. But oh god, *It's like you know me*. And asking when he's around. Ugh, and *xo*. So stalkerish.

The subway car has fresh graffiti: *Fuck you Nazis. Fuck Antifa. Take back our country. Assassinate Sweeney.* I close my eyes and imagine Murray's message in his soft, massaging voice. Then I picture him reading my reply. Tap—block user. Bland Sandra Sandwich, watch out, she really wants to know you.

Janelle and Cliff drink coffee in the staff room. The urge to share my news is overwhelming. I want to tell everyone, shake awake the sleeping bodies in the cafeteria: Look! See what can happen! But right now, it's only for me. It's okay to have things just for oneself.

Sandra, Cliff says, take you long to get home last night?

Good morning, Cliff. About forty minutes. I walked.

My bus took three hours, Janelle says. Everything around High Park was shut down. It's where the bomber lived, apparently.

Oh, that must have been exhausting.

Cops and dogs everywhere.

Some people have it so hard, I say. You wonder what happened for them to choose that path.

Poverty and desperation lead to radicalization, Janelle says.

And if the government gave a shit about poor people, Cliff says, they'd help out instead of scapegoating minorities.

She must have been so lost. Makes you realize how lucky we are.

Janelle crumples her coffee cup and chucks it in the garbage can. I feel exposed, like my fly is undone. What did I do now? Oh, I didn't hop on the misery town bus with her. I hear there's a three-hour delay.

Velma's head appears in the doorway. Sandra? A quick word?

I pause at Velma's office, but she gestures me past it. We

go out on the fire escape. She dangles her legs off the edge and lights a cigarette.

I thought you quit smoking, I say.

She takes a deep drag.

I mean, don't feel bad. You can quit again.

Sandra, you're a really hard worker, you know. We're lucky to have you.

Thank you.

And things are really stressful right now. I've worked with different non-profits over the years and it's always a hustle. But it's never been this rough.

Velma's hand trembles as she inhales. The morning light exposes dark circles under her eyes.

Anyway, Sandra, what I'm saying is, with times this tough, your state of denial is concerning.

Denial? There's no denial. I'm very aware of current affairs.

Okay. What you're not getting, Sandra, is no one wants to hear it. You're kind-hearted, but you're pissing people off.

I haven't received any anger from anyone.

But you don't receive much pleasantness, do you?

I turn so she won't see me blinking. Across the alley, a woman pins T-shirts on a clothesline strung off her balcony.

It's your knee-jerk response. Someone expresses frustration and you neutralize it. People are scared and upset, Sandra, they want to release their feelings, not have someone stick a plug in them.

A plug? No, I care about how everyone feels.

Want to know how they feel? They're scared. They want to feel like you're in the trenches with them.

But I am. We're all together in The Dimming. And if

we project positivity, we can end it.

Velma taps her cigarette. How does that work? she asks.

Okay. So, everything people make and do begins as ideas—things people imagined, right? So, if we imagine a happy, prosperous world for everyone, it can become reality. We must visualize that reality, believe in ourselves and combat negativity. Because negative energy does the opposite; it sabotages those good things.

So, good thoughts equal good things. Tit for tat.

I wouldn't put it—

It sounds like religion. And although St. Jude's was originally a Catholic organization, we're non-religious. There's a safe-place clause in your contract, remember?

Yes.

So. Please refrain from placing your spiritual ideas on others. If someone's venting, fight it in your mind without verbalization. Okay?

I stare at my coffee mug. A layer of scum floats on the top. Budget cuts mean the cheapest brand.

Okay, Sandra?

Yes.

I have to get back to it. Velma stands. She puts her hands on my shoulders. The tobacco smell is overwhelming.

If you ever want to talk, Sandra, I'm here. I meant what I said, you're a great part of the team.

I nod. Velma steps back inside. Across the alley, the woman pins a beige brassiere to her clothesline. As she pushes it out, a blouse unhitches and flutters to the ground.

Hey, I call. You dropped something.

She looks up at me, mouth full of clothespins. She gives me the finger.

The rest of the day is processing housing applications. Eating salad at my desk. Catching laughter in faraway conversations. Feeling my ears heat up, like they're picking up on any toxic waves of gossip in the atmosphere.

I should not be angry. Velma is only expressing her truth. But *her* truth makes huge assumptions about *my* truth and how can she call it religion? How can she compare a scientific theory, which has never had an opportunity to be proved wrong, to faith systems based on ancient myths? How can she dismiss something she knows nothing about? It's like throwing away an unchecked lottery ticket.

At five, I exit from the back door. The new subway security procedures add an extra twenty minutes to the commute. I wouldn't mind if I was listening to Murray (Christ, calling him Murray now, like we hang out on the weekends), but he tweeted a selfie from a yoga studio on Queen West just after four, which means he's checked his account and didn't respond to my message. I can't bear to hear his voice. So ridiculous to feel like I've lost something.

My mailbox is full of flyers and scams. A notice from the landlord: TO ALL HEDGEGLOVE TENANTS: RENT WILL INCREASE BY 12% ON MAY 1ST. PAYMENT INCREASE IS RESULT OF NEW TAX LAW FOR THE PROMOTION OF PERSONAL HOME OWNERSHIP. DIRECT ANY QUESTIONS TO YOUR LOCAL MP VIA EMAIL.

My paycheque is already a mosaic of commitments, a hundred shattered, pre-spent bits. What do these assholes expect me to do, sell my eggs? I squeeze the notice into a ball, tight, tighter. I crack a nail. Fuck you, Hedgeglove fucks.

Maybe it's time to leave. If I'm *pissing people off*, I might as well get out of non-profit work. Like Father says, bleeding hearts eventually run out of blood.

The Pinot Grigio in the fridge is cheap, but ice cold. I drink two glasses while the microwave popcorn pops.

I wake at 6:43 a.m. Still on the couch, work-skirt twisted around me. Didn't make it into post-work soft pants. It's okay. Getting sad sometimes is okay. Horrible hangover self-hate can happen. MHD may be in order.

I'm about to text Velma about not coming in when I see the Twitter notification. One unread message. From @MurrayDove:

> Dear Sandra,
> Your message made me smile. Even this long in the game, it brings me pleasure when I hear someone who's been helped by Murray Dove Inc. We're a small, but persistent army these days.
> I'm doing a book promotion tomorrow afternoon at the Royal York. Would love to meet you and brainstorm about improving our world. Hope you're free. My assistant will put your name on the door.
> Blessings,
> Murray

Wednesday afternoon

The sign outside the Royal York's Imperial Room reads *Murray Dove: The Science of a Better Life*. There's a life-sized cut-out of him for photo ops.

I consider sitting near the back, but there's one empty chair in the front row. Has to be a sign. I sit and calm myself with self-congratulations: drank fruit smoothie hangover fix this morning, called in sick, went running to steam off anxiety, treated myself to a full regime of hair removal, moisturizing, and precise makeup. The black wiggle dress was originally intended for the annual work supper, but today requires my very best me.

The lights dim. Murray Dove enters in his signature black jeans and T-shirt, *You Are Your Attitude* emblazoned across his chest. His hair is soft coils. I imagine it feeling like goose down.

The PowerPoint presentation is from Murray's third book, *Think It, Be It*. His hands beckon and emphasize as he clicks through diagrams: *the brain = a muscle, positive thinking = exercise.*

When we practise a new skill, he says, like playing the guitar or perfecting a slam-dunk, our brains change with our bodies. Exercising positive thinking has the same effect.

A red-haired female assistant in a similar black T-shirt and skinny jeans appears. A large model of a human brain glides before her. It is motorcycle-sized, made from frosted glass. The audience exhales.

Murray taps the front of the model. It lights up yellow. Different areas of the brain have specific jobs, he says. Memory and problem solving are functions of the frontal lobe. He taps the back, turning it purple. The occipital lobe controls vision and movement.

He plunges his arm into the top of the brain. The audience gasps, then chuckles as we realize there's a rubber slit. A blob in the centre lights up pink. This, he says, is the ventral striatum.

The blob pulses like a lava lamp. The audience coos.

When we experience something wonderful, he says, like a gorgeous sunset or a great meal, this is where we continue to feel happy later. For positive thinking, this is the big muscle. The glutes of happiness. He gives his bum a little pat. The audience laughs. He's so cute.

We hear a lot about how hard it is to stay positive, he says. This is why the ventral striatum is so important. Prolonging positive thinking requires exercise. My upcoming book, *The Happy Muscle*, reveals how we can become *athletic* positive thinkers. Olympic-level athletes! Together, we can lift ourselves out of The Dimming and into the light!

The audience rises. Whoops and cries. Murray Dove smiles and bows. Our eyes seem to meet. Does he recognize me? I imagine it to be yes.

Afterwards, there's a long lineup for book signing. I act consumed with my phone, pushing my heels into the carpet to fight my flight response. When the crowd thins, I wait behind a group of middle-aged ladies trying to get just the right selfie with him. Then it's my turn.

You are Sandra, Murray says.

I stick out my hand. He takes it and kisses my cheek. He smells like nutmeg and honey. His eyes are turtle-shell hazel with gold specks, and I imagine his heart as a burning ember of goodness. I tap his book in my hands. Steady voice now: I can't wait to read this. Will you sign it?

Of course. Paige—he gestures to the red-haired assistant—Ms. Somers' copy is comped.

Sandra, you can call me Sandra. I mean, you just called me Sandra and you can keep calling me that. And thank you, so much, for the book.

You're very welcome, Sandra. What did you think of the presentation?

It was wonderful. It's so important to reveal the scientific truth in your work—what a great idea with that wonderful big brain! The one you used on stage, I mean. I was trying to explain positivity theory to a co-worker yesterday and it would have been great to whip out a miniature of those . . . brains.

I'm sputtering like a broken hose. Paige the Assistant blinks at me.

Really? Murrays says. What did you say to your co-worker?

Oh, she wasn't receptive.

See, this is why we must publish the science. In The Dimming, positive thinking seems futile. But that's how fear works, isn't it?

Murray writes something in the book with a flourish and passes it to me. I restrain myself from reading it.

Sandra, he says, this is last-minute, but would you like to get a bite? I'm always too excited to eat before a presentation and right now I could chew the leg off the Lamb of God, as my dear old grandmother used to say. I'd love to pick your brain about your work and how we can confront the resistance you encountered yesterday.

Yes. I can go for a bite.

Relax. Don't babble. Don't gush. Don't let affection turn pesky, like a newly hatched spring fly, sullenly swatted away by another handsome man.

In the elevator Murray presses the button for Epic Lounge. He discusses the presentation. He was nervous about the technical aspects, but the Royal York staff are great and Paige made sure it went smooth as butter, so wonderful to have trust-renewal experiences such as this. I nod and smile. If the elevator jammed, I could die right now and be happy.

We are alone in the restaurant. Murray smiles, a little sheepish. Bit precious, isn't it? he says. The owner is an old friend. He understands I need to recharge after a session.

Oh no, it's wonderful.

He pulls out my chair for me. What if I missed my seat, fell right on my ass? God, so much perfection, ruined.

We don't have much choice in meals, but they make lovely bruschetta if that's okay.

That's one of my favourites! Yes, please.

And then champagne and here I am in this opulent room with the man I listen to five days a week—the only man who has ever improved my life. We clink glasses and the liquid down my throat is nectar of pure gratitude. The bruschetta appears pre-cut in sensible morsels. We eat with subtle bites.

He asks and I tell him about St. Jude's, about how, when I started, the housing crisis was the main issue, but now we're overwhelmed: US refugees forced out by Sweeney's anti-immigration laws, the Rent Control repeal, fugitives from neighbourhoods occupied by New North American Nationalists. And Velma's List: how it was a joke initially, a way to use up an old scroll of dot-matrix printer paper as she began tracking her petitions and letters. Now if the scroll unrolled, it could wallpaper her entire office. Murray's fingers play across his lips.

She's discouraged, he says. Sounds like a major negative

energy blockage.

Yes. And I feel like I try to conduct positive energy, to help people see something bigger, but also smaller, those little things which bring so much life to life. I mean, it's hard right now, but it's always hard times somewhere, you know? But it just bounces off her.

Murray slaps the table. Sandra, dead-on! Exactly the phenomena I write about. He pours more champagne. Interesting you use the word *conduct*, he says. When I saw you in the audience, I thought, she's so beneficent. Electric.

You saw me?

Of course. I thought, there she is, ready to help. And you did, through your positive presence. I was so nervous.

You didn't seem nervous.

Well, thank you for saying that, he says. He looks around. A server appears with more champagne. Maybe tomorrow will be another MHD for me.

So, he says, tell me about Sandra Somers.

There isn't much to know.

Well, that's unfair. You know about me. It's difficult to make new friends when you have your own Wikipedia page.

Oh, you're so funny.

I mean it. Most people don't share easily. And I want to know you. Where did you grow up?

Mississauga. But now I live in Broadview North.

You have family around?

My father's in Mississauga, but we're a little estranged. It's not a bad thing; he can be toxic. I also have a brother, but he's much older. He lives in Iowa with his family.

Are you close?

Not lately. He married an American and revoked his

Canadian citizenship. He's been quite open about supporting Sweeney. We don't see eye to eye.

I mean to sip my champagne in a dainty way, but my cheeks fill and it's too good not to gulp. Murray refills my glass.

It's trying when families disagree, he says. Can I ask where your mother is?

She left when I was six.

Oh, Sandra. That's tragic for a child.

My mother suffered from anxiety. Father's moods made it worse. She left for her own well-being.

And she left you with him?

It's a long story.

I stare at my hands on the table. I don't trust myself to get into this. I'm too nervous and happy and want to unbutton my soul, tell him how much he's helped these three years, tell him about finding the stack of letters—Christmas cards, birthday cards, train tickets—stuffed in the tear in Father's stinking recliner, his regular spot for drinking, smoking, and ranting about traitorous, psycho-fucking-bitches. Finally meeting her at the Second Cup across from Union Station and we sat like two alien life forms, me in Occupy Wall Street badges, she in her dangling Progressive Conservative Conference lanyard and blood diamond wedding band. And I burned my tongue on my cappuccino and the table wobbled and I thought how it was unlike everything else between my family and me, our solid mutual resentment, and wouldn't it be nice if we were more like this table, something with a little give, as clumsy as it is.

Murray's hands encompass mine and I admire them together, a nest of belonging. His eyes are golden in the late afternoon sun. We join in understanding, in this moment of shared vision and appreciation.

Thursday

As soon as I arrive at work, Velma pulls me aside. For a second, I imagine she knows; maybe someone spotted us, maybe Royal York staff tweeted about Murray Dove and a new lady friend. Spill the beans, she'd say, and we'd sip coffees on the fire escape and after I told her everything, she'd have to smoke a cigarette. And throughout the day, we'd share sly glances and sneaky remarks about my special glow.

Cliff got jumped by Nationalists last night, Velma says.

Oh no.

Right on his own street. They travel in gangs now, in broad daylight. I'm waiting to hear from his husband, but I know there was head trauma. No arrests of course.

Janelle approaches us, tears streaming. Goddamn fucking pigs.

Shh, Janelle, Velma says. Half the clients are off their meds. All I need is agitated homeless maniacs losing their minds. At least when they're drunk, they're quiet.

Velma—

Sandra, leave it alone. Christ, I'm exhausted. I could murder someone just to make a nice warm pillow from their corpse.

Janelle and Velma convulse into giggles until they're holding themselves up. Despair laughter—Murray writes about it in the second chapter of *Think It, Be It*, which I read on the subway this morning. The instinct to laugh during hardship proves the natural state of our minds is seeking joy, producing a positive reaction. Amazing how I just read this and here it is happening. The universe speaks.

I tell them to keep me updated and retire to my stack of housing applications. At this point, it's all data entry. Every subsidized housing project, housing co-op, and temporary shelter in the city has a waiting list. All I can do is enter names in the system and tag categories: refugee, victim of NNAN, mental health overflow, vagrant.

And today is trying because I must resist replaying last night: Murray's arm around my waist, my legs like tightly coiled springs, trying to walk sensibly to his suite. The door swinging open to his private oasis, all polished mahogany headboard and Egyptian cotton. Murray's taut body, his body hair in elegant patches like it was painted on with a horsehair brush, and the way he peeled my dress off, the appreciative sounds deep in his throat. And how he took charge with no hesitation: move this way, head down, tilt up, show me, that's it. And afterwards, I said I feel so good about my body and he said, I feel so good about your body too, and we laughed.

Today I will be productive and present for co-workers. Will purchase get-well card for Cliff. Will help Velma however she needs and will keep quiet. Will keep it for myself anyway. My own secret joy.

What's up with you today?

Velma peers at me from the staff refrigerator. I'm staring out the window with my coffee halfway to my lips.

Me? Oh, nothing.

You've got the goofiest smile. If you have good news, share it. I could use a perk.

I pull out my phone. She reads Murray's last text message:

Hello Sandra,
What a blessing to meet a kindred spirit like you. I
would like to see you again. Hope you feel the same.
xo

Who's it from?

Murray Dove.

The motivational guy?

Yes!

Sick day, huh?

I'm sorry, Velma, I should have said.

Don't worry about it. Glad you had a good time.

Oh, it was magical. I mean, I've been following his work for so long and—

Be careful though. I hope he's not like that guy who messed up Rosemary Betts.

Who?

Client from a few years ago. School teacher, lived in a condo. She developed this crippling anxiety disorder. Turns out she got involved with this crazy New Thought Movement guy who convinced her to microdose on LSD. He thought it would enhance her output of good energy, or something like that. Except he gave her stuff cut with something nasty and experimental.

Oh, that's terrible.

Anyway, when she was here, she'd been evicted. Her anxiety kept her from work and she ended up hiding in her condo until they threw her out. We found her an affordable apartment. But yeah, poor ol' Rosemary Betts.

Murray would never do something so awful.

I'm sure. But you know. Sometimes it's not worth it to meet your heroes.

Then she's off to pass the hat for Cliff, her head bobbing in its colourful wrap. Velma only wants me to be safe. I appreciate her approach. Even though it wouldn't kill her to microdose herself on a drop of enthusiasm, maybe a little pat on the back for people who are finally receiving some nice karmic payback. But whatever. Cliff is in the hospital. It's a bad day. Poor Velma.

I finish the forms, sign Cliff's card, and donate ten dollars. No news of arrests, but witnesses in his neighbourhood took photos, which are circulating online. I retweet the images and get a like from Murray.

And later, at home, another text:

Would you like to visit me this weekend? We can arrange a train ticket. Please say yes?

I've never been this happy.

Saturday

Murray can't come to the Cobourg train station, but Paige is there in a slim grey suit and sunglasses. She manoeuvres my bags into the trunk of the silver Mercedes sedan.

We pass lush fields with red barns and everything is painted electric by my excitement. Must remember to accept everything as it comes, be in the moment. I should have meditated this morning.

Paige opens the gate via security code and we turn up an arcing road flanked by tall hedges. The house is dark wood, tall windows with a solar panelled roof. Clever and full of light. Murray meets us in the foyer, dressed in linen pants and a white cotton shirt, so clean and neat in his element. He smells amazing.

The two of us tour the compound, strawberry mojitos in hand. He shows me the greenhouse, the garden, and the guest lodge. I'd like to accommodate larger retreats, he says. Right now, we can host about six people. Any more would restrict space and opportunity to till the soil. But during my research for *The Happy Muscle*, I started considering large group-focusing sessions, forty, fifty people. Imagine the potential of that much concentrated positive thinking.

Wonderful, I say. My cheeks are flushed already. Slow down on the mojito.

We stop at a long brick building. A generator hums to the side.

I'd like everything off the grid, he says. Carbon footprints and all. But this idea moved faster than perfected construction.

We enter a long white room. A row of computer monitors lines one wall, parallel to an installation of framed photographs of psychedelic-looking clouds. At the end is a large round machine painted like the night sky. A stretcher beside it.

It's a CT scanner, Murray says. In children's hospitals, they give them murals, like underwater sea worlds—makes it a playful experience instead of scary. I thought, why not have our own? Paige designed it, she's quite an artist.

It's amazing.

I step forward. The entrance hole looks small.

What do you do with it? I ask.

Murray spreads his arms towards the wall of photos. This! he says.

Each image contains a blob of peach-coloured light, varying in shade and intensity. Tell me, Sandra, he says. Who is the most positive person you can think of?

You.

You're sweet.

We kiss. Our lips are sticky with strawberry rum. How sturdy is that stretcher.

Okay, second most positive.

Um. Oprah, I would think.

Murray points to a photograph near the top. The colour is almost neon.

Really?! Her CT scan?

Yes. All these images came from the minds of positive thinkers. Mapping brains is a major part of my research. All subjects meditate first. In the scan, they visualize what makes them the most happy. And they're very comfortable. We even pipe in the music of their choice.

I move along the brain scans. So many varying shades of pink. Whose is this? I ask. I point to a pale one, like the inside of a clam shell.

He signed a confidentiality agreement, I'm afraid.

Oh, okay.

But let's just say the name rhymes with Cheap Rack Dopra.

My laugh erupts like a hiccup, which makes him laugh too. What about this one? I ask. It is particularly beautiful, all different shades like a sunset.

Oh. Shelly. An ex.

Oh. Is yours here?

Ah, yes.

Murray points to the one beside Shelly's. It's also like a sunset, but with more detail: subtle glimmers of gold.

I'm sorry, Sandra. I hope this isn't making you uncomfortable.

He places my glass by the monitors and takes my hands. I just want to show you my passions, he says.

I really love it.

Because you feel like you could be a real passion as well.

The stretcher proves itself sturdy. Afterwards, Murray dozes in my arms. I let my eyes take in the room. I must cherish these moments all weekend: Murray's breath on my collarbone, the glow of a hundred positive thoughts basking on the walls. My eyes catch on the sunset pair, third from the top, fifth column across. Side by side, like beacons for each other.

Monday

With Murray, it's like as soon as I imagine how wonderful it could be, he grabs those expectations and makes them multitude. When was your last vacation? he asked yesterday. I described my three days at Christmas; Craig and his family visited from Iowa. His wife drank too much on the plane and slept through dinner. Craig and Father bickered over Canadian health care and the kids played Grand Theft Auto V on their PlayStation Vitas.

That's no vacation, he said. Can you stay the week? And an email later, he'd made an anonymous donation to St. Jude's to make up for my short notice. Then Paige brought us breakfast in bed and I barely had time to pull up the sheets when she arrived with the waffles.

On the compound, everything is both serenity and stimulation. That morning we meditated and strolled along the pond. Details stand out: choruses of insects in the grass, perfect apples in the orchard. Everything is simple, peaceful, brimming with life.

I've been too joyful to consider Shelly and her stunning ventral striatum. But I imagine someone with that level of inner glow made him very happy. It is hard not to wonder if they created this place together, born from their matching energies. If they could make something this magical, what split them up?

What's happening in Sandra's beautiful mind?

Oh, nothing. I'm so happy.

You can tell me. I didn't ask you here to be the demure house guest.

I'm just . . . curious about the CT scans. Yours and Shelly's are so interesting.

I think all the CT scans are interesting.

Yes, but yours are very similar. Like kindred spirits.

He spins me by the waist so I face him. He kisses my forehead.

And for all you know, Ms. Somers, whatever you've got in there could be even more interesting. I can't imagine it not being so.

I can't imagine it at all.

Sandra. You are here because I'm crazy about you. I know it's impulsive, but when I like someone, I can't suppress it. It's my downfall, really. Most people would say it's uncool.

It's my downfall too! I could never play the hard-to-get game.

I know, it doesn't make sense! If I like someone, I want them to get me.

We kiss and I want to tell him this is more than *like* for me. He's got me. I am so very, very gotten.

And if you are curious, my summery Sandra Somers, he says, we could run your CT scan. Just say the word.

After supper, Murray has a Skype meeting. I take a bubble bath and list pros and cons on my pruney fingers. What if I panic in the machine? Worse, what if my ventral striatum is nothing special? Like the shade Father painted my bedroom. I was eleven and in love with purple, but Palm Desert was on sale at Home Depot. It's pink, he said. Girls love pink. The bedroom drab and plain, like a tuna fish sandwich.

And why risk it? What is all this? How many women can Murray Dove summon at a moment's notice? Five hundred? Ten thousand? His Twitter followers are well over two hundred thousand, at least 80 per cent women, estimated age range 27–42. Yogis, hippies, open-minded women. Maybe for him we are walking, talking ventral striata, peach splotches he can get to glow a little harder. Velma's voice comes to me, some quip about an unsavoury ex of Janelle's, a musician who invited her over to show off his extensive vinyl collection. Bet he has other collections, she said. Headboard notches. Special picture folder on the hard drive.

So why am I eager to be a souvenir? Is it the hope that years later, he'll look at my mind and miss me? Why am I scared to see my mind for myself? This is a fine example of negative thoughts suffocating Potential for Discovery.

Murray enters the bathroom with a gentle rap at the door. His hair is tucked back behind his ears, like in his YouTube videos when he's being serious.

Just wanted to see if you need anything—wow. You look lovely. Like you're in a nest of clouds.

Want to get in?

Very tempting, but no. I have a little work to do and I was wondering if you'd like to have a drink at eight o'clock. I'm sorry. I'm not the most entertaining host.

I'd love to.

Good. Sorry to do this. My latest project is making exciting advances.

What's it about?

Sandra, have you ever dreamed of something so much, it feels like speaking it aloud will reveal your inner delirium? Does that make sense?

I know what you mean.

He scoops up a mound of bubbles from the tub. For years now, he says, I've conducted task-based experiments with positive thinking. For example, a participant does a number of positive-thinking exercises, then completes performance-based activities—games, math tests, job interviews. Every time, the positive thinker outperforms the control group. And in our longitudinal studies, those who continued to practise the exercises saw continued success in their lives. All from regularly visualizing what they want for themselves and the world.

He blows on the bubbles so they flutter over the tub.

But then we publish our findings via social media and it's ignored. Like telling people to avoid sugar or get more sunshine. So I've taken a different approach. What are barriers to positive thinking? Negative thinking, of course.

He scoops up more bubbles. Imagine a brain, he says. Here—he taps the front—in the right prefrontal cortex, this is where negative thoughts happen. And like exercising any muscle, if someone tends to think negatively, the prefrontal cortex becomes hyperactive. It's like baseball pitchers—their throwing arm gets bigger.

Wow. Yes, I get that.

So we're trying to give the positive muscle a fighting chance. Have you heard of TMS?

No, what's that?

Transcranial Magnetic Stimulation. TMS induces a small electric current to specific parts of the brain. They use it to treat depression. It sends pulses through the forehead. Very mild. Patients usually need four or five treatments a month.

Is it like electroshock therapy?

Much less severe. They don't even need to sedate patients. So our science asks, what if you gave your prefrontal cortex a break? Calm it in order to strengthen the ventral striatum? Athletes do it all the time: change focus to develop necessary muscles. So we've developed a TMS treatment which instructs the negative thought area to relax. During this break time, the candidate focuses on working out those positive-thinking joints. When the prefrontal cortex returns to normal, the rest of the brain is better equipped to handle negativity.

Murray blows the bubbles away and dabs the last bit on my nose.

What do you think? Crazy, or what?

I think it's brilliant.

Really?

Yes. And . . . if the CT scans are involved, I'd like to see mine.

There. Decision made. I just want to give him something of myself.

Are you sure, Sandra? Please don't feel obliged.

Consider it my contribution to science.

Tuesday

In the CT scanner, music (I asked for Pink, so ironic) plays into my headset, but I can still hear the blaring drones. Murray is just outside. He joked about me going to Mars because of Paige's night sky mural, but it makes me think of the first Alien movie, when Tom Skerritt's character dies and they shoot his body into space.

And then I'm retracted. Murray hugs me.

We have a picnic lunch by the pond, fresh air flushing out the claustrophobia. Murray pulls bagels, lox and cream cheese from the basket. More of my favourites.

I received news during your scan, he says. But it must stay between us.

Of course.

And unfortunately, it will interfere with our visit. I'm sorry. It has to happen right away.

I understand.

So, for months now, we've been working with TMS experiments. By we, I mean my team and Dr. Sasha Lee. Have you heard of her?

She doesn't sound familiar.

There's this great *Science Today* article on her. She's both a TMS and mood disorder expert. We found a willing participant a while ago, this young man named Joel, but the project's been in limbo, waiting for approval. And we got it! They're both going to be here by Thursday to run the TMS treatment!

Oh Murray, that's wonderful! You have a lab here?

Yes, Dr. Lee put it all together. I can't believe the red tape's finally cut.

Of course it is. You thought it, you believed in it, and now it's so.

Murray beams. Look at you, he says. The student becomes the teacher. I know it puts a glitch in our time, but their schedules won't be free again for a while.

It's no problem. I can go back whenever.

Oh no, I wasn't suggesting you leave. I mean, if you want to—I don't want to keep you from your life.

No. I mean, I'm having a fantastic time, but I don't want to be in the way.

Sandra. If you don't need to go and you're interested, I'd love it if you stayed. God, you'll keep me sane, that's for sure.

I'd be honoured.

Mr. Dove!

Paige speed walks towards us. She holds a large piece of paper. Sorry to interrupt, she says. But I think you should see this. Ms. Somers, your CT scan.

This is it. The moment I learn there's a brain tumour. A shadow, a spreading mass. A bird chirps over the pond.

Murray gapes at the image. I've never seen anything like it, he says.

The scan resembles the others: spirals, blobs. But in the centre, someone has placed what looks like a pool of lava.

It's so vibrant, he says. Alive.

Like a volcano, Paige whispers.

And this as well, Murray says. He points to a greyish area to the side.

Wow, she says. What a combo.

What is it?

It's hard to see in contrast to the ventral striatum, but it's your frontal cortex. Also very developed. Your mind contains two powerful muscles at odds with each other.

You mean I'm really negative?

No, not at all. But your negative thinking is very toned. Likely a side effect of The Dimming.

Oh.

Sandra, don't be disappointed. You are a well of positive energy.

He hugs me to him. It's just a hurdle for it to get out, he says.

I hold my mind's image in my lap. The blob seems to pulsate like a heartbeat.

Wednesday

Dr. Lee arrives this evening. Paige says Dr. Lee is gluten-free, so I'm making cornbread. The pantry is stocked with several alternative grains. Murray prepares for all dietary restrictions for retreat participants. Sometimes new eating sensitivities emerge through rigorous personal introspection, he says. Lots leave lactose intolerant. I nod in agreement, even though I could never give up cheese.

I stir butter and eggs into the blue cornmeal, turning it a rich indigo. I imagine it as my well-defined negative-thinking muscle, sleek like an eel, flexing my insecurities, grudges, fuck-ups. Even this, the making of thoughtful snack food, is busywork while Murray and Paige prepare. This morning I helped myself to a bagel as he set off to the lab with a printout of instructions. The guest house is ready for Dr. Lee with a fresh bouquet of orange day lilies, her favourite, according to Paige.

I read my messages while the cornbread bakes. Velma has written twice, once to state that a week off without notice is usually only okay in emergencies, especially since they're run ragged, but she'll let it go this time. The second is to say Cliff is still in the hospital but improving. There was another incident on his street with the same NNAN group. Counter-protesters have moved in. The media call them Antifa, even though only some of them are. I'm not impressed that you've run off with a stranger, she says, but even if he is a crazy cult leader, you're probably safer there than anywhere in the city. She signs off *Don't Drink the Kool-Aid, xo*.

And suddenly I want to see Velma, see St. Jude's, return to the locked hovel of my apartment, my bed, my intention board, the clamouring hum of the Don Valley Parkway. Get up, go to work, drink bad coffee, and have purpose, even if it's only data entry. At least there's hope of helping, performing my small, comfortable part tapping keyboards and daydreaming and Murray wouldn't be something real I can lose or have to acknowledge as impossible to really have.

I start an email to update Velma but stop myself. We could fit five families here. We could feed the whole shelter. Instead, I write *Thank you* and press send. When the cornbread is ready, I leave it out to cool. Upstairs in the bedroom, I lie close to Murray's side of the mattress. I close my eyes against this perfect space.

When I come down for supper Paige is busy in the kitchen and there's no sign of Murray. But Dr. Lee has arrived. I am grateful for napping. The bit of sleep makes me more prepared to deal with her.

Dr. Lee is compact and immaculate in a grey Chanel suit. Her black hair is cut in a 60s bob, her high cheekbones like ivory cliffs. She's Chinese, I assume, but I won't. Her accent is British and posh.

Sondra, yes? Murray's friend from Toronto. I'm Dr. Sasha Lee. She slides her hand into mine. Her skin feels smooth and expensive.

Mississauga, originally, I say. Like it makes me exotic.

Murray tells me you manage a homeless shelter.

Oh, that's not accurate. I help process applications for those in need.

And there are so many. You run a vital resource. Unfortunately.

Paige appears with a tray of stuffed mushrooms which I recognize as Costco brand and shouldn't feel satisfied, but I do. Dr. Lee pops one in her mouth and chews with gusto. The food on the plane was awful, she says. Even in business class.

You must be excited about tomorrow, I say.

Yes. But my schedule doesn't allow me to see the experiment to completion. After the procedure, Murray's team takes over.

Murray's team? I imagine an army in white lab coats

appearing at once, strolling out of the orchard, emerging from the pond.

They'll be here Saturday, Paige says. Friday is rest and recovery for Joel.

Wow. Busy times.

I chew a stuffed mushroom. I imagine the headlines: *This Is Your Brain on Positivity. Fitter Minds, Better World.* I swallow the mushroom and my own petulant stirrings. He will not have time for a woman he's known for a week. I will not maintain expectations. I've had a wonderful time. Too early to pin my heart on him. Stop it stop it stop it.

Murray enters with a bottle of wine. Sasha, he says, fantastic to see you. He and Dr. Lee kiss each other's cheeks in greeting. He kisses me on the mouth and I am ridiculous to keep track.

Over supper, Murray goes over the plan: Joel arrives tomorrow. He will complete surveys and activities designed to gauge his positive and negative reactions. One involves reading about world events and responding.

I don't know how anyone can react positively when reading the news, Dr. Lee says.

It's not just emotional reaction, it's solution finding, Murray says. Our hope is once the trigger of negative thoughts is lessened, one recognizes the bigger picture and envisions the best options for the most people.

He strokes my leg under the table, but his body stays angled towards Dr. Lee.

After supper, we visit the CT building. Murray moves a curtain at the back—I had assumed it was a dressing area—and reveals a small elevator. What a sweet little lift, Dr. Lee says.

The elevator lowers and opens into the downstairs lab. The room is white, with stainless-steel cabinets and monitoring equipment. A small crane-like mechanism dangles a helmet-shaped contraption over a chair. The air smells lemon-fresh with earth tones, like new soil.

Would you like to see how it works, Sandra? Dr. Lee sits in the chair and lowers the helmet-thing over her forehead. Inside is an electromagnetic coil, she says. It sends vibrations to areas of the brain. In normal TMS treatments, the patient would receive several sessions. But we're only doing one.

Why just one?

We don't want any chance of permanently inhibiting the prefrontal cortex. After all, both positive and negative thoughts are necessary for logic.

What do you think, Sandra? Murray asks.

It's fascinating. I point to the helmet-thing. It reminds me of the Tin Man's hat in *The Wizard of Oz*.

Dr. Lee's expression remains stoic, but Murray claps his hands: Brilliant! My favourite book. *I shall take the heart . . . For brains do not make one happy, and happiness is the best thing in the world.*

And he swings me around in his arms and we laugh and I could be this, I could help him make his dreams reality. I close my eyes and send a single, powerful intention into the universe: *Us.*

That night, we all retire early. But I wake shivering in the dark. The air conditioning is on bust and I'm alone. There are extra blankets in a hallway closet. As I go to fetch them, I hear voices from the kitchen downstairs. Murray and Paige.

Murray's voice is a moan. I creep to the stairwell. If I look down, I'll be able to see part of the counter and stay hidden. I brace myself for the worst: naked shapes, sweaty dishevelment.

But it's not a sound of pleasure. Murray cradles his head. Paige paces.

What if we pay him? she says. Throw money at the problem.

No, it ruins the theory. The subject has to be a volunteer. If there's financial motivation, my critics will claim bias. People have to want to exercise their minds.

Goddamn Joel. Paige pours a glass of wine. I had a bad feeling about him.

And now he won't answer his phone. Such cowardice.

Murray rubs his hands through his curls. Okay, he says. In the morning, we reschedule with Sasha. We find another subject. Subjects. We'll get backups, like understudies.

It took us a year to find Joel.

We'll try harder.

The grant committee expects a report in two months.

I know, Paige.

She drinks her wine and stares at the glass. There is an option, she says.

Like what?

Silence. Paige faces Murray. She points up, meaning upstairs. I can't see his face, but she raises her eyebrows.

No way, Paige.

She believes in your work. Deeply cares about it, I'd say.

This is not up for discussion.

And her scan? She's ideal. Big positive muscle blocked by—

Absolutely fucking not.

Look, I understand you have feelings. I mean, I've never seen you like this. It's great. Christ, some of the others—at least she's nice. She's an actual activist. But we're in a bind and we already know there won't be damage—

This conversation is over. I will regard any attempt to bring up Sandra's involvement as a highly negative, possibly toxic, contribution from you.

He takes his glass and leaves. Paige curses softly. She pours her wine in the sink and walks away.

I tiptoe downstairs. Murray is on the front steps. With his head hanging low, his back and shoulders resemble a perfect oval. His curls lie defeated at the nape of his neck. I want to sit beside him, comfort that posture.

Instead, I go to the bathroom. I turn on the faucet and stare at myself in the mirror.

When I arrived on Saturday, I realized I'd forgotten my hair straightener. Now my hair is wavy, rich with new highlights from being outdoors. Five days of fresh air and clean food look good on me. Plus all the sex. *Radiant* comes to mind. No one has ever called me radiant. Here comes Sandy Sandra, Father used to say. She's like a sandy beach in summer. Nice under your feet, but can grate on your ass.

I turn off the faucet. I exit the bathroom quietly. Paige's space is in the other side of the house. A hallway leads to one door, her light is on. I clear my throat and knock.

The door opens. Paige looks puzzled. Everything okay? she asks. Do you need anything?

I overheard you and Murray talking. About Joel.

She exhales hard. Okay, she says. Damn. I'm sorry you

overheard. I didn't mean to suggest—

Would I be sick afterwards?

Sick? No. It's not like that.

Tell me what it's like.

I push past her. The room is softly lit and surprisingly sparse. A desk, a bed, a bookshelf. A faint smell of lavender. Books and binders cover the only chair, so I perch on the edge of the mattress.

Why do you want to know? Paige asks.

I'm not making any decision until I have all the information.

She stares at me. I avert my eyes. Framed photographs clutter the bookshelf: she and a red-haired man pose in Niagara Falls. Maybe a brother. A twin.

Shit. I'm definitely getting fired for this.

She pulls a burgundy binder from the bookshelf. This contains an overview of everything, she says. Joel read it before he signed the waiver.

Waiver?

We need one for legal reasons.

She opens to a page with bulleted points. During the session, the TMS transfer coil delivers two Tesla pulses, twenty-five vibrations per second, she says. The subject may experience the following: a deep peaceful sensation, a series of clicking sounds, headaches, and facial twitching. Most serious risk is a seizure, but it's a low possibility.

And afterwards, it's just tests?

Yes, to collect your responses.

Paige flips to the back of the book. The last page is a contract. Take the binder if you want, she says. I mean, if you're serious, you should know what you're getting into.

There's an edge in her last sentence. Of course I'm serious, I say. I wouldn't be here discussing it otherwise.

Or, you know, you're curious. I get it. It's all pretty intriguing. You're a long-time fan. And he's magnetic. Believe me, it's been a problem before.

The plastic edge of the binder digs into my thigh under the bathrobe. How many times? I ask.

What, you think he's never been stalked? Harassed? God, it's either some infatuated fan or a fascist posing as a follower. I mean, he wanted to invite you, but it wasn't spur of the moment. No one comes here without me checking them out.

I get it. I figured.

Look, I'm sorry you heard what I said. Don't feel pressured. You're a decent person with a fulfilling job. You live in the heart of Toronto the Good. This is a great free vacation for you.

You make me sound like a groupie.

Well. There's been groupies. They come, they have fun, they get a kick out of his big ideas.

Paige sighs. Sorry, I'm exhausted, she says. I've been working with him for twelve years. People come and go. He persists. I'm not trying to be a bitch.

No, I understand.

Anyway. Here's the details. Enjoy.

She stands and stretches. I need a few good hours sleep before facing Dr. L, she says. Take it with you. Just don't let Murray see you reading it. He's upset enough already.

I step into the hallway. She shuts the door. The line of light underneath vanishes.

In the kitchen, there is no sign of Murray, nor is he outside. I open the binder on the counter. Electromagnetic coil. Pulses. Peaceful sensation. Seizure. What the actual fuck am I doing? Is this what I want to do or just a desire to please?

I close my eyes. Deep breaths. Focus.

When I made my first intention board, there were directions. *Clarify Your Intentions: What do you want? What do you need? How do you want to feel when your intention becomes real?*

I want to be a positive force. The kind of person who helps people discover their way in a manner that betters the world.

What do I need? I need love in my life. I want to feel like someone who can be loved, who is *something*. Not a bland lady at a computer, not an annoying presence.

I want Murray and me to be *us*.

A blue pen is tucked in the binder's inside flap. I sign my name.

Thursday

In the morning, I wait until I hear Paige moving around. I bring the binder to her. She signs the witness section: *Paige Farthing*.

Like a penny, I say.

What?

A farthing, like a copper coin. Your last name fits your hair.

That's a sweet way of seeing it. I used to get Paige Farting in high school. Didn't help that my twin's name is

Rolm. Here comes a rolm-page of farting.

We both laugh. It's nice.

We should tell him together, she says. This won't be pretty.

Let's do it.

Murray checks his tablet at the kitchen counter. His hair is a frenzy of stress.

Murray, I have something to say.

He blinks at both of us, his eyes pink and tired.

I overheard you and Paige last night. I've decided to take the place of Joel in the study.

Goddamnit, Paige.

Don't be angry with Paige, it's my decision. I've gone over all the details—

Sandra, no. Absolutely not.

Why? Why not?

I refuse to disrupt your life like this.

My work in Toronto is a job I do because I want to help people. Helping you do your work will be more than I could ever do at St. Jude's.

She really wants to do it, Murray.

Stay out of it, Paige.

What's going on?

Dr. Lee stands by the counter, head to toe in black lycra running gear. Is everything okay?

We have an issue with today's plan. Joel cancelled.

But I'm volunteering to be the subject—

And I was just telling Sandra, it's inappropriate for her to take his place. She's new in my life and this is not a casual decision—

I've read the information. I've signed the waiver.

What's the problem then? Dr. Lee says. Murray, you showed me Ms. Somers' CT scan last night—he was bragging about you, my dear—and she has both the ventral striatum and prefrontal cortex of an ideal candidate. Better than Joel's.

Sandra should not be—

Murray, you always say to ask for what you want. I want this.

She's got a point, Dr. Lee says. You also tell people to consider the big picture. What helps the most people? The science is our main concern; she's provided a solution. And you know she's in capable hands.

Sasha, I don't doubt you, he says. But—

But you are letting your feelings get in the way.

Murray's eyes shine with emotion. In this moment, I could hand over my heart to him.

So, Dr. Lee says, are we settled? Paige, you prep the lab. I'm off for my five K. We'll reconvene in two hours.

Paige darts out before anyone speaks. Dr. Lee exits to do warm-ups on the step. Murray puts his arms around me and rests his head on my shoulder. We stand like this for a very long time.

Dr. Lee is all business. No water for an hour beforehand. Remove any jewellery, change into the hospital gown. Go to the bathroom. The lab is chilly and I get goose bumps under the thin gown. The vinyl-covered chair squeaks with every movement. Dr. Lee smooths a cotton pad soaked in something cool over my forehead and temples.

We'll be starting momentarily, she says. Murray wants a word first.

Yes please.

She leaves and he enters. He's showered and shaven, tamed his curls behind his ears. He kisses my cheek and lips. I breathe in his honeyed scent.

You can still back out, he says.

I've made up my mind.

I'm overwhelmed you're doing this.

Why?

I've had the best week I can remember. It's been a long time since I really connected with someone. And now here you are, deep in my crazy life. He takes my hand. I just don't want to scare you away, he says.

Scare me? Murray, the more I learn about you, the more I want to be a part of what you do. And, see, me telling you this scares me—that I'm scaring you away.

He kisses me, long and soft. I'm not scared, he says.

And then, because it's so present and heavy, like overripe fruit, the words fall from my mouth: I love you, Murray.

He stares into my eyes. The golden flecks in his pupils glitter like lost stars. Oh Sandra, he says. Me too. I love you so much.

We kiss again. I'll see you in twenty minutes, he says. He steps back as Dr. Lee scurries in.

The coil lowers over my cranium. I close my eyes and savour the bliss, the pure joy of requited, wholesome love. The machine whirls and the beats begin, a click, a winding up. I let Murray's love and my love and the world's love, all the love in this beautiful, broken universe fill me up like a living storm of pulsing, perfect pink li—

PART TWO

Days are pictures now. Like a projector.

Here is Velma. Her mouth makes slow words.

Here is a nurse. She holds a spoon.

Velma talks to a police officer. She shakes a finger in his face.

Janelle, in a chair. Looking at her phone.

Father's silhouette in the doorway. Hello. Hello, Father. My mouth is sealed. Feels duct-taped shut.

Then longer pictures. Velma's voice. Cat. Cat. The card has an orange cat. Try, Sandra. Cat. A sound, a voice, from somewhere underneath. *Cag. Cag.* Good job, Sandra. Now this one. Boot. Boot.

It all makes me tired.

Think, Sandra, Velma says. The Pickering Nuclear Station. They found you there. Do you remember anything about the Pickering Nuclear Station?

No. I don't think so.

She leans close. Today her head has a pink scarf. Her head has many scarves: blue, black, red dots. Your message said you were with Murray Dove, she whispers. Was that true?

Murray loves me.

And then I want to shut my eyes and think of him, because I cannot dream and the light in the room is so bright. C'mon, Sandra, Velma says. Try to remember. But when I try, I fall asleep.

Changes occur in shifts and creaks, like termite trails. I walk outside. Sit on a bench. Look at grass. I can talk and listen for five, nine, thirteen, twenty-four minutes without exhaustion. I can go through the cards and remember the ones we did from the day before, from two days before. The crease between Velma's eyes isn't constant.

I can put my finger on the calendar and know the day. Velma gets me to show the police officer. Then she waits outside. The police officer has thick eyebrows like caterpillars and a deep voice and he says it's been six weeks since I was brought in.

Workers at the Pickering Nuclear Station found you, he says. You couldn't talk. You were dressed like you were hiking. Do you remember going for a hike?

No.

Did you get there by train?

I only remember being with Murray.

Certain groups are targeting the Pickering Nuclear Station lately. Break-ins mostly. Do you recall seeing anyone there?

It was just us four. Paige, Dr. Lee, Murray and me.

His eyebrows ripple. Mr. Dove gave a statement. He says he was at the Lansing Institute doing research at the time. They've backed him up.

That's wrong. We spent a week together.

Mr. Dove doesn't have property in Cobourg.

Yes he does. It's a beautiful place.

The police officer makes a note. Mr. Dove says you met after a speaking engagement at the Royal York Hotel.

Yes, he invited me there.

He acknowledged that. He says he often invites fans to events.

It was wonderful. His talk, and then dinner.

He says you met at the book signing. No dinner, no other socializing.

Did he or Paige say that? Paige is probably just scared they'll get in trouble. They didn't mean to hurt me.

Sandra, there's an ongoing investigation with the Pickering Station. It seems like you were hiking and found your way onto the site.

No, I was with Murray Dove.

What did you do during your week off?

I just told you, I was with Murray. At his place.

Okay. What did you two do? Any drinking? Drugs?

We drank, but no drugs. Not even when Dr. Lee ran the machine on my head.

Velma McAnespi says you emailed her from your phone, which we can't find. Do you know where your phone is?

It's in my jacket. I hung it up in the lab after I changed. I'm very tired now.

I close my eyes. I want to stop talking. When Murray comes, he'll clear all this up.

The police officer opens the door. She's asleep, he says to Velma.

The doctor says her rationality is returning, Velma says. Maybe this is a blip on the way to recovery.

Or it's PTSD and this story helps her cope.

If so, it's her kind of story. She was always very optimistic.

Optimistic. Glass half full. Even though things are confusing, I am recovering. I count up the pros: I have no scars.

People care about me. My dreams are returning in flashes and droplets. Last night, I dreamed of a pool of bright beating liquid light, like peach sherbet. It's warm and alive and it lives inside me. It's ready to work.

Velma tells me we're leaving the hospital soon. Hedgeglove claimed my apartment. The provincial government has established temporary control over all non-profit shelters, as they suspect they're potential hotbeds for terrorist conspiracy. Since Velma is working from home, she says I can stay in her spare room until I'm back on my feet. I think this is nice and it's nice of her. I tell her this and she frowns a little.

Today Cliff visits. A thin red scar etches from his hairline to the centre of his left eyebrow. The shape of his nose is slightly off. A cane rests beside his chair.

I'm here twice a week for physiotherapy, he says. Velma said you were doing better. Figured I'd stop by.

It's good to see you.

Good to see you too, Sandra.

Cliff's smile doesn't reach his eyes. His sadness makes me move to the edge of the bed. Cliff, always so handsome and charming. The hair is shaved along the side of his head, his dark skin paler where the stitches have healed. My body tips a little as I settle.

I'm sorry this happened to you, Cliff.

I'm sorry this happened to you, Sandra. Are you okay? If you fall, I can't catch you.

I'm okay.

Cliff passes a hand over his face. It's so fucked up, he says. The fucking Dimming. Anyone with a drop of hate in them has licence to set it on boil.

It's a very difficult time.

Those New Nationalist fuckers and the Pickering Station. They steal chemicals, anything they can use. Genocide scavenging—their own fucking words and the media still won't call them terrorists. I'm so sorry you were a bystander.

It's a misunderstanding, actually. I was helping Murray Dove with an experiment.

Oh. Shit. Velma said—so that's what happened, huh?

It is what happened. I know it sounds terrible. I feel bad Murray had to talk to the police. But it will be straightened out soon.

A spot pulses in Cliff's upper jaw. If that's the case, he says, aren't you angry? He hurt you.

Good question. Whatever happened was definitely a big mistake and it's not right to cover it up. But I don't feel upset. I think it's all going to be okay. Like it's for a reason. And if Murray doesn't come explain, when I get better I'll go to his house and we can fix it. Because he loves me. And I love him.

Cliff rubs his hands together. There are faint scars on his knuckles, but otherwise his hands are smooth and elegant.

I don't know whether to envy or pity you, he says. Faith in humanity would be a reprieve for me right now. All I do is try not to feel scared at every strange noise, every stranger. Try not to be constantly angry. But I want them to pay. I want those fuckers flattened.

His hands form fists. I lean forward and touch them. My mind feels like the source of a conveyor belt, churning feelings into thoughts into words into what I want for Cliff.

No one blames you for feeling this way, I say. But maybe, Cliff, what would be the best for you is to try and remember what you loved in life before this incident. Seek out beauty and goodness. We are in The Dimming, but there is still light left. Chase the spark.

Cliff's head rises. He frowns. His dark eyes gleam with a hazy acknowledgement.

You're right. I mean, it's just trying. What is anything if you don't try?

He grabs his cane and stands. He moves to the window.

Look at those clouds. It will rain soon. This world could use a good, hard rain.

My hands still hold the compact heat of Cliff's fists. I watch the rise and fall of his back as he breathes. When he turns, he smiles, then blushes.

Sandra, thanks for the advice. I feel—I don't know. It's a new day. Thank you, Sandra.

He limps out the door. I can hear him greeting nurses: Hello. Good day. Nice scrubs! What's the print, little frogs? Frogs are my favourite amphibian. He giggles, hard and abrupt, like a gunshot.

The air in the room flutters somehow. I did not expect him to react this way. But I'm happy he did. It feels good to see him understand the big picture.

Monday

Velma's house in Scarborough has a wonderful garden. She's coaxed vines into growing over the chain-link fence separating her backyard from the railroad tracks. When the

GO Train passes, the leaves do an excited little dance and the off-breeze sways the sunflowers. There are so many flowers, particularly bee-friendly ones: coneflowers, hyssops, black-eyed Susans. Even when landscaping, Velma dirties her hands doing the good work.

The GO Train makes me think of Murray. Ninety-three kilometres to Cobourg from here. These days, I can stay awake up to seven consecutive hours. My mind is clear. He hasn't returned my messages and his phone is out of service. The last thing he tweeted was an article on the importance of taking a break from social media. *Going on a brief hiatus for self care. Much love.* So tomorrow, Cliff's driving me to his house.

What if he won't speak to you? Velma asked. Or sends out security guards?

There's a security system, but I didn't see guards. His only staff was Paige.

So he lives in a gated compound with gardens and there's only one full-time staff member?

When I was there, yes. But the people on retreats perform a lot of upkeep.

Sounds pretty sketchy, Sandra.

It's natural for Velma to be concerned. She's so nurturing. When I'm all better and get my own place, I will host a dinner party. Velma, Cliff, Murray, all the people who care about me will come. What a wonderful night it will be.

Cliff arrives early the next morning. We hug hello and I realize we never hugged during our time at St. Jude's. But now, we're close through our parallel experiences. It just goes to show how good things arise from crisis. I say this to him and Velma. Cliff agrees. Velma lights up a cigarette.

I pack an overnight bag. I imagine Murray's quite busy, but I should be prepared to stay. Velma is waiting at the car.

I'm coming, she says. I was going to stay out of it, but I'm too worried.

That's great, Velma. The more the merrier.

Yes, Sandra's right, Cliff says.

Velma stares at Cliff with her eyes squinted. I call shotgun.

Traffic is backed up near Port Hope. The police have closed off part of the 401. A group of refugees were caught crossing Lake Ontario by boat. The police line them up near the vans. A young woman closes her eyes and mouths words. When her eyelids open, her pupils are dark fear. I reach for Cliff and he holds my hand.

A police officer stops the car to provide updates. He is boyish, but his chest and arms bulge with muscles.

Sorry for the delay, folks. Once we move the current detainees, the highway will be clear.

Thank you, officer, Velma says.

What are you going to do with them? I ask.

They'll be processed at the nearest internment station.

Processed? Sounds like a factory.

Sandra, let the officer do his job.

Well, ma'am, we don't know who these foreigners are. Once we learn their backgrounds, they'll be dealt with according to our laws.

Backgrounds? They've been chased out of the US.

Thank you, officer. We're good.

Why lock up people seeking sanctuary?

Ma'am, the stations are a result of the current housing crisis. You can read about it on the federal government site.

Velma pushes the close button on my window but stops when I lay my hand on it. I lean out a little to see the police officer's eyes. They are blue like old denim.

Perhaps what you can do, officer, I say, is try to see these people as human beings instead of problems. Perhaps what would be the best for you is to regard them as no different from your family or dearest friends. What a world it could be.

I lean back inside. The window slides up.

Jesus Christ, Sandra, Velma says. He has trigger-happy written all over him.

The car in front moves ahead and we follow. In my side mirror, the cop stands frozen. I feel warm all over. It's like Christmas, when someone appreciates your thoughtful gift.

The compound gate is closed. I press the intercom. No answer. The fence is high, but the wrought iron is sturdy enough for a foothold. I step up and hoist myself over the gate.

Sandra, don't! Security cameras!

I land on the other side. No alarms. I knew it would be okay. I'm going up to the house, I say. I'll get Paige to let you in.

Goddamnit. Cliff, help me over this fucking fence.

Velma and Cliff climb while I walk up ahead. My legs can't stop speeding up. I cannot wait to see Murray. Touch him, hear his voice.

The house is dark. I knock and call out. Everything is locked. Maybe they're out on errands.

Velma and Cliff arrive, panting. Let's check the lab, I say. Then you can see the garden and the greenhouse. You'll love it. Velma starts to speak, but I push on.

The greenhouse is locked. Most of the garden has been harvested.

Sandra, look at this.

Velma points to a sign: PROPERTY OF THE AAFC.

What's the AAFC?

Agriculture and Agri-Food Canada. This is government property, Sandra.

Murray's probably letting them use it.

I move to the lab. A hot grinding invades my stomach. I don't know what it is. If it was anger, I would feel angry. If I'm prepping for disappointment, it should feel more familiar.

The lab is closed up with a padlock, but the screws in the bolt are loose. Pulling on them doesn't work. I use a rock to knock it out. By the time Velma and Cliff catch up, I've got it mostly knocked off. Cliff yanks it free in one hard tug.

The door swings open. The CT scanner and monitors are gone. A frayed cable dangles from the wall.

Lab, huh? Velma says.

I step inside. Glass crunches under my shoe. A broken picture frame.

On the walk back, Velma says things like this place feels sketchy and we should leave, and Cliff says things like are you okay and what do you want to do now. I keep going. I'll check the windows in the house. I'll go around the pond. The sour emptiness inside me sends signals, but my head is clear. I have to decide my next move. I need to show him I'm okay. I just have to find him.

A man is by the house. He's stocky and bald and wears a large tool belt. The pouches are full of heavy things. He pulls out a phone when he sees us. Oh shit, Velma says.

This is private property, the man says. How'd you get in?

No need to worry, I say. We're looking for Murray Dove.

This area is part of an experimental farm. You can't be in here.

Sorry, Velma says. This whole thing is a misunderstanding. We're leaving.

Murray Dove was staying here, I say. Do you have his forwarding contact number?

No one's stayed here for over six months.

You must be confused, I say. I was a guest here two months ago.

Sure, lady. You all need to leave now or I call the police.

When I step towards him, his hand moves to his tool belt. But my stomach pains vanish and I'm suddenly light-headed. This poor, hostile man. He has to protect this place from The Dimming all the time.

I understand being scared of strangers, I say. But we're on a quest to find Murray Dove, who loves me very much. I believe if you look deep inside yourself, you'd see we're decent people. Being afraid of us just causes more stress. It wouldn't take much to lend a hand. We're only looking around after all.

The man blinks. His rubs his cheeks in circular motions.

I am scared of strangers, he says. So many freaks. Every week, there's another bunch trying to contaminate the area. I'm sorry.

It's okay. Do you have a key to the house?

He pulls a key chain from the tool belt. I do, he says. He regards it in his palm. You seem like decent people, he says. Why don't I help for once? He holds it towards me. These days, he says, everyone is so afraid.

I unlock the door. The man follows, his hands folded behind his back. Inside, the kitchen is bare. A cupboard door is open; one package of gluten-free crackers inside. I check Paige's space. Empty.

Okay, Sandra, Velma says. Can we please leave?

You don't have to be afraid, the man says. I'm not scared of you.

What do you want to do, Sandra? Cliff says.

I stare at the carpet. Murray is gone. He knows what he did to my mind was a mistake. But these feelings of clarity and ability, it must be his intention. I suddenly know I can find him, wherever he is.

In the corner on the floor is a jar full of something copper. I scoop it up. Pennies. The first currency to be abandoned in the ongoing succession of soaring prices. A memory flashes. This room. Paige's copper hair. Farthing.

I know where to start, I say.

Monday afternoon

In the car, I sit in the back seat with my new phone. A Google search for Rolm Farthing produces his Facebook profile and LinkedIn. Studied at Ryerson. Works as a Project Management Consultant in Niagara. I try a 411 search.

What happened with that guard? Velma asks. Did he

have a mini-stroke or something? It's like his whole person-ality switched.

He realized helping us was a good idea, Cliff says.

The guard. His harsh face, the hard line of his mouth. Like Father, solidly stubborn with stifled emotion. But when I spoke, he listened.

He saw we weren't there to cause harm, I say.

Velma says nothing. She changes the station from CBC to top forty.

We stop at a Tim Hortons. It's nice to get out of the car. Velma closes her eyes as she sips her double-double.

So Paige's brother Rolm is in Niagara, I say. He'll know where Paige is.

Janelle's parents live out there, Cliff says.

Maybe they can help us?

Great idea, Cliff says. I'll contact Janelle.

Wait, what? Velma says. It's a two-hour drive. You want to go to Niagara, impose ourselves on Janelle's family, and then track down some stranger?

Yes.

And you're certain he'll help?

Yes. I have faith.

All we can do is try, Cliff says.

Sirens wail. Several police cruisers fly past. The woman behind the counter raises the volume on the flat screen above the sandwich area: RCMP are currently pursuing an alleged rogue officer after an incident at the Ajax Refugee Processing Facility.

The screen changes to a shaky video. A cop pointing a gun at other cops. The reporter continues: Here we see

Officer Dylan Hazeline forcing the release of Facility occupants.

How can you treat them this way? Officer Hazeline screams. You're monsters! I won't let you!

A cop steps forward, arms out, reasoning. Officer Hazeline fires his gun in the air. Everyone ducks.

RCMP are in pursuit of Officer Hazeline as well as over forty refugees who escaped when Hazeline opened the gates.

Holy shit, Velma says. That's the cop from before. He's lost it.

Or he had an epiphany, I say.

Velma's expression is a myriad of emotions: confusion, fear, wonder.

It's three o'clock now, Cliff says. Janelle's at her parents' too. They've invited us over for a barbeque.

How generous. People are so nice.

They are, Cliff says. It's wonderful.

Janelle's parents live in half a duplex, a comfortable red brick house with a water feature in the backyard and a large cedar deck. Photos of Janelle and her sisters are framed on the wall. Janelle has a big smile in all the photos and even though I've never experienced that smile directly, it's nice to see so many happy faces.

Her parents hand us wine and invite us to fill our plates. It's good to sit and eat. According to my Google search, Rolm Farthing's office is twenty minutes away. I tell Cliff this and he agrees to drive me after supper.

Sandra, Velma says. It's after five. He won't be there.

Go tomorrow, Janelle's mother says. You can stay here

tonight. It's dangerous after dark.

I push potato salad around on the plate. Velma is right, of course. But I know the grinding in my belly won't disappear until Murray and I work this out.

Janelle's mother makes up a couch in the basement and I retire early. I lie down and fold my hands over my stomach. I take deep breaths until I fall asleep.

When I wake up, I have to think hard to remember where I am. It's dark, but Janelle's laugh rings clear. She and Velma are still out on the deck. The side window is open a crack. Their voices are boozy.

But everyone's bananas these days, Janelle says. Mom and Dad can't even watch the news. Retired teachers and suddenly they're saying stuff like humanity is poison.

It's different though, Velma says. Cliff follows her around, not questioning. Commenting on how pretty everything is.

He probably just feels sorry for her.

I tiptoe to the window. I can see up through the grass outside. Velma pours wine.

No, something's off, she says. She spoke to those men and they were overcome.

So, you think what, Positive Sandwich got zapped with nuclear energy and now she's the Purple Man?

Shh, not so loud.

Janelle stands silhouetted under the patio lights. So at ease in her comfortable home with her functional family. She sips her wine and smacks her lips. Janelle in her nice childhood home, no Father drunk on the lawn every Mother's Day. No witnessing your brother's Twitter followers call him out for abusive trolling.

I return to bed. My stomach flutters. I understand Velma's concern. It's unfortunate she finds it so surprising I could inspire people. She should really try to be more positive.

I wake up early. If I speak with Rolm first thing, I might find Murray by lunch. Cliff and I snack on leftover pineapple from the barbeque while the coffee perks. Janelle appears looking tired.

You guys are up already?

Yes, we're heading out to find Rolm.

She fetches a coffee mug. Sandra, she says, please don't be offended. But showing up at a stranger's office to ask about his sister is creepy.

When I explain, he'll understand.

This guy could be anybody. And Cliff's been through a lot. Think twice for his sake.

I want to help Sandra, Cliff says.

See, Janelle? He wants to. Anyway, assuming Rolm would harm us is unproductive. Just because the TV news scares your parents doesn't mean all strangers are dangerous.

Her eyes harden. Listening, were ya? she says.

Well, you were loud.

Janelle pours coffee into her mug. Look, Sandra, she says. I told my parents about your accident and they agreed to let you stay. But really, go home. See your doctor. And yes, I've always found you a little unstable and it's not fair to rope Cliff in.

Unstable? I think that's you being unfair.

Don't take it personally. I think you're a good person.

How should I not take it personally, Janelle? We've worked together for years. It's like you don't even know me.

Well, if you think about it, that's how it is with most co-workers.

But if you don't know me, Janelle, how can you consider my perspective? Maybe, Janelle, what would be best for you is to look inward. Try to be more empathetic.

The fresh pineapple burns its taste into my cheek. Janelle's face turns indignant.

Be more empathetic? I bust my ass at St. Jude's.

She drops her mug in the sink with a splash and clatter. Her eyes fill with tears.

I mean, there are so many of them. All homeless. All complex. It never ends.

Velma walks in with wet hair: What's going on?

Cliff and I are leaving. Do you want to come?

You should go, Velma, Janelle says. I understand how worried you are.

Rolm Farthing is busy, according to his secretary. But when we discuss my situation and how making up excuses for other adults is probably not what she dreamed of doing with her life, she lets us in. And Rolm refuses to give Paige's location, but after we talk about what she and Murray did and how protecting her is not his duty, as she's capable of handling her own life, he writes an address on one of his business cards and hands it to me. His face pinks up and I can tell he's pleased with his choice to help.

The house is a bungalow with dingy beige vinyl siding. Velma starts on about more sketchy, dangerous places, but when I turn to her, she goes quiet.

There's no answer at the door. The backyard is surrounded by a tall wire fence. And like serendipity, as we're considering climbing it, Paige appears. She pads across the backyard, picking up beverage cans.

Paige. Hi. It's me, Sandra.

She turns. She drops the cans. She has sunglasses on, so it's tricky to gauge her feelings.

Can I help you?

Good to see you again, Paige.

I'm sorry, this is private property.

Rolm gave me the address. I need to speak with Murray. I understand things became confusing, but it's time to talk.

Paige waves a cellphone. Leave, she says, or I call the police.

She's so far away, I say. She needs to come closer.

Sandra, Velma says. We should go.

Cliff scoops up a rock from the ground. Come over here now, he says, or I start smashing windows.

The cops will knock the shit out of you, Paige says.

Cliff hurls the rock. A window shatters. There is a screech from inside, a woman's voice.

One broken window is better than two broken windows, Cliff says.

Jesus, Paige says. Okay. I'm coming.

She stops about ten feet away from us. Make it quick, she says.

My hands clutch the gate. I search for her eyes through the dark glasses.

Paige, I understand this situation wasn't planned. You're trying to protect everything you and Murray worked for. But mistakes were made. I believe if you look inside yourself, you'll realize the best thing right now is to tell the truth. It will set you free.

Paige snorts. Clasps a hand over her mouth. She runs towards the house.

And then all I can think is *up*. My hands yank and hoist and all that's behind me are Velma's cries and Cliff's cheers. I'm better at climbing than I imagined. It's so nice when you discover new areas where you excel.

The yard is all patches of grass worn down to dirt. Paige sits on the ground. When I get close, she starts laughing.

I hate hiding out here so much, she says. We tried, you know? Murray and Sasha and I. We talked to researchers, we networked with scientists. Too radical. Too dangerous.

Sasha?

Dr. Lee. And Murray never wanted neutral candidates anyway. They should already be trying to be positive, he said. They should want to volunteer. But come on. Who's going to sign up for that? So we looked at the followers. Who's a big fan? Who's single? Who never has friends or family in their photos? Ideally, a lonely woman with a lot of hope. Murray's words, not mine. We thought it would work. But fucking Sasha messed up the wattage. You were a walking coma. We had no choice but the Pickering backup plan. I told Murray that in The Dimming, one more drop in the chaos soup doesn't get noticed.

Where is Murray?

It's top secret. In the house.

The screen door squeals open into a damp-smelling porch. Voices in a distant room, sounds of glass being swept up. The porch leads into a kitchen, three cereal bowls on the counter, one box of organic Kamut flakes.

Dr. Sasha Lee appears in a grey T-shirt. Her '60s bob is dishevelled in the back. What are you doing here? she asks.

Hello, Dr. Lee. I'm here to sort things out.

And then, there he is. Bare-chested Murray in plaid pyjama pants. His curls in a ponytail. His mouth open.

I step forward to hug him. He hops backwards. He and Dr. Lee exchange a look. The lies and fear are so sad to see.

Paige told me about the experiment, I say. How you chose me.

Look, Dr. Lee says, if it's money you want, you already signed the release. You consented.

Shelly, I can handle this.

Shelly?

Sha-lee. Paige sways in the doorway. Sa-sha Lee. Shelly. Pet names. Hey, Sandra, your friend took off. She looked scared shitless.

I'd like to speak to Sandra alone, Murray says. Please.

Dr. Lee folds her arms. The hem of her T-shirt shifts, exposing the pink elastic of her underwear. I don't think it's a good idea, she says.

My stomach churns with disappointment. Her. She and him.

You said you loved me, I say. Murray, it meant something.

Shit, Dr. Lee says. You poor thing.

Please, Sash, give us a minute, Murray says. He shuts the door to the porch and Paige. Dr. Lee shuffles out of the kitchen, tugging her T-shirt down.

Sandra. I was hoping to spare you this. Yes, we had a nice time and I'm sorry we misled you. But I knew you believed in the science that was the goal. For the greater good.

I clutch my stomach. Hot dissonance buckles in my core, spreading to my chest. In his face there is no love, no kindness. Resignation. Caution. Displeasure.

What's your plan, Sandra? We've been on the down-low because of all of this. But if it comes out, the contract you signed absolves us. There's no real proof we left you in Pickering. And we're still working on my theory. We're still fighting to brighten The Dimming.

I really love you.

I'm sorry, Sandra. I can say don't take it personally. But it's understandable if you feel like a pawn.

I realize I want to cry. Or release somehow. His face, his blank insincere face. I want his old face back.

Murray, you chose me because you knew I'd love you. And I did. I let you do this to me because I love you.

Sandra—

I've loved you more and better than anyone else. I gave myself to you. You put me to sleep, you cast me out, and I came to find you. You locked yourself away in a box and I tore it open. I believe, Murray, if you look inside yourself and consider what you do and what you've done, you'll see accepting my love and returning it is the best thing to do.

Murray stares at the linoleum. I move forward and take his hands.

Because the experiment worked, I say. What more do you really want? Maybe the best thing for you and your dreams is being with me. Because you know I'll make it all happen.

His chin rises. His hazel eyes meet mine. They are soft with golden flecks.

Everything you say makes sense, Sandra.

I kiss him, once, twice. On the third one, he responds. And as he kisses me back, I know everything will be alright.

Three Weeks Later: Monday

It went as smoothly as could be expected. Right away, it was important to get Murray out of that house. Cliff kept Sasha calm as we gathered Murray's things. He held my hand in the back seat as we drove away.

We stayed in a hotel at first. It was lovely to be together again, even though it took him a couple of days to clear himself of his stagnant mindset. He said he wanted to be with me, but he and Sasha had been part of each other's lives for so long—can't she remain part of the project somehow? We finally came to a mutual understanding once I explained how important it is we be a positive, united front together. He agreed we should avoid any opportunity where our energies may be misdirected. Then he made a post on his social media on how revitalized he felt from his time off: *Recharged and clear-headed!* With a selfie of us together. #nofilter, all glow.

I was able to get a meeting with Hedgeglove and explain how we needed an affordable place. They were able to see how providing reasonably priced housing was beneficial in the long run. And now we have this beautiful apartment on Avenue Road, walking distance from flower markets and cute restaurants.

Murray says he's never been so productive. His book sales are up. At speaking engagements, he introduces me as his partner and we talk about making a positive world from the ground up. He describes me as a natural life coach with an instinct for encouraging self-improvement. He experiments with quirky terms: Instant Insight. Intention Athlete. Gladiator-Level Positive Thinking Champion.

So much progress already. We convinced the provincial government to loosen their grip on shelters. On the municipal level, I've spoken with several members of city council and they've managed to quash plans for three new condominium projects. Now funds are earmarked for affordable housing. Hope grows in Toronto.

But poor, exhausted Janelle, basically running St. Jude's now with Velma on leave. I have not seen Velma, but she has sent several text messages. She repeatedly asks for an explanation as to what I am doing. I invite her for lunch, coffee, opportunities to talk, but she refuses. A whole career devoted to social justice and she cannot fathom change happening through words, through positive energy, through a little friggin' faith.

Next week, we meet the premier. Each day is ascension: more smiles, more safe places, more Twitter followers. Each night I sleep in Murray's arms, tucked in place like a bookmark.

Tuesday

A rough morning. New Nationalists and Internment Camp protesters clashed at Queen's Park. Riot police broke it up. Two protesters killed. *Do not be disheartened*, Murray tweets. *#loveoverhate*.

The New Nationalists need to be stopped, I say.

Freedom of expression, my dear, Murray says. There

are a lot of grey areas around what's considered hate speech.

I watch him busy himself with the espresso machine. Post-meditation Americano is a new routine. Refugees don't deserve to be treated like criminals by these hypocrites, I say. No one is safe as long as NNAN and other Nazis spread propaganda and infect those already poisoned by negativity.

You're right, my love.

Sometimes, I feel bad for not expecting more of Murray, but he's a healer and motivator, not an activist. Not like at St. Jude's, where we did what we could with so little, everything a small but steep step. I miss Velma and working in the trenches.

And then it comes to me. I kiss Murray goodbye and head to the centre. Janelle, Cliff and I lock ourselves in Velma's office. Her dot-matrix wallpaper is still there: the list of everyone she's written and petitioned over the years.

We stretch it out so it covers the floor and attack it with highlighters: names, roles, issues. Here are those in charge of low-income housing in the GTA. Here are the top human rights lawyers in the province. Here are corporations with political influence. We list them in columns, who does what, who knows who. Velma's tireless activism is finally paying off. First, we find them, then we make them see.

Wednesday

Cliff drives, Janelle directs, and I relax. What a day. We began with the Minister of the Status of Women. After a conversation where I said if he wanted to do his job well, he'd consider the lives of 50 per cent of the population before making poor economic decisions, he agreed to open more shelters for abuse victims and fight for increased funding.

Then we crashed a political fundraiser at the Metro Toronto Convention Centre. Getting in was straightforward and the Attorney General and Minister of Community Safety were so gregarious, it was easy to strike up a chat. Once inspired, they were on board. No to internment camps. Yes to punishing those who hate.

Afterwards, I treated us to champagne. I texted Velma to inform her of our activities and show gratitude for her inspiration. She hasn't responded. I hope she's doing well.

Thursday

By evening, we're a third of the way through Velma's scroll. Our spreadsheet is a checklist of positive accomplishments: warnings issued to anyone participating in hate-crime behaviour, promises of a stronger police presence in NN areas, a review of current regulations regarding internment camps for US refugees.

But there is backlash. The Chief of Police questions the Attorney General, lawyers threaten lawsuits. Everything is red tape and financial rhetoric. No wonder people get discouraged. Even when you get through to someone, they can only do so much.

At home, Murray calls out from his office. His Smart-board swarms with diagrams of brains, energy waves, and facts on thought-blocking. The newest CT scans of my mind are displayed, my prefrontal cortex now paled to a grey smudge.

Oh Sandra, I missed you. Do you want a glass of wine?

Yes please.

So nice to come home to him, all cozy with the twinkling lights of the city off our balcony. Murray hands me a glass of Pinot Grigio and we settle on the couch. On the new flat screen CNN shows President Sweeney's brassy hair and fleshy face. He poses before one of his New York real estate ventures. I mute it. Murray's phone on the coffee table dings.

A new text message appears: *Please talk to me*. Unknown number.

Is Sasha communicating with you?

Yes. She tracked down my new number. Paige is still on her honesty kick. She gave in to Sasha's requests.

Perhaps we should talk to Paige.

Yes, good idea.

The wine is cool down my throat. Murray places a throw pillow behind my lower back.

Thank you, Murray. It's been a long day.

You're doing a great job.

But every person I reach can only do so much. So much *no* out there.

Negative energy forms a tightly coiled resistance.

Yes, that.

Maybe we should shift the target? Take you, for instance. Before the procedure, you were working hard to help the world, but your own thoughts could trip you up. That didn't change until we affected the origin of your negative ideas.

Well, until you almost killed me.

But that's what I mean. Until we dampened the negative muscle of your mind, it trapped you.

I'm not seeing your point, my darling.

You're talking to stakeholders in the region. But they don't hold all the cards. You need to go to the source.

On the TV, CNN posts shots of Sweeney's status updates. A throng of protesters on a Brooklyn street.

Murray, does your agent have American connections?

Saturday

On Monday, we will leave for New York City. Murray, Cliff, and Janelle are coming. Such a great feeling of community and purpose. And Velma has agreed to see me. I think she'd be a wonderful addition to the America trip.

We meet at a small café in Little Italy. Velma's black hair hangs in ringlets around her face, Pre-Raphaelite-like. When she has time to do her hair, it's quite something. She sits straight-backed at the table. She's treated herself to chunky new headphones; they dangle around her neck. Her fingers hover to them as I sit. She's wearing gloves. It's disappointing to witness so much distrust, but it's still good to see her.

How are things? I ask. I've missed you.

Things have been concerning. I'm concerned. It's why I want to talk.

It's good to clear the air if you're concerned.

Sandra, what's going on with you? Murray describes it as instant insight—

Oh yes. Or Positive Thinking Athleticism. He's a bit silly sometimes.

How are you getting people to follow your advice?

I'd be happy to tell you. Murray's performed some tests

lately. His original treatment worked, but we didn't realize it at the time. They shocked the section of my brain responsible for negative thought. So now, negative ideas don't interfere with the power of my intentions.

Your intentions?

Yes. Positive energy attracts people and heals the universe. My positive-thinking muscles were already quite fit, so now when I try to help others, they recognize my positive intentions. They see what is good for themselves and others, through me.

Velma bites her lip. It seems difficult for her to maintain eye contact. But, she says, how do you know what's for the best? Because Cliff and Janelle, they're not the same.

They seem fine to me.

What advice did you give Janelle?

I told her she could be more empathetic.

Sandra, that's all she is now. She owns every hardship she sees. She's crying all the time at St. Jude's. And Cliff, it's like he's lost his critical thinking abilities. Everything is how nice, how beautiful.

Janelle and Cliff are very positive, helpful people.

You have politicians simply changing their minds and not using appropriate channels. And now you want to meet Sweeney—what do you plan on saying to him?

I plan to talk about important world issues. Things I know you believe in, Velma.

But I never ask people to blindly change their minds. When I wrote those letters, I knew the requests wouldn't be met, but I hoped for compromise.

Isn't this better than compromise?

If you *persuade* Sweeney to do an about-face after all

the fear-mongering he's concocted, it will get dangerous.

Things are already dangerous. Anyway, if someone was bent on stopping me, I could help them see things differently.

That sounds sinister.

Sinister? My intentions are good. Honestly, Velma, maybe what would be best for you is to have a little fa—

No!

Velma slams the headphones on. Her gloved finger shakes in my face. Don't you do that to me.

Velma, c'mon. You're being dramatic.

She bolts out onto College Street. I watch her black ringlets ricochet off her shoulders as she rushes away.

Tuesday

A whirlwind. I'm not even sure how it all happened. Murray snores in the hotel bed and I can't stop watching Cliff's video of Sweeney and me. It's been sent to me in all formats, including in an email from Velma with an all-caps subject line: YOU CAN'T SAY THIS ISN'T FUCKED UP.

It starts with Murray and me moving through the hotel with the manager, Karl Jarvis. Murray introduced us and after I explained I wished to have a quick word with President Sweeney, he took us through security. The video captures the pause outside his suite as Secret Service get involved. At one point, one of them gets up in Cliff's face, demanding he turn off his phone. But after I speak with him, he calms down.

We enter a wide golden space. President Sweeney sits at a gleaming desk, perusing documents. He is surprised and frustrated to see us; he even jumps up and backs away. But everyone is calm and Sweeney and I have our moment. Cliff didn't catch the audio, but what a beautiful shot: the two of us in the window, silhouetted by downtown New York City, my chin raised as I speak into his face. As he listens, his hands rise to cover his mouth before he falls to his knees. So moving to witness such a powerful figure finally aflame with realization.

He immediately wanted to tweet: apologies, confessions, a denouncement of all his literal and figurative walls, but we convinced him to resist. And then there was a meeting with the vice president and officials for the new health-care bill. Such a high to explain how everyone deserves free health care and watch their pupils dilate with insight. They wept and tore up the legislation, agreed to start fresh. Murray's hand on my shoulder; *you are the oracle*, he whispered.

Tomorrow, Washington. They can't wait for me to address Congress. I've already considered the priorities. Once everyone's on board with making a better world, they'll see the best way to stop gun violence is with strict gun control, ASAP.

Wednesday

So nervous. Murray tries to relax me with shoulder massages, but nothing can lessen the magnitude of what we are attempting. I've never done group work. All the meaningful moments so far have been one on one. Can a whole group listen and change? Murray says address their philosophy: they're motivated by money and power. Focus on undermining that.

The atmosphere outside the Senate is frenzied: reporters, protesters, security. The media recognize Murray and me. Headlines buzz with drama: *Sweeney Abandons Christian Right for New Thought Gurus? Has Sweeney Become a Hippie?*

We are led into the chambers. Sweeney will introduce me and then I'll have the floor. My cue cards dig a sweaty wedge into my palm. I take deep breaths. I will smile and engage. I will speak of the long-term gains of empathy, compassion, and a healthy, accepting population.

Sweeney stands at the podium with his arms raised. His chin juts out in that manner I always considered smug and prideful. But now it's for me.

Last year I promised to transform the USA back to glory, he says. And you know, I thought we were doing a great job. I felt pretty terrific about it. But I gotta say, I was wrong. It's really great to know you're wrong and own it. Smart people do that, admit when they've made mistakes. And my actions have caused tremendous troubles for the American people. Tremendous, terrible troubles. I've defended some real losers, the kind of people who would like to cast out anyone different than them. You can't get a job? Maybe it's not because of the Mexicans or Muslims or gays or someone who isn't you. Maybe you're stupid and should be fired.

The room barks in shock and complaint. Sweeney raises his open palms. So, this is why, oh look, you're mad now, this is why as of this moment Immigration Reform is cancelled. We're getting rid of it.

Yelling now, furious roars. Outside, a wave of whoops, reactions from the protesters.

So now, I'm going to introduce you to a great lady. I tell you, she's so smart, so classy. I know she's going to help me put us back on track. We'll be winning again with Sandra Somers.

I step up to the podium. The crowd is a boiling pot of business suits. The microphone squeals on my first word.

Hello.

And then chaos. An army of black suits enter. Someone with a megaphone: Attention everyone! Cover your ears! Now!

So many of them. They pass around small, neon orange packages. There is another loud squeal. My microphone stops working.

FBI, Sweeney says. Morons.

Everyone stay where you are. You will be handed disposable earplugs. Apply them immediately.

Two familiar faces appear. Velma and Dr. Lee approach the person with the megaphone. It's handed to Velma. She wears black, like the rest of the FBI team, but a black jeans–dark jacket pairing. It's a good look for her.

Sandra, she says, this must stop.

Dr. Lee yells into the megaphone over her shoulder: Murray! She's destroyed your mind! We're here to save you!

Oh goodness, Murray says. Isn't that a shame?

Come with us now, Velma says. No one wants to hurt you.

But it doesn't seem that way. The agents have weapons. There are so many of them. Velma, I shout, there's no need for this. Velma shakes her head and covers her ears.

I turn to the nearest Secret Service agent. This is a big misunderstanding, I say. Do you know what I mean? Everyone's being very reactionary. Your job is to help. Could you do a good job and help me and my friends leave safely, please?

Of course! There's a special passage.

He takes us out a side door. An agent charges. He shoves them aside. We race out. Dr. Lee's voice screams at Murray: Come back. It's not real.

Everything in the hallway is madness until the agent pulls his gun. Then we're in a back door, a narrow hallway. We channel out in a straight line, quiet except for our breaths. We emerge into daylight. A car waits. The noise from the Senate is distant thunder.

Thursday

Once again, I am in some new, strange place. Sweeney's aides say we can stay here until things die down and then he'll secure passage to Canada. The Baltimore apartment is neutral and basic. It is a challenge to find things to occupy ourselves with besides checking social media.

The Anti-Internment-Camp movement calls yesterday a triumph, which feels very nice. But others hurl names: witch doctors, cult leaders, brainwashers. Velma and Dr. Lee convinced the authorities and media to investigate everyone we helped: the Attorney General, Toronto city council, Officer Hazeline. There are videos of interviews where they all sound clear-headed, but uncritical. An indoctrinating effect, some expert calls it. Likely a kind of hypnosis. Likely involved drugging the victims.

Murray says it will pass. He's been saying it all day. This is temporary, we'll get back to our good work soon. I stare at him in his clumsy drawstring pants.

Obviously, they're collecting evidence for their case, I say. If they find us, we'll be going to court.

They just don't know you, Murray says.

Murray, maybe we jumped the gun. Sweeney was too much, too fast.

I think you're right, my love. We'll scale back when we start over. It will be wonderful.

I excuse myself and go out on the balcony to exhale my annoyances. *Sweetie. My Love. Dear.* Catchphrases for him.

My phone rattles with notifications. News on Sweeney now, the latest firings in his administration. His anger over claims of his dementia, insanity. New calls for impeachment strengthened with most of the GOP now rallying against him.

And a new message, from a strange but official-looking account: *Ms. Somers. We know where you are. We want to keep you safe. Please call this number. We have a project we feel is a good match for you.*

Two Weeks Later

Fresh starts and reflection. Things with Murray were a bit troublesome. Hard to admit the magic we shared was fleeting. He is a kind, brilliant man, and I love him. But it is the kind of love one has for a historical bond, for a mentor or childhood friend. I still value his companionship, but I wonder how long he can be unproductive. It's a good thing my new work is lucrative and we don't need the royalty payments from his books—those dropped off after Dr. Lee and Paige's confessions. But he seems content. He tinkers with his theories and praises my talents. He has no visible regrets.

At this moment, my situation fits my long-held beliefs: how life is happening *for* me, not *to* me, the hardest moments are a calling to something greater, and elevation may require isolation. These are lonely days, but it's necessary to stay safe and focus on the future. I miss Toronto and St. Jude's. I miss Cliff and Janelle. I especially miss Velma, but she's on her own journey.

I count my blessings. I am in a warm safe place, protected by those who recognize my worth. I have people invested in me—in my health even, a personal chef, a trainer. And even when my body tells me it's sad and bothered, I have a full schedule of new ventures to keep me occupied and focused.

Good things are coming. The Dimming will be vanquished by light. And it will be a light that encompasses the world, one moment at a time, one day at a time, and for me, one language at a time. The Russian tutor says I'm doing great, but in Mandarin class, I have to work on my vocabulary.

But I can do it. I know I can.

ACKNOWLEDGEMENTS

The stories in *No One Knows about Us* took shape here and there over the years, and there are many who lent an ear and an eye to get them where they needed to go. Much gratitude to Eva Crocker, Michelle Porter, Tracey Waddleton, and my writing group, The Naked Parade Writing Collective: Violet Browne, Diane Carley, Terry Doyle, Penny Hansen, Matthew Hollett, Jim McEwen, Jen McVeigh, Kelley Power, and Heidi Wicks.

To Kate Kennedy, thank you for your wonderful editing skills. It was a joy to work with you again. Thanks to Rebecca Rose and the whole Breakwater team.

Thank you, Lisa Moore. Your guidance and support with this collection means the world to me.

Thank you, Jason Sellars, for telling me about the lobster and the eagle. Thanks, Jim McEwen, for the info on tree-planting shovels.

Thanks to my lovely, supportive family, Mom (Barb), Liz, Jason, Mary Anne, John, Patrick, Michelle, and Malcolm. Thanks always to Jon Weir.

SOME NOTES

In "The Lobster," the book Gaby is enjoying is *Us Conductors* by Sean Michaels.

"Apartment 312" was originally published in Issue #23 of *Riddle Fence*.

"Colleen's Birthday" won an Arts and Letters Award (Senior Fiction) in 2015. It was later published in *Galleon III*.

The first story in the "Gutless" series was published in the *Word Hoard*, Nov. 2016.

"Bradley and Molly" was originally published as "Bradley+Molly4ever" in *What's Written in the Ladies: Photographs and Scribblings*.

"Hands in Pockets" was shortlisted for the 2015 Cuffer Prize and published in the *Telegram*.

"Seventeen Minutes" was a winner in the BC Federation of Writers 2017 Literary Writers competition and published in *WordWorks*.

Author photo *by* Ritchie Perez

BRIDGET CANNING has published two novels: *The Greatest Hits of Wanda Jaynes* (2017) and *Some People's Children* (2020). In 2019, she won the CBC Emerging Artist Award with ArtsNL. *No One Knows about Us* is her first collection of short stories. She holds an MA in creative writing from Memorial University and a master of literacy education from Mount Saint Vincent University. She grew up in Highlands, Newfoundland and Labrador, and currently lives in St. John's.